(S)WITCHBOARD

ANDREW POST

JOURNALSTONE
YOUR LINK TO ARTIST TALENT

ISBN: 978-1-950305-16-2 (sc)
ISBN: 978-1-950305-17-9 (ebook)
Library of Congress Control Number: 2019953552

First printing edition: February 28, 2020
Printed by JournalStone Publishing in the United States of America.
Cover Design and Layout: Mikio Murakami
Interior Layout: Lori Michelle
Edited by Sean Leonard
Proofread by Scarlett R. Algee

JournalStone Publishing
3205 Sassafras Trail
Carbondale, Illinois 62901

JournalStone books may be ordered through booksellers
or by contacting:
JournalStone | www.journalstone.com

(S)WITCHBOARD

I

THE NEEDLE &
THE DAMAGE DONE

1.

THE ALLEGED CHEMIST had entrenched himself in a lonely tower. Strip malls crowded the interstate to the north, while a cemetery-like plain of dead factories lay to the south. Tenants within the Dunsany Arms building whose windows faced north could go on ignoring the sprawling deadlands. Out of sight, out of mind; the wastes might not metastasize if they aren't regularly glimpsed. But what the alleged chemist felt when he peered from his sixth-floor window didn't interest Lieutenant Dwayne Spare: he only wanted to take *alleged* chemist and make it *convicted* chemist. And having met the man, Dwayne could only imagine that when Gerald Metzger looked out over the wasteland, he probably considered the desolation something to which he'd directly contributed, and was pleased.

After dihydrodesoxymorphine—street name "krokodil"—had slithered over from Eastern Europe, possession charges for meth and heroin had plummeted. Those who'd given the newcomer a try had found another ticket to the void, one that was cheaper than crack but packed a kick comparable to uncut smack. Though krokodil had wasted little time spreading its blight across the Rust Belt and soaking in deeply, with Erie, it couldn't have arrived at a worse time. Half the plants and mills had departed for sunnier, more economically stable pastures, and the unemployment rate had never been higher. Hopelessness and spare time never pair well—and the vultures, as they are wont, descended.

The mayor got behind his podium and wheeled out the word "epidemic"—then after, at the state police luncheon, took Dwayne and his captain aside. "Find who's making this shit. The DEA isn't getting the satisfaction of cleaning up our backyard for us." The ides of March approached.

Before Metzger surfaced as a person of interest, Dwayne had spearheaded a dozen krok-den raids. The smell was the worst. When a user injects krokodil, the blood vessels surrounding the injection site erupt and the area turns necrotic and, before long, an addict will begin to resemble someone with advanced leprosy. Though the life expectancy of a krok addict hovers, for most, around three years, a majority live to watch themselves fall apart.

Last summer, Dwayne had kicked in a bedroom door and found a man lying cocooned in a tainted bedsheet, I WILL HEAR HIM smeared on the wall in engine grease. On the nightstand, between candles burned to pale puddles, stood a neat pyramid of burner phones.

With untold days of its wearer soiling himself, the sheet had become brown and brittle, crackling dryly as Dwayne ripped it from over the cadaverous husk underneath. A needle remained jutting from a thigh shrunken and rippled with rot, but he was breathing. When the man remained unresponsive after being ordered to stand up, Dwayne grabbed him by his wrist and hauled him to his feet. This was before Dwayne knew how fragile a long-term krok-user's composition could become—the man left a considerable portion of himself upon the mattress. Back flayed, the wraith wrenched himself free, leaving Dwayne holding three of the man's grayed fingers. With the ones he had left, he hunched in the corner and pecked feverishly at each of his burners in turn, tears spilling. "I didn't hear him. You kept me from *hearing him.*"

When the man charged, screaming about being interrupted from *hearing him*, Dwayne swung. Screams from a jawless mouth sound very different.

Though he died minutes later, the man's scream echoed in Dwayne. It exhumed his insomnia first, and soon it deafened him each time he dared to sit alone in a quiet room. Sarah was a light sleeper, so Dwayne took the couch at night, the TV keeping him company. Sometimes he'd scream himself awake, as if his dream-self was a dog howling to equalize away a painful note. Soon, three glasses of whisky would nightly follow whatever explicitly meat-free dinner he could stomach. Then it was four glasses, then five. Sarah took Jamie away before it became six, and he couldn't blame her. But when a trio of dealers were caught with ten pounds of krokodil apiece, each claiming they slung for one Gerald Hain Metzger, the name replaced the scream.

* * *

Captain David Cleckley looked over the proposal and sighed. What Dwayne was suggesting certainly wasn't on the up-and-up, but two search warrants had gotten them nothing. It was like the alleged chemist knew to purge his apartment hours ahead of time. And there he sat on his only piece of furniture, a moldy lawn chair, hands in his lap, smiling as Dwayne and his team failed to pull so much as a trace off the walls. Nothing under the carpet that'd soaked through to the pad underneath, no residue on the vent covers, nothing. Pristine.

Watching them work, the alleged chemist matched the view outside the window behind him. Gray and silent, abandoned. Dwayne pegged him to be around ten years his senior, but running his ID, not only did Metzger possess a record as spotless as his home, he'd only just turned thirty on Halloween. Of course.

The lab results came back from the latest batch making its way around town. It wasn't the standard dihydrodesoxymorphine they'd previously seized. *Atropa belladonna* extract had been added to the new mix. Dwayne learned online that belladonna—known also as deadly nightshade, which at full bloom produces a deceitfully beautiful flower of five-petaled purple—had been a common component in the ointment witches of yesteryear would slather on broomsticks to "fly" and, in more recent history, held the ill repute as a favorite controlled substance among the Manson Family. What was the alleged chemist's goal? To have a customer shoot up and suffer dark dreams about their body falling apart, only to wake up to find exactly that was happening to them?

Metzger maintained his position that he held zero knowledge of dihydrodesoxymorphine or *Atropa belladonna*, but thanked Dwayne emphatically for the, quote, "fascinating history lesson."

The DA nudged. They had to cut Metzger loose. The only prints on the intercepted baggies of belladonna-laced krokodil belonged to the three dealers. The chemist—Metzger or not—had been careful. Apparently it'd been a total coincidence that the three dealers had given the same name and the same address of a completely innocent man. Life's funny like that sometimes. Almost as funny as how those three dealers each caught a sharpened toothbrush to the throat mere minutes after receiving their peel up in county.

Dwayne didn't think Metzger was gifted with any kind of ESP. If the three slingers weren't bullshitting about how much money they were pulling down hustling for the alleged chemist, it'd be tough for a cop with some steep child-support to resist trading tips for tastes. But an empire, secret or no, needed a system of communications—unless the alleged chemist was going up to the roof and dispatching orders via carrier pigeon. Dwayne didn't think that was likely, so bugging Metzger's apartment would be their opening move, as detailed in his proposal.

"If you do this," Cleckley said, "you're taking some time after. You aren't looking well."

Dwayne shoved a pen at him, his hand tremulous.

"When was the last time you ate?"

"Sign it, David."

"Have dinner with me. We'll talk."

2.

"ARE YOU GOOD around blood?"

The young woman had parked her wheelchair so close to Jack he could smell the coconut shampoo lingering in her long midnight hair. She had intricate ink running up and down both her arms and two purple lightning bolts tattooed in place of her eyebrows—which crashed together when she looked him in the face. He might've been staring.

"Sorry, uh, am I good around blood? Honestly, not really."

"Then I'd recommend not watching," she said, pulling on a surgical mask.

In a chair that looked like it'd been stolen from a dentist's office, she had him tipped at such an angle that the blood was settling in the back of his head. The spare bedroom-turned-OR of apartment 308 was small and a few degrees warmer than his liking, but his jitters may've been from the painkillers she'd given him—picked from a rattling, colorful assortment she kept in a mint tin. Then she'd shaved his armpits and administered a local anesthetic, left side, right side. One thud of his heart, and his arms felt like they'd dropped off.

"The worst part of this process," she said, "is going to be when that hair starts to grow back." The corners of her eyes crinkled, smiling under her mask. "I'm Connie. Did I say that already?"

He shook his head. "Jack Cotard."

"Oh, we're doing last names? Trusting. Wieczne."

"Wieczne?"

"Let me guess, you have the one Polack joke I *haven't* heard."

"No, sorry." He laughed, an unintentionally anxious titter. "I like it."

Connie ran her eyes over his body, lying naked to the waist, as if inspecting a used car for dents. "A few scars but no piercings, ink, or pockets, huh?"

"These will be my first." And only, hopefully.

She pulled on latex gloves and angled a light's yellowish beam on him. He could feel its warmth, a lizard in a terrarium. "Which side would you like done first?"

"Does it matter?"

"Not to me," she said. "I like to offer whatever small sense of control I can. Makes for less fidgety patients. So . . . ?"

"The left then, I guess."

"Splendid. Go ahead and roll over and we'll get started."

On his right side, her hard, small fingers took him by the elbow and raised his arm above his head. "Stay just like that," she said. "Still as possible. We're going to be working near your axillary artery—not to freak you out or anything. We good?"

Hearing metal tools rattling on a metal tray, he broke out into a cold sweat, but managed to nod.

"Take a couple big, deep breaths for me."

"Okay."

"Actually do it. Don't just say okay."

"Sorry." Jack took two deep breaths.

"And look at the pretty picture." With a gloved hand, she steered his attention to a print taped to the far wall.

Trying his best to ignore the sounds of cutting, Jack peered into the night scene, the golden-eyed goat ringed by a prostrating crowd. Sitting upright like a person, the goat seemed to be offering a laying-on of hands. One child that'd been brought forward was a skeletal husk with withered legs, held aloft by a craggy-faced old woman. Her offering was ignored by the goat in favor of the healthier-looking spawn brought by healthier-looking mothers, with radiant skin and overjoyed expressions. Other small, gray bodies littered the image, with one lying discarded on the ground as if kicked aside. An odd choice of decor for a doctor's office, even one such as this.

"Goya could certainly command the eye, couldn't he?" she said—half-engaged, working.

"It's something."

She sniffed a tiny laugh. "That it is."

"Is the goat making the sick kids better? Is that what's going on?"

"Looks like we have an optimist in our midst," she said. "Not to be a downer, but if the goat is making the kids better, explain the dead ones hanging from that pole in the background."

Jack couldn't explain that, but he could smell blood.

"Maybe that's what makes it a great piece of art, you know?" Connie said. "Nobody but the artist knows what happened first, what happened after, only that one moment locked by brush strokes in beautiful ambiguity. Hell, maybe *all* those chicks were doe-eyed innocents before they wound up the goat's groupies. Or the busted-looking ones, even though they look old, are his *new* recruits."

He wished she would talk to him more or put on some music or something. He didn't like feeling the faraway tugs and pulls on his body, hearing all that *slicing* and *peeling* and the wet *pop* as his skin layers were teased into separating.

"Are, we thinking about getting anything else done today?"

"Like . . . what?" Isn't this enough?

"I doubt you're with child"—that small, sniffing laugh again—"but I could make you with*out*, if you were. Or, to prevent future whoopsie-doodles, you could walk out of here only shooting blanks. Could get a tramp stamp, get something pierced. Or bifurcated, if we're feeling adventurous this morning."

"Bifurcated?"

"Yeah. Tongues are the norm, but I've split a couple dicks before too. Interested?" Connie asked.

No anesthetic had been administered to his crotch, but the area still numbed. "I think I'm good. People actually ask to get that done?"

"Nobody asks for things they don't want, Jack. Actually, scratch that. They do. Case in point." She rapped gloved knuckles on her wheelchair's armrest. "I mean, you're getting pockets cut into your skin so Gerald Metzger can extend his customer base to the Great White Way. Can't imagine that back in first grade, you put that down as your 'What I want to be when I grow up.'"

"I wanted to be a fireman."

"That's cute," she said. "You probably go, what, a buck-forty soaking wet?"

"Around there."

"Mom couldn't kick the Virginia Slims for nine months?"

"And a few other things," he said. "What about you?"

"Nah, Mommy Dearest preferred her poison in liquid form. And before you ask, no, that's not why I'm in a wheelchair."

"I meant what you wanted to be when you grow up."

"Heh. Right. Well, if you know anybody who'd pay someone to sit around, drink red wine, and watch horror movies all day, I have tons of experience."

"This isn't what you wanted to do?"

"Don't take this the wrong way, but what the fuck do you think?"

Jack looked again at the three small bodies hanging from a pole in the painting's background. Goya hadn't given them much detail, which may've made them more unsettling. How had she put it? Beautiful ambiguity?

"Shit. You didn't feel that, did you?"

"Feel what?"

A sudden *shhk* of tape. "All done on this side. Shall we flip?"

Arms numb, he clumsily twisted over onto his left side. He was lying on his wound, but only detected a faint warmth in his armpit. There weren't any paintings to look at now—only his surgeon. Connie's wheelchair appeared to have some miles on it. She'd plastered band stickers on every available inch, and the armrests were badged with scratches and scuffs.

Against his better judgment, he looked—and saw she was stuffing cotton balls into the bloody, toothless mouth she'd cut into his side.

"Your breathing changed," she stated. "We holding in there okay?"

"I'm all right."

"You looked, didn't you? Or was it all the talk about split dicks?"

Pain spread across the top of his skull and knotted the nerves behind his left eye. "My head hurts."

"Yeah, that'll happen with blood loss. Turns out, the brain doesn't care for that."

"Am I bleeding a lot?"

"No more than anybody else," she said. "After we're through, we'll get you a big glass of OJ and some Oreos—if there's any left."

"Was that your kid?" he said. While his surgeon had been prepping her workspace, covering everything under layers of Saran wrap, Jack had sat in her living room waiting area with this shirtless, dirty-faced kid gawping at him. He wouldn't smile back when Jack accidentally made eye contact with him, and wouldn't engage in the smallest of talk, not even hello. They sat in silence watching *The Price is Right*—or, more accurately, the kid watched Jack watching *The Price is Right*—the whole scene feeling like some bleak and inscrutable indie movie, the kind Jack's ex-girlfriend used to drag him to all the time.

"What kid?" Connie said.

"That kid out there on your couch."

The wet sounds of surgery paused. "This happened just now?"

"Yeah."

"You saw a little boy, in *this* apartment?"

"Yes. Why?"

"Huh. You met Sam. He died alone in this building a long, long time ago. You must have *the sight*."

"Are you . . . serious?"

"No, dingus, I'm not serious. His name's Sam, but he isn't dead, he's just weird as shit. He lives upstairs with his dad." Connie laughed her sniffing little laugh. "Your face."

"Jesus. Might not speak too highly to your skills, making patients think your apartment's haunted. Just saying."

"I only do it when I get the impression they'll look if I say gullible's written on the ceiling." She returned to working on him. "Don't actually look. In fact, you should be like *super* still right now."

Only moving his eyes, Jack looked up at her, a strange feeling suggesting there'd be something other than his surgeon to see. On the ceiling a flower bloomed among the water-stains, giving Connie a spreading halo of five pointy petals in lush mauve.

"Do you see that?"

"Nice try," she said.

His silence that followed might have suggested how serious he was, but as if the star-shaped flower was only for him, it faded away before she'd twisted around in her wheelchair to look. When she faced him again, her lightning-bolt eyebrows were furrowed sympathetically.

"Maybe *two* glasses of OJ might be in order," she said. "Deep breaths. We're in the home stretch. Breathe in. Breathe out. In, and out."

3.

THE WAD OF ground chuck hissed when the fry cook tossed it onto the griddle. Dwayne watched from his stool at the counter as the formless mass skittered and screeched as if still alive. The cook crushed it flat under a spatula before it could escape, forcing it into the shape he wanted.

Dwayne looked down at the grilled cheese on his plate and made himself take another bite, chewing mechanically. At least the coffee here was decent. It could use a little splash, but he didn't dare, not with his captain sitting right next to him.

Cleckley, apparently unbothered by the greasy smells and the fog of cigarette smoke, sawed into his ribeye. "Tell me again why setting up another surveillance team first would be a bad idea."

"It's in the proposal." Dwayne was unable to look at his friend's meal a second longer, that wrinkled skin of congealing grease and watery blood.

"I know," Cleckley said, "but I want you to tell me. No statistics and time tables, a simple explanation why you feel *this* approach, this time, will actually get us somewhere."

"We can't risk spooking Metzger again. This needs to be done with precision, and fast. Getting in close, I'll get what we need and get out before he catches on. Or before someone has the chance to let him know what we're up to." Dwayne glanced around the diner, distrustful of every ear, every set of eyes. "You know this will work."

The captain set down his fork and knife and worked a napkin through his hands. "So you're planning on waltzing in saying you're the meter man?"

"I'll rent an apartment. I'll need somewhere I can listen in, after the wiretap is set up."

"When's the last time you talked to that kid of yours?"

"Last week." Is that right?

"She like her new school?"

Dwayne turned to look his captain in the face. "What are you getting at?"

"I'm asking you how your kid's doing."

"She's doing fine, David."

"That's good. I'm glad to hear it." Cleckley put his attention back on his steak, his knife grating sharply on the plate. The noise set Dwayne's teeth on edge. "My boys are doing fine too, in case you were curious."

"How's Suzanne?"

"Good. She asks about you."

"Tell her I appreciate that."

"I will. Let me send someone with you."

"Out of the question. I don't know who Metzger's gotten to in the department." Dwayne leaned in, ignoring the reek of his captain's meal filling his nose. "I only typed up the proposal as a formality—and because I know, with you, once a bureaucrat, always a bureaucrat."

Spearing it with his fork, Cleckley steered his next bite around the plate to mop up the blood and grease. "I fed it to the shredder before I left tonight."

Dwayne leaned to take out his wallet. "Thanks for wasting my time."

Cleckley snapped a Pennsylvania driver's license onto the counter that, while it had Dwayne's picture on it, bore a different name.

"Who's Daniel Owen Wells?" Dwayne asked.

"You."

The name was hazily familiar. "Was this somebody?"

"Not anymore." Cleckley tucked a twenty under the corner of his plate and stood. "One week. Do *not* let yourself lose track of time."

* * *

As far as the rest of the department was concerned, Dwayne was just taking a personal leave, no need to worry. This meant he'd need to gather his equipment off the books. The day his "vacation" was to begin, he went down to Evidence.

They'd busted a guy who'd installed waterproof micro-cameras in his bathroom to record his stepdaughter in the shower. The creep's trial was in eight months. Dwayne hoped he'd have the cameras back long before then. From another bin, a lock-pick gun that'd been bagged after a liquor store robbery left both clerk and mugger dead. It wouldn't be missed. Some seething electronics whiz got caught tapping his ex-wife's landline. Dwayne pocketed the homebrew wiretap device and its tangle of wires.

13

He stopped shaving, and dyed his hair dark as a raven's wing. He bought some clothes from Goodwill and washed none of them. He'd wear them stinking of the cologne of dead old men and mothballs. It took work breaking the ramrod posture the sisters at Saint Anthony's had beaten into him, but nursing a glass, he paced his living room in a sore, shuffling gait until it was habit, whisky helping to quicken the metamorphosis.

He attempted to take in his surroundings, his home, how a stranger might. As if he'd just wandered out of the night to the one-story house and found the door unlocked. This was the home of a lonely man, Dan Wells determined about Dwayne. He studied the scars people will give a house, the evidence of lives lived. The height chart in the pantry doorway that recorded the incremental growth of a little girl named Jamie, starting at age four. The marks stopped after age ten, but she still existed somewhere. Taller than this, just not here. All pictures of her are in boxes, put away. Dwayne loved her, Dan Wells knew, but that love hurt him, and now he only thinks about his daughter when he's in the state where he's willing to risk traveling to the memory minefield—which is to say, not very often. The number of empty bottles in the recycling bin under the sink speaks to that. He self-insulates as often as he self-isolates. He has no actual friends, no family. He does not enjoy his own company but has learned over the years to tolerate and ignore himself, like a bad smell one eventually gets used to the more time they spend steeped in it.

The number of deadbolts on the front door suggest how his job, day by day, showed him in vivid detail how ugly the world could be. The thought that some of that ugliness might find its way to his door and slink uninvited into his family's sanctuary scared him more than anything. Living alone now, he seldom locks the door. He does not think about this. This is non-deliberate negligence. Though he prefers to be alone, he does not care who or what may visit, regardless of their intent for him. To be shot while asleep would be an end more pleasant than many police officers he'd personally known had received. Back when the front door didn't have so many deadbolts and chains, Dwayne had carried Sarah over the threshold. Thirteen years later, he watched her stepping over that same threshold, carrying boxes of her things out to the car. Each time she came back in to fetch another load, he wished she'd stop, look at him, and say she'd changed her mind, that was she was going to stay, but she didn't. When she was done and pulled the door closed behind her, with half of the house empty of its belongings and two-thirds of its people, the final click of the bolt echoed—and it still echoed, he felt, if he only listened for it.

There were dark squares on the living room wall where the afternoon sun had faded everything around the pictures, now gone, leaving the stain of their shape. The nails waited to hold up new snapshots but Dwayne, it seemed, hadn't experienced much lately that he wanted to be reminded of. In the master bedroom, the paint was damaged as well. A spot where the headboard had rubbed some of it away from rhythmic scraping—scraping that had become infrequent, then nonexistent. Love's abandonment of this house had been gradual. A slow leak. Maybe it'd been quicker for Sarah. Dan Wells wondered if there was a specific moment she'd stopped loving him; if she'd looked over at him while they were grocery shopping, or lying in bed, or driving somewhere with hopes of being reminded what fun was, and thought, It's gone.

Running his finger down the scratched portion in the paint, feeling the house's sub-dermal layer, Dan Wells wondered what the walls might say about Dwayne and his family if they could speak. Or if the walls weren't capable of forming opinions or divulging any gossip, what they might repeat instead, things overheard. Flimsy reassurances that life was going to be okay once Dwayne got Metzger put away—and similar flat platitudes and outright lies—probably made up the bulk of what the man told his wife. Dan Wells imagined that Dwayne probably often told his daughter how much he loved her, and meant it. His wife probably issued a fair amount of warnings and pleas for him to get himself together, with patience and care sometimes and, when things got particularly dire, without the softness he didn't deserve anyway.

The kitchen walls would probably echo a fair number of "Happy Birthday" renditions (to go along with the height chart in the pantry doorway, as was the tradition), maybe Dwayne whistling a jaunty tune while making coffee the morning after a night of good, deeply connected lovemaking with Sarah. The living room walls might reiterate dozens of arguments while simultaneously, in the first bedroom on the left up the hall, those walls would recall a young girl's muffled weeping.

If they could, what might the walls replay of the last two years of Dwayne's life for Dan Wells? After refilling his glass, he glared at the nothing he'd tripped over and put his ear to the living room's floral-print wallpaper to try. Silence, which made sense. Dwayne didn't strike Dan Wells as the kind of guy who goes around talking to himself. Maybe twice a week a metallic crack as a fresh bottle was broken open, another half-gallon in the tank for his fifty-year sojourn toward cirrhosis. Or maybe some brief laughter when something on TV hit Dwayne on just the right day in just the right mood—but it didn't seem like that happened all that often. Silence, then. Silence while Dwayne went about his nights performing his thoughtless after-work routines alone, trying to convince himself that when he caught Gerald Metzger, he'd stop drowning himself—as he sloppily poured himself another. It'd be a waste not to finish it, do I look like I'm made of money? Silence as he told himself how, once clean living seemed like it'd stick, he'd start calling Sarah and Jamie more often, get those communication lines open and flowing again. Once that became ingrained in his routine and Sarah ceased giving the impression she was in a hurry to get off the line, maybe he'd suggest they come back home, see if giving things another try might be possible. If so, he might put in a request to change departments. Ride a desk, punch a clock, come home, be Dwayne the husband, Dwayne the dad, make *them* the priority over work, and become the family man in cop's clothing and not the other way around, as things had been since . . . however long it'd been since he'd started losing himself.

This had to work. If the walls could give Dan Wells their opinion about things they'd seen and overheard in the last few weeks, they might say they're growing concerned. How when he cleans his gun every Saturday afternoon he'll sometimes pause with the reassembled, reloaded firearm in his hands, stare ahead at nothing as if he's briefly shut off, and without fail issue a tiny gasp as he snaps back into himself, then promptly puts the gun in another room and closes the door on it, out of sight, out of mind. Again, this had to work.

"Dan Wells, pleased to meet you," Dwayne told his glassy-eyed double in the bathroom mirror. "Dan Wells," the man on the other side of the looking glass said. "Pleased to meet you."

✳ ✳ ✳

On an overcast morning in February, he took a car from the impound that was nearing its sheriff's sale, crossed town, turned onto Bergen Street, and pulled into the Dunsany Arms parking lot. A place where nineteen missing persons cases, all filed in the last year, came to a dead end, trail cold, and had provided the setting for fifty-five homicides since it started taking on tenants in 1984, one occurring only three days after it'd opened its doors— the starter pistol, as if the place was always meant to be shadowed.

A prolific arsonist had called Dunsany Arms his home. Torching himself to avoid apprehension, according to what Dwayne overheard in the precinct break room, the firebug got halfway into singing "Gloomy Sunday" before his vocal cords snapped from the heat. An online trafficker of illegal digital material had been backtraced to Dunsany Arms, where nine terabytes of stomach-turning photos and videos were discovered across a well-organized archive of external hard drives. The first victim of the Millcreek Mangler had the misfortune of calling Dunsany Arms her home. On the stand, sobbing as he angled for an insanity plea, the Mangler claimed he'd been a model citizen up to that point in his life, a person who'd never even lied on a job application, but while out driving around one day, "Something said take this next left, then the next right. And I parked there, at the curb. It felt like I was supposed to, *had* to. Minute I saw her come out of the building to get in her car, it was like a movie. I saw everything I'd do—to her, and the other . . . thirty-five. It was like I'd been led there by something that wanted me to catch up to what I was always going to be. And things just sort of . . . started happening around me, to me."

Crossing the lot through the ankle-deep snow, Dwayne looked up the building's gray face, feeling eyes on him from every window. Entering through the front, he noticed that while there was a buzzer, the glass door had been helpfully chocked open with a car battery. Inside it was as cold, if not colder, than it was outside. He'd forgotten the pervading smell of urine until it hit him like a wall. The lobby was barren save for the neck of a security camera mount hanging severed, wires dangling. And though the call button was still aglow, it seemed the manager had yet to get the elevators fixed—the hand-written sign reading *I called the guy* hadn't moved. Graffiti artists had incorporated the walls' deep gouges and impact-dents into their tableaus, unsavory images all. Most of the fluorescents were out; the rest stuttered and droned.

Dwayne knocked at the door marked MANAGEMENT. A dog barked from within. Quite a large one, given the power behind its throaty, angry woofs.

Having met the building manager during the two previous failed raids, this would serve as Dan Wells' trial run. The door opened a crack, and a lined, leathery face let its glare ask what Dwayne wanted.

"Dan Wells. Pleased to meet you. I called earlier?"

No sign of recognition surfaced on the old man's mug. He turned away to whisper kindly into the apartment, "I'll be right back, sweetie," before snatching up a ring of keys the size of a Buick's engine block.

Leading Dwayne up a dim staircase, every few steps a glass capsule would pop under their feet, sending shards tinkling toward the basement. The manager—whose name Dwayne took to be Leslie Rider, given that was what was stitched onto his jacket's breast in red thread—offered no explanation as to how his building found itself in such a wanting state, instead only pointed out which steps were untrustworthy and best avoided.

"Got a dog?" the building manager said.

"No, but it sounds like you've got one big fella, though. Rottweiler?"

"Pit bull. And I only let me keep mine for security purposes. I don't want any cats in here either. Fish, snakes, gerbils, none of that shit. We clear?"

"Understood." What about crocodiles?

On the second-floor landing, they passed a slim, barefoot individual in sweatpants and a T-shirt so threadbare Dwayne could count the bumps of their spine. In a hushed conspiratorial tone, they were quietly informing the space where the walls joined, "He said *she* said that the little boy said the woman had said then *he* said then she said then he said . . ."

Leslie gave the person a wide berth and continued up the stairs, as if this was nothing unusual. Only once at the door to the third floor did he tell Dwayne, "Don't waste any time worrying. They live with their mother here. According to her, they used to write kids' books or some such."

Dwayne glanced back down the stairwell at the former author whispering their endless yarn to the wall. "Then she said then *he* said then *she* said . . ."

Passing door after door on the third floor, various stinks hit Dwayne. Forgotten food blackening on a stove, baby shit. TVs blasting studio audience laughter, action movie mayhem, and one sound that was too clear to be coming from a TV. A young man, crying behind the door of apartment 305. Apparently, they would be Dwayne's across-the-hall neighbor.

RIP had been spray painted on the door to apartment 306 in red letters, Dwayne couldn't help but notice.

"I'll come up and sand that off when I get time," Leslie murmured, sorting through his keys.

While he waited, Dwayne looked down the hallway. Three floors above, apartment 603. The den of the krokodil.

"You want to see it or not? I don't got all day."

Following the manager in, Dwayne breathed 306's musty air. Leslie flipped the light-switch, and a single florescent halo above gave a faltering blue-white radiance to the cracked walls and grimy, well-trod carpet. A sliding glass door let out onto a leaning balcony that overlooked a courtyard boxing in a leafless black gnarl of a tree, a rusty swing-set, some wind-tossed plastic furniture, and a grill being held hostage to a pipe by a bike chain.

Remaining near the exit, the building manager used one of his many keys to pick at a clump of dried plaster on his thumb that resembled a miniature head of cauliflower. Maybe my new landlord's a sculptor in his spare time. Flicking the dot of dislodged plaster onto Dwayne's carpet, Leslie said, "Rent's four-fifty a month. Utilities aren't included. Elevators are on the fritz right now, but laundry's in the basement. I can show you that too, if you feel you need to see it."

"I can find it."

Leslie looked Dan Wells over again. "Just get out?"

Dwayne put on his best "crestfallen," and nodded as if self-ashamed.

"Working, I hope."

"Sorenson Steel, out off fifteen."

"I know it," Leslie said. "What do they got you doing?"

"Lathe operator." Dwayne knew Dan Wells' make-believe life inside and out.

The building manager's wattle crinkled under his chin as he nodded, satisfied. Perhaps remembering something, Leslie's small, watery eyes flicked to something above Dwayne. Following his gaze, Dwayne saw the nicotine-yellowed ceiling bore a patch the diameter of a basketball, the plaster bright white, recent. And under him, a wide pink ring amid the filthy carpet. "If you start feeling blue," Leslie said, "you go and you *see* somebody about it. Can't always think yourself better."

"All right."

"Don't go punching holes in the walls and shit, no loud music." As to the high-tempo beat currently bleeding through the wall, thrumming Dwayne's lungs, the manager either chose not to hear it or was so acclimatized he was immune. "Well? You interested?"

"I'll take it."

From paint-spattered dungarees, Leslie produced some crinkled forms and plucked the pen from over his ear.

While Dwayne put down Dan Wells' false information, he thought he'd test his cover's resilience. "Police come here often?"

"No more than anyplace else." Roughly taking the agreement back, Leslie dragged open the warped door. "You go back in, I won't hold your crap." Sending three keys bouncing across the kitchen counter, he rattled off as he exited, "Other two are for your mailbox and the building herself, don't make copies. Rent's due on the first by nine PM, no excuses. And even when you're in, wouldn't be a bad idea keeping this locked." The door closed.

The kitchen and bathroom faucets would only drool yellow water that smelled like eggs. The floor of the shower was ready to collapse into the apartment below. The electric stove's burners wouldn't turn orange. There was a mount *for* a microwave. The fridge's interior was thickly lined with black mold.

"Home, sweet home."

Returning outside to haul up his things, Dwayne found it snowing again, his borrowed transportation already half-buried. He'd gotten a buzz from going successfully unrecognized by the building manager—but it was broken when he closed the car trunk, seeing a boy no older than eight watching him through the rusting spindles of a balcony railing a few floors up. Dwayne freed a hand to wave. In reply, the boy—shirtless despite the plunging temperatures—closed one eye for better aim down the barrel of his finger.

Dragging in the trash bag he would've used for a suitcase whether he was playing a role or not, Dwayne tugged on the closet light's pull-cord and surveyed its emptiness. He noticed marks in the far back corner, near the floor. Drawings in blue crayon. Cadet blue, if he was right recalling the trademarked shade from his daughter's Crayolas. Birds in flight, simplified to M-shaped waves, the same way he himself had drawn birds as a kid.

Even something as innocuous as a drawing of a bird dragged a memory to the surface, one he didn't hesitate kicking back into its grave. Not now. Not tonight.

From the trash bag, he retrieved a wrinkled T-shirt and started pulling it over his head, momentarily blindfolding himself with the faded cotton that stank like strangers. When he emerged from the shirt's neck hole, up the short hallway, someone inside his apartment side-stepped from view.

Dwayne froze, the shirt only halfway on, one arm through. He couldn't be sure he'd seen what he'd seen, it'd happened so fast. Even with every light on in the apartment, shadows remained abundant in the corners.

"Is someone out there?" he said. Before joining Narcotics, he'd investigated a number of B&Es that'd yielded bloody results. He wondered how many deaths immediately followed a homeowner asking the same question he'd just asked.

From the bedroom doorway, he could see his bottle of Maker's on the kitchen counter, making him briefly consider if now, at the worst possible time, he was starting to develop DTs. What a great fucking venue for hallucinating. He also noticed his gun, in its holster, was out there in the kitchen as well—closer to them than to him.

Frustrated he'd let something like a trick of the light get under his skin, Dwayne stomped out into the living room, letting them know he was coming, but no one was there. He'd kept the front door locked as the building manager had advised. Same with the sliding glass door. He joined his reflection in the glass, cupping his hands around his eyes to see past himself. Nothing but unblemished snow on the balcony.

Dwayne told Dan Wells, "You're all right. Just some pre-game jitters."

He set an alarm on his phone. He'd sleep away the remainder of the afternoon to be sharp for his all-nighter.

Using his jacket as a pillow, he lay looking up at the living room's buzzing fluorescent halo until its blue after-image floated everywhere else he looked—even eclipsing the oblong ceiling patch that, to Dwayne's eye, appeared to be the work of a twelve-gauge. Realizing he was lying in the pink-stained portion of the carpet, he shifted over. It didn't mean he wasn't lying where someone else had died, but out of respect, he'd avoid the most obvious.

4.

CONNIE WIECZNE COULD hear her new next-door neighbor through the wall, walking around, talking to himself. When he'd gone quiet, she figured he was likely taking a nap. After all, from the glimpse she got of him out the window earlier as he lugged in his things (he wasn't fooling anybody dying his hair that dark), he looked old, maybe around her dad's age. Old enough that naps were probably something the new tenant looked forward to, maybe even served as the highlight of his tired days. Connie didn't care for naps. Most people who suffer from night terrors don't like allowing their unconscious mind to take the wheel. But when she'd surrender to the fact that sleep was necessary, *anywhere but here, anywhere but here* was her before-bed Dorothy mantra. She couldn't move her feet enough to click her heels anymore. Maybe that's why she kept waking up in apartment 308. Alas.

Out of courtesy for the new neighbor and the self-escape she assumed he was presently trying to obtain, she lowered her stereo's volume and, with a forward throw of her arms, moved her wheelchair to the window that overlooked the building's parking lot. She watched the man, right on time, exit the building and crunch through the ankle-deep snow, stop under the lamp post, turn around, look at her a moment, then get in his car and leave—as he always did. There was something familiar about his face this time, though not necessarily because she'd watched him leave every night at the same time for what felt like forever. Without fail, he always looked up here, at her window, before getting in his car and driving away, leaving a perfect black rectangle of bare asphalt where his beat-up car had denied the snow to collect. She remained at the window, watching the black rectangle get filled in one flake at a time—a correction.

The city of Erie gets lake-effect snowstorms, which can be real fuckers if you're not accustomed to them. Take the forecasted snowfall for anywhere else in the state and double it. Then, once the lake's frozen over

22

and you happen to be facing the wrong way at the wrong moment when a strong wind comes blasting down from Canada, your eyes will freeze to marbles in your head. Why the fuck do any of us live here, stuffed inside a snowman's asshole? Maybe it was the fear of departing from the cozy box in which we were hatched, like most people Connie went to high school with (three of whom, last she heard, were still trying to make it as hip-hop stars, using their parents' basements as impromptu recording spaces), or maybe we end up fastened to a place because of family ties, family ropes, family cast-iron shackles, family cement shoes. Or work does it—as was the case with Connie. Why couldn't she have gotten trapped someplace where snow's something only seen on TV? Well, Connie can hear them now, "That's what vacation is for," those happy in their cages will merrily whisper with their faces pressed between bars hewn from vulcanized student loans and mortgages and car payments.

A nice idea, absolutely, but Connie couldn't take a vacation. There was nothing but the job, these four walls, and the ceaseless toil to be tended betwixt. The word "prisoner" was never used in her presence, but that didn't mean anything; labels can be stuck on invisibly—like KICK ME on your back, but more permanent than a tattoo. Especially if you happen to be remotely good at anything. The mules need body mods. The minute a junkie has two nickels to rub together, they want a tattoo. And when they have *three* nickels to rub together, they'll need to be vigilantly shepherded back from the edge of death so Metzger can shove them toward it again. The pounds of necrotized tissue she must've scraped off her patients and sent down the garbage chute, poured into repurposed bodega bags.

She had a recurring nightmare that would start in a kind of floaty, disembodied POV peeking into the dumpster down in the basement. Another bagged load falls from the chute, slapping heavily upon the others, another tithe of sacrificed flesh that addiction and dedication to Metzger demanded be sloughed from the flock. Then the bags of bad begin to split, letting the loose, stinking contents pour themselves out in a slow-motion tumult of wrecked skin. Together, they form a flesh-collage homunculus. It gasps in horror of itself as it comes awake within Connie's dream. An inky hate sloshes in its wrong heart. Fueled by it, it gracelessly climbs from its trash-bin womb, a toddler escaping a crib, and, blind and moaning, it ploddingly ascends the stairs to the third floor, rage its only compass. It has kicked down her door many times over many nightmares. On lucky occasions, Connie wakes before the abomination can squelch across her living room to her, her chair's wheels refusing to turn, denying her escape. Other times, when her REM cycle decides to play the mean-spirited jailor, she can only stare up at the reanimated krok-rotted viscera as it takes its time pushing a gray finger against her throat until her enviably unblemished skin gives. A hollow snap and all her life trickles down her front and dribbles off the sides of her wheelchair.

Connie didn't require any deep-dive journey of introspection to get the point her subconscious was trying to make. Oh, she was aware, but there'd been stories about people who broke Gerald Metzger's trust. They don't even look human when they're found, floating in the lake or wrapped inside a carpet under an overpass. *I'm exactly where I led myself.*

Maybe she'd been a little judgy, she considered. The wannabe hip-hop stars at least likely have fun while they waste their time. She didn't even have that. Had she ever, at any point, enjoyed her life? Jesus, what a fucking question to ask yourself. No wonder she kept the radio or TV on all the time, if *this* is the kind of shit that'll pop into her head when it's quiet.

She turned away from the window and looked at the parallel lines her chair's wheels had pressed into the carpet's worn pile, tracing from the kitchen to the sofa, sofa to bathroom, bathroom to window, sofa to bedroom, bedroom to bathroom, bedroom to kitchen, bedroom to sofa, all the miles she'd traveled one throw of her arms at a time within this homely box of less than five hundred square feet. The patch of carpet near the door to the hall was less traveled. She couldn't remember the last time she'd even gone down to the lobby, or upstairs to see Gerry in person instead of just taking orders from him over the phone. She had her hands clamped on her wheels, ready to steer herself toward the door, to leave the apartment, but then removed them and idly scratched at the armrest, frozen in fear and indecision. *You're okay. You're home.*

She'd tell her patients when they started freaking out, "Breathe *in.* Breathe *out.* In, and out." She tried it now, and it worked. For the most part.

Following the parallel ruts in the carpet that strung from the window to the kitchen, she turned the little plastic spigot on the box of merlot, filled a coffee mug, and savored the pleasant burning in her nose as she exhaled after the sip. She paused with the cup lifted halfway to her lips again, thinking about how odd it was that the wine didn't taste corked even though she'd bought the box, whenever that'd been. By their own volition, her thoughts began considering if "corked" would even be the correct term for wine that comes in a box, because boxed wine doesn't have a cork, but she forced herself to focus, to remember when *exactly* she'd bought this particular box—but she couldn't recall the last time she'd left her apartment, much less the building.

Let's think. It wasn't uncommon for her to have upwards of three glasses a night—all right, fine, lately it'd been more—but right there, printed on the front of the box, it says it contains five liters, the equivalent of thirty-four glasses. She picked up the box by its cardboard handle, weighing it and giving it a shake to hear the contents slosh around within. Without tearing open the packaging to check the plastic bladder inside, she couldn't be certain, but it still felt full. Usually it's when the box became disconcertingly light that she worried about herself, but now, it's how unnaturally heavy it was that bothered her.

Maybe it wouldn't be the worst idea to take a break, she thought, and ripped open the box and draped the bulging bladder over the edge of the sink. It resembled a kidney, red and plump. She opened the spigot all the way and watched the river of cheap merlot go down the drain, the kidney-shaped bladder collapsing and wrinkling as it slowly disgorged itself.

Watching the crimson whirlpool spin, she thought about her life before she'd gotten wrapped up with Gerry Metzger through a friend of a friend. The day she met him, he sat across from her in that crowded Starbucks, smiled, and asked, "If you could wish for one thing, what would it be?" Going back farther, she thought about her life, and who she used to be, before she'd dropped out of veterinarian school after half-assing her way through two years of it, and even her life before the wheelchair. High school. Connie had been a two-fold teenage entrepreneur who sold loosie cigarettes in the student parking lot after class for a quarter a pop, and to cater to the non-smokers, she'd offer palm readings. She took both business branches seriously, only shoplifting brand-name cigarettes and studying up every night to ensure she'd be giving accurate palm readings. It didn't take her long to learn it was helpful to approach face-to-face transactions with a sense of showmanship. Selling a loosie cigarette couldn't be made all that lively, except maybe through some sleight-of-hand, but that could easily backfire if a customer was in the throes of a serious nic-fit (which did serve as a lesson on how best to wrangle junkies later in life). But with palmistry, adding a little drama would often lead to a decent tip and some good word-of-mouth. (Example: If the pad of a person's thumb is flat, that might mean they handle cash wherever they work. You can also tell if a person handles cash if you saw that individual manning a cash register at the local grocery store over summer break.) Sometimes it pays—literally—to have a forgettable face. She knew so many of her classmates' names, what neighborhoods they lived in, what kind of car they drove or what number bus they took, even though many of them probably couldn't have even given you her first name. She didn't mind. She liked watching people, witnessing from afar doomed courtships playing out beginning to end over a single week, the cliques congealing and disbanding, *solve et coagula*.

"The hash marks on the first and second knuckles of your fingers mean you like blondes. Is that true?" And she'd smile as the boy's friends elbow each other and go *ooh* and *ah*, never mind that Connie had furtively watched the quarterback systematically break the heart of every tow-headed cheerleader on the school's squad. For those interested, those little marks actually mean you tend to recklessly charge into relationships—romantic, business, or otherwise. If you have those marks, you're probably broke and/or have an STD.

"You heard right, it's a quarter a smoke—but I'll give you five for a buck. Good deal, right? Thanks for your patronage."

"The more triangles you have in your hand's grooves, the more psychic you are. Rumor has it Miss Cleo has like a *thousand* on her right hand."

"This is the hand you write with? Okay, hold it loosely, like you're asleep. Let the fingers curl a little. Now, see these little lines on the outside edge of your palm here, directly below the crease of your pinky? Each of those lines represents a kid you'll potentially have in your lifetime." Connie told this to a girl who, she remembered, *really* liked that section in home ec where everyone had to take care of a robo-baby—to the point she'd openly bawled when it was time to surrender her adopted circuit-hearted progeny at the assignment's end. The girl was overjoyed to learn she'd possibly have up to six kids, and gave Connie double her usual rate of five dollars for the news. That one hadn't been a lie. That's what those lines actually mean. Go ahead, look.

Of course, as word started to gain traction around school, there were some who started remembering Connie's face. Years later, Connie would become intimately familiar with the sad fact that the mind will reliably hold the imprint of those we despise much more clearly than those we favor. Even now she can see them—lips curled in that haughty, disgusted sneer, contempt burning in their eyes for she who dared to step off the assembly line. She'd think about what they said to her many times, long after graduation. Including the overcast Thursday morning when she tried to kill herself a few years ago, a period in her life when the opinions she held about herself were even crueler than the cutting words of those awful, awful girls.

Anyway, when she had enough profits from the smokes and decrypting heart-lines, she'd walk to Waldenbooks in the strip mall near her house, pass the mushy young adult fare without a second look, and weave her way to the back corner the store seemed to be intent on hiding, the same section in which she'd found *Palm-Reading for Beginners*. Shelf by shelf, she devoured books about the most haunted places in America, books about UFOs, books on Tarot that came packaged with a deck ready to go, and biographies of famous occultists such as Aleister Crowley, Gerald Gardner, Eliphas Levi, Austin Osman Spare, Algernon Blackwood (who also wrote some stellar fiction she enjoyed), and the indomitable Helena Blavatsky. Connie had no qualms about procuring her inventory of cigarettes illegally, but she'd never steal a book. One has to have standards, after all. Otherwise, what are we?

During one semester, she went from being a tree-whispering green witch to a hedge witch, learning she could brew certain kinds of herbs together and, in lieu of a broom handle in order to "fly," soak a tampon in the concoction like one would a tea bag. She had many interesting afternoons communing with the cosmos before her parents got home from work. She dabbled in universe-tweaking chaos magick, drawing and burning sigils. She went up to the roof and chanted at the moon. She started squirreling away crystals all over the apartment—one of which she'd forgotten to remove from under her bed, resulting in the untimely death of the vacuum cleaner. She couldn't stop learning. But she still felt, all along, she hadn't found quite what she was looking for, though with every loosie cig and palm reading she sold to buy another book, she was getting a little bit closer to catching up with her true self waiting patiently ahead.

The day after her sixteenth birthday, with some money from Grandma burning a hole in her pocket, Connie entered Waldenbooks for the first time with a feeling of dread instead of the usual joy. She approached the spine of the one book she'd been avoiding during her months of witchy self-education. Given its strikingly audacious title, the blood-red pentagram on its cover, and the infamy it held, the book, by all rights, should've been irresistible to her. She still hesitated, speculating whether some notoriety was well-placed. With nothing else left to read, it was either complete the New Age section by buying this final book, or return to the tedious arena of the more age-suitable *Tiger Beat*. Learning it was foolish to think she could place the volume face-down so the clerk would only scan the barcode on the back, Connie gave the clearly disappointed Waldenbooks employee her money and, on the bus ride home, cracked open the work of Anton Szandor LaVey.

Hiding the cover from her fellow passengers with her jacket, in less than twenty pages she discovered this was, of all the New Age she'd read, where she should've originally started. There was nothing frightening inside. Instead, Connie found that much of what LaVey had to say were things she'd secretly been holding up as personal truths for so long. Sadly, a great deal of those secret truths she'd felt ashamed for harboring, but now she knew that shame had been needless, because marking a human being's most natural inclinations as bad only benefitted those who trafficked in the wonder salves, drug-peddlers of their own kind who only wanted to keep the world obediently cowed. LaVey made it clear he was appalled by that ilk. He wrote passionately, occasionally wrathfully, toward those deserving of it and, to Connie's surprise, some of the passages were genuinely funny. She hadn't expected to be laughing while reading such an infamous book. Sins, she learned, were perfectly okay to indulge in, because for each sin there is a counter-sin that will automatically balance out the other. Pride will counteract gluttony, because Man's the only creature that suffers from vanity. And lust will naturally counteract sloth, because when you spend any time lazily lying around you'll eventually want to engage in the greatest indoor activity—either alone, with another, or with multiple others—and after the deed's complete, nobody wants to lie around in the mess once the afterglow's dimmed.

It wasn't about worshipping any red-skinned, horned antagonist with a pointy tail. There was no baby-eating, no bathing in the blood of virgins. That couldn't be further from the truth. It was about worshipping *yourself* as a god, relying on your *own* inner strength to buoy you while wading through life's bullshit, instead of begging an imaginary friend to throw down a golden rope. Self-reliance, self-actualization. Determination. Harnessing your integrity and strength and cranking your take-no-shit attitude up to eleven. Be a reliable, upstanding person *despite* the fact there's no goodies waiting for you in the afterlife. All of this, and packaged in a very heavy metal aesthetic too. This she liked, a lot. The inconspicuous mass market was a compact library of blazing insights that could fit in her pocket. Before the bus had reached her stop, it felt like her own adamantine gates had opened and now, bathed by the heretofore trapped light of the Morningstar, she was comfortably crowded around by like-minds, because anyone who picked up this book and lived by its knowledge was a friend. When she returned upstairs to her parents' apartment, a skip in her step and her heart singing, out went the crystals and the dream-catchers—though she held on to the Tarot cards. She'd found her path.

Seventeen years later, much changed, she pulled down from her bookshelf the battered, dog-eared mass market with its torn cover, fuzzy with Post-It notes sticking out all over. It'd been with her during her time in the hospital, though she hid it under her pillow whenever the nurse came in or her parents visited, and it was with her now. Though the unenlightened might accuse that reading Anton LaVey was why she'd ended up in Dunsany Arms as a prisoner-but-not-a-prisoner, Connie did not. Failing to heed his suggestions about holding on to one's integrity may've actually resulted in her agreeing to things she shouldn't have—all of which, naturally, had sounded very appealing to her at the time. It was almost like Gerry had used her trick against her. Peered into her palm and given a pitch-perfect rendition of precisely what she wanted to hear. She let herself, day by day, get further tied by him, roped, shackled, fitted with cement shoes. There'd been no punishment for cutting off communication with her mother and father, but if she tried to do the same to Gerry, there would be. She knew this. Swift and catastrophic.

Eyes closed, she shuffled her Tarot deck and snapped down a single card on her chair's armrest. And with a dread more powerful than that which had chewed at her heart before picking up that final book on the New Age shelf, she flipped the card over.

The Ten of Swords. Fuck. Something horrible is soon to happen, is in the process of unfolding, or has recently happened. She may also be hesitating to accept a painful change, to her own detriment. At this, her dread did not abate. Instead, validated and bolstered, it sharpened to a hot, bristling mass between her lungs.

As was also part of her nightly ritual before bed besides the single-card draw, after she'd changed clothes and brushed her teeth, she unfolded the knife she kept hidden under her unfeeling left thigh and cut another mark on her bathroom wall among the purple flowers of the wallpaper, marking that day's death of the sun. She made the mark out of habit, though she'd stopped counting them some time ago. As much as her eyes wanted her to sit in here and count them all, she flicked off the light and wheeled herself back to the window again, seeing that the car had reappeared sometime when she hadn't been paying attention. The man who always looked up here had come back, but his vehicle had left no tracks betraying either his return or his departure, though the latter had occurred only a few minutes ago. The snow was falling steadily, yes, but it couldn't have erased deep tire tracks that quickly. It was like he'd never left, though she'd seen him do so, same as he did every night, the one part of her before-bed ritual she had no influence over but felt she'd miss something if she didn't witness it nonetheless.

The dread remained, unchanged.

Connie set her chair's brakes, transferred herself onto the couch, and dragged her legs to join the rest of her, manually crossing them at the ankle. She lay, holding close the book she'd bought when she was sixteen, looking up at the water-stained ceiling. Of course, she wasn't safe in her dreams either. The homunculus, in pieces, was waiting to rebuild itself. Please, one night without it. If I can't take a vacation for real, let a night with an empty head serve as one. Please. She closed her eyes and imagined her dream-self clicking her ruby-red heels, listening to the boxed wine trickle down the drain, being drunk by the building the same as it'd leached so much of her life.

Anywhere but here. Anywhere but here.

5.

H I S H E A R T W A S pounding when he woke, but he couldn't recall the dream. Maybe that was for the best. Careful of his back, Dwayne rose and went out onto the balcony. Across the courtyard, some silhouettes sat on sofas or recliners, motionless and backlit to shadow people by flickering TV screens, while others ranted and raved at one another. Though the shouts were diluted to near incomprehensibility by distance and wind, the weighty anger in the voices still rang clear. Dwayne let himself miss Sarah and Jamie a moment. He hoped Jamie was liking Cleveland.

He checked his phone. 2:21 AM. As promised, Dwayne sent a text to his captain: I'm starting.

Cleckley must've been burning the midnight oil. Keep me posted.

Wrestling himself into his shoulder-holster, Dwayne checked his pistol and stole three deep pulls of Maker's. Stomach warm, he put his eye to the peephole. Seeing no one, he stepped across the hall and stuck one micro-camera above his neighbor's door—who was sobbing again, or was *still* sobbing.

Back inside, door locked, Dwayne checked the feed on his laptop. Grainy as hell, but he'd be able to see who, and how many, were outside his door if anyone knocked.

He filled his jacket pockets with everything he'd need for the next set of tasks. One last swallow of Maker's for the road, Dwayne locked up, and Dan Wells headed up the hall, head down, hands in his pockets.

Encountering no one in the stairwell, he climbed to the sixth floor. There weren't any whiffs of baby shit or stale cigarette smoke, but something else. Bad meat, chemicals, a bouquet Dwayne recognized immediately. The jawless man skulked in the corner of his mind. You kept me from hearing him.

Silence from each door he passed. Either Leslie kept the top floor largely unoccupied to avoid having to climb all the way up here every time something broke, or these tenants were some serious church mice. Dwayne glanced at each peephole he passed, feeling watched. Heel-toeing up the hall, he recalled Metzger's composure during the most recent raid. How he'd tracked everyone who passed before him, rarely blinking. To meet his gaze, it was like staring into the injection-mold face of a mannequin; nothing was felt. He couldn't help but imagine that Metzger saw everyone as ripening circulatory systems, ready to receive his product and become his customer, slave and, in time, monster.

Dwayne paused at an intricate labyrinth of wobbly black lines that'd been drawn onto the wall. It stretched from floor to ceiling and was wider than the span of his arms. It must've taken days. Abundant in dead ends and complex patterns colliding into other mad designs, there didn't seem to be any way for someone to *begin* an attempt at solving it—there was no break in the line making up the maze's outermost wall, which also meant there was no exit. But at the unreachable center, the impossible goal, were two words written so small and crushed in so tightly by the madness wreathing them, he almost hadn't noticed—and probably wouldn't have if his eye, like anybody's, hadn't naturally been drawn to see what lay at the labyrinth's dead center.

Mtahsab Belsharh.

He had no idea what that meant, or even what language it could be. He moved on, feeling like he had to drag his eyes away.

Turning the next corner, a short hallway crooked off to his right. The finger of winter caressed his unshaven cheek, and he saw a rickety set of stairs leading to a hatch above, propped open with a brick. City noise and a manic cawing of birds drifted in with the cold. Maybe Metzger did use carrier pigeons, he mused. He pressed on, reached the hallway's next corner—and the door to apartment 603 fell into sight. He sneaked up and jammed the second micro-camera onto the wall directly opposite, just above the doors of the defunct elevator.

Dwayne should've headed down to the basement and set up the wiretap, but before he'd even fully thought about it, he had his ear to Metzger's door. The smell of chemicals wafting out from underneath seared his sinuses. He wanted nothing more than to kick the door down, gun drawn. When a phone trilled, he recoiled as if heart-shot. Measuring his breaths, he leaned in again and listened.

A plasticky clatter, a phone receiver being snatched up. Metzger hacked, spat. "What."

If Dwayne had done the wiretap *before* the cameras, he could've recorded this conversation. Now he could only eavesdrop, listening as Metzger paced, drawing close to the door to the hallway.

Heart crashing against the roof of his mouth, Dwayne cleared the range of the peephole and unclasped his holster.

"I don't know," Metzger said. "Maybe tomorrow, late. Ryan needs time to recover." He moved away, into the deeper reaches of the apartment, maybe to survey the industrial ruins outside his window, his kingdom. "I said I don't know. They've been quiet this week. But you three can still come up if you want."

Shit. Come up?

Fighting his rising inclination to flee, Dwayne listened a moment longer. Metzger was saying, "—still the same shit, nothing new. But if you feel you gotta give the latest handful a listen, I'll buzz you in. Hold on."

Dwayne rushed back down the hall. He turned the corner—and stopped dead, hearing a creaking door hinge. From ahead or behind, he couldn't say. Sound carried strangely in Dunsany Arms. The roof access hatch stood at his left. Footsteps echoed from up the hall, more than one set. Mumbling conversation. He'd just gotten started; he couldn't alert Metzger. Not now.

Wind tore at his face, brought tears to his eyes, burned his lungs. He eased the hatch down and ducked to peek back inside. Six legs in dark denim scissored past.

Dwayne stood, scanned his surroundings. Steaming exhaust vents, a swarm of satellite dishes on the northmost tip of the Dunsany triangle—and beyond, Lake Erie glimmered in the distance, frozen and reflecting his hometown back at itself. He turned, facing what lay past the building's southern edge. Moonlit ruins, hard edges blunted by the blanketing snow. This was how the entire city would look, if Metzger got his way. A wasteland peopled by the krok-afflicted who, in their amaranthine wandering, would leave footprints and whatever had rotted to the point of sloughing off, begging for their next taste and the reassuring touch of Metzger, their god of chemicals.

The crows' infighting took an uptick. This wasn't the idle cawing for the sake of making noise, like the crows that populated his quiet cul-de-sac. These birds *screamed* at each other. The manic beating of countless wings disturbed him. When the wind rushed at Dwayne again—making him painfully aware of how high up he was—with it came the unmistakable scent of decay.

He crunched over the icy gravel and was momentarily blind, stepping through a wall of steam. The undulating oily mass scattered skyward, the crows vanishing instantly against the night.

Feathers danced across shallow red wells in the ice, drilled by spilled bird blood. The shredded lump was unrecognizable until he brought out his flashlight. A pecked hand and six inches of forearm, cleanly cut. The curled fingers had received the worst, with the remaining unpecked flesh carrying the deflated, corrugated texture of a habitual krokodil user.

He could quit his one-man surveillance mission and call in the arm. And if Metzger was responsible, maybe he didn't stop after relieving his victim of the one limb. It could be an arrest, a conviction of *something*— but it wouldn't be for the krok. Dwayne took a picture with his phone and used the edge of his boot to form a cairn of snow and roof gravel over the arm. He'd come bag it later.

Struggling down through the hatch, he found the sixth-floor hall empty. Peeking around the corner, Metzger's apartment door was closed, no activity. Dwayne hurried to the stairwell and started toward the basement, steps squeaky with melting snow, his huffing breaths steaming out ahead of him.

He passed the former author on the stair, murmuring again with their face crushed into the corner of the second-floor landing. "Then he said and she said that they said then he said then *she* said then he said . . . "

If they regularly occupied this spot—and it seemed they did—there was no telling what they might've overheard.

"Excuse me," Dwayne asked their turned back. "Could I ask you something?"

" . . . he said then I said *leave me alone* then she said and the little boy said the woman said that he said and . . . "

"Thanks for your time."

As he continued his descent, the incongruous mixture of mildew and flowery detergent thickened around him. Directly across from the stairwell door was the cramped, humid laundry room. Only one dryer was running, its load badly unbalanced. It wildly canted forward and back, sending violent clangs about a basement comprised of low, narrow corridors—oil-black puddles pooled in low spots, while pale fingers of calcium build-up dripped from above.

His flashlight beam settled on an ashen face leering at him, three empty voids making up its eyes and mouth. Dwayne looked at the plaster head resting on the seat of an abandoned wheelchair, and was initially angry at himself that it'd given him such a start. He could assume the head was homemade given that it appeared to be papier-mâché, perhaps formed around a balloon, then given its graven pallor first with craft paint then years of dust, abandoned like the many art projects Sarah had half-started, still occupying Dwayne's own basement in plastic totes, though his ex-wife's craftwork was mostly stuff to arrange about the house around Christmastime—so many goddamn pinecones—not leering ashen-faced heads with the eye sockets raggedly cut with what must've been an awfully dull blade.

Junkies just do weird shit sometimes, he concluded—but he didn't feel like he could move on just yet. He ran his flashlight over the wheelchair the discarded art project sat upon, noticing that the paint of both armrests had been scratched away in places, about where someone's hands might lie. He imagined a forgotten person sitting in the wheelchair, scratching out of boredom, waiting for a visitor that never came. He wondered if the owner had passed away or moved somewhere else—because with the building's elevators having been out of commission since his initial visit to Dunsany Arms over a year ago, someone in a wheelchair would have no easy time getting around. Unless, once they'd moved in, they never left until they were borne down the stairs by EMTs. That mental image added to Dwayne's jitters a heavy drop of sorrow, something this place seemed to excel at provoking.

Passing the basement's elevator doors, in old man hand *Out of order* had been scribbled onto a scrap of cardboard. A metallic twang from within halted Dwayne. When the sound didn't repeat, he continued tracking a wrist-thick bundle of cables trailing along the wall, stopping when his flashlight wobbled upon where they terminated at a large metal box. He brought out the lock-pick gun, turned an ear over his shoulder—hearing only the unbalanced dryer and the contents of someone's toilet surging through a pipe next to his head. The padlock put up little resistance. Biting his flashlight, Dwayne picked through the confusion of dust-coated wires until he found the one marked 603 and readied his wire-cutters.

If he's using the line again and it goes dead on him, he'll know something's up. And don't forget he's got friends over.

Dwayne snipped the line, shucked the insulation from both ends, and spliced in the tap screwing the raw connections to the device's copper pads.

He was worried that all the concrete and metal might interfere, but its light finally flashed green, having successfully paired to his laptop upstairs. He plugged his headphones into the device. Static. Was that good? Before trudging back upstairs, he'd wait until Metzger got a call to know for sure.

6.

I T'S STRANGE REALIZING your body has new orifices. For Jack, this naturally conjured some nightmares. Namely, Connie giving him even more unwanted holes—and bifurcating parts of him. His dick, his tongue, *his entire head*. Thanks to nightmare logic, he survived to live out his days scaring dogs and making children cry with his skull grotesquely clamshelling open and closed whenever he tried to speak, brain matter collecting about his feet. It was one of those times, no matter how bad things were in his waking life, that he was relieved when the dream released him.

He lifted his left arm, tucked a pack of gum into the pocket, and turned one way, then the other, studying himself in the mirror. Invisible. Walking around the duplex, casually swinging his arm as he strolled, he could barely feel the foreign object.

He called Metzger.

Without so much as a hello: "Did you know, though kangaroos are the most commonly associated with having pouches, a lot of other animals have them too?"

"That's what makes them a marsupial, isn't it?" Jack said. Whenever Metzger went into a lesson about whatever random topic that'd become this week's obsession, you could only play along until he'd regurgitated all the data he'd amassed.

"That's correct," Metzger said. "Koalas, wallabies, Tasmanian devils. Possums too."

"I didn't know that," Jack said, trying to sound genuinely fascinated.

"Did you know possums are the only creature besides man with opposable thumbs—albeit possums' thumbs are on their back feet? Ninety percent of them are immune to rabies and the bites of most venomous snakes. People think that when a possum plays dead it's something they control, but it's not. And when they do, they automatically shit and piss to make themselves a highly unappealing treat for would-be predators. Female possums are called jills, and males are called jacks." Metzger paused. "Your name's Jack. And you have pouches too now, I hear."

The back of Jack's neck tingled. Was the chemist merely reading factoids off the internet, oblivious to when he became inadvertently scary on the phone? "Um, that's right. I do."

"Does that mean you're ready to work?"

Jack swallowed. "Yes."

* * *

When its engine stalled at a red light, Jack made a bargain with his Mazda. Get me to Toronto and back, then you can die.

He reached Buffalo a few minutes into the witching hour, pulled into the parking lot of a dead car wash, and once clear of easy view from the street, fired up a smoke and sat reviewing his life's choices in the dark solitude of his car, determining he was only pleased with two or three. A battered old Mercury grumbled up behind him and flashed its brights. Jack pumped his brakes three times, pulsing the vehicle behind with red light.

A shape, lost to shadow, stepped from the second car, came up to his passenger side, and knocked. Reaching across, Jack cranked down the smeary window, incrementally giving him sight of his visitor. Receding hair dyed black, an inch of silver showing. A deeply lined forehead over a set of bloodshot eyes. An aquiline, gin-blossomed nose. A fortnight's worth of a salt-and-pepper beard. Not the usual guy.

"Who're you?" Jack said.

"Happen to be headed to Toronto tonight?"

"Yeah." Jack could breathe again.

The old man maintained steady eye contact while digging through the pocket of his ragged flannel jacket. Every time he moved, Jack caught a whiff of mothballs, reminding him of his grandmother's house. The old man retrieved a wrinkled piece of paper.

Turning on his car's dome light, Jack reached to take the note, but the old man pulled it away.

"No. Just look at it." Cough. "Memorize it."

Though the old man's hand constantly shook, Jack studied the hand-written address until he had it down. Without asking if he had it, the old man crumpled the note and stuffed it in his mouth. "They'll test what you brought," he said, chewing. "So if you do something stupid like step on the shit thinking they won't notice, they will."

"I've done this before."

The old man swallowed. "Never up to Toronto, not according to Gerry." Cough. "Heard you got cut."

"Dress for the job you want, right?"

The old man scoffed. He held up two fingers in a tremulous V. "Second thing. If you get stopped and decide to roll on—"

"I won't."

As punishment for the interruption, the old man gave him a long, impenetrable stare. "If you get *stopped* and you decide to *roll* on us, you're fucked when you get to county. Fact."

"Yeah, yeah. You giving me the shit or what?"

The old man made no moves to do so. "Half a pound uncut belladonna extract. Powder, as agreed." Cough. "Run it back to me."

"Half a pound of powdered, uncut belladonna extract."

"A dab will do you. Tell them that."

"All right" Jack said.

"*What* will do you?"

"A dab."

Cough. "If they like the results, we can have another half-pound to them in a week."

"I'll pass that along."

"So, *where* are you going, again?"

Jack said the Toronto address again.

The old man tossed onto Jack's passenger seat a lumpy plastic bag lashed with bands of duct tape. "Do *not* let yourself lose track of time. Again, do *not* let yourself—"

"Got it, thank you, goodnight."

The old man stepped back from the car and was absorbed by the shadows from whence he'd coughed and shuffled. When Jack left the parking lot, he looked over at the old man who'd remained sitting behind the wheel, hands at ten and two, staring ahead at nothing—as if now that his job was complete, he'd simply shut off.

Down a couple blocks, Jack pulled into an abandoned K-Mart's lot and lifted his shirt. He pulled the first thumb-sized baggie from the load, tilted the rearview mirror, and fed it to the hole in his armpit, then another, comfortably squeezing four baggies on his left side and four on his right. He tweaked the rearview mirror to look himself in the eye, told himself he was fully capable of doing this (his reflection seemed unconvinced), and left the lot, following signs for the Canadian border.

7.

HE WAS STARTING to get cold standing in the damp basement waiting for someone to call Metzger, but it gave Dwayne time to think—though that wasn't necessarily the best thing.

The minute they'd become available, cheap pay-as-you-go phones became the best friend to the drug world. Dwayne didn't think Metzger would conduct business any differently. He'd already proven himself a real crafty son of a bitch by making his entire operation disappear *twice,* so it'd be a shock if he did something as stupid as talk shop over his landline, but maybe—just maybe—burners had become *so* ubiquitous within the trade, Metzger believed the police wouldn't bother with his home phone. It was worth a try. They might get something. Christ, *anything.*

Like any other still moment, the jawless man's scream returned, and Dwayne involuntarily recalled the pile of burners on the nightstand and the engine grease decree on the wall *I will hear him* as he'd stood there, holding three gray fingers in the palm of his hand. Hear who? Typically, the user calls the dealer, not the other way around. And if not their dealer, or Metzger himself, who were they wanting to hear from? Odd, also, was why they'd apparently done a hit and wrapped themselves up like a mummy. Wouldn't you want to be conscious—and *not* cocooned in a bedsheet—if you were expecting a phone call? It was a series of questions Dwayne had revisited countless times, and found he could only sever the loop with, Junkies just do weird shit sometimes. Like the papier-mâché head, or that unsolvable maze up on the sixth floor. Exhibit A, Exhibit B. Don't try to understand it, you'll just end up like the lost soul on the stairs unspooling their nonsense to the wall.

It couldn't be fought. Feeling the words over inside his mind no longer satisfied. "Mtahsab Belsharh."

Metal rumbled. His earbuds tore themselves free when Dwayne spun, one hand flying to his holster. He trained his Maglite's shaking circle up the hall—and saw Leslie's hand-written sign had fallen to wick up a puddle on the floor. The elevator doors stood parted a crack, an old sneaker wedged in place to maintain the divide. Darkness, within, stood in place of the elevator car. "Leslie?" Dwayne called, but only his echo replied.

A faint puttering came from his dangling headphones. Keeping a grip on his gun, Dwayne shoved in an earbud just as Metzger picked up.

Click.

"Hey, uh, it's Ryan. Um, sorry it's so late, but I just wanted to let you know—"

"Careful . . ."

"No, yeah, I know, but we've got a new guy. Guess he took 306."

"306?" Metzger said. "Sure hope ole Les cleaned it up for him a little." [*laughter*]

"No shit. That shit went *every*place when—"

"Ryan."

"Shit, sorry. So, I uh . . . "

"Take your time. You weren't interrupting anything."

"So, uh, Sam was out on the balcony, right? He told me he seen the new guy dragging in his shit."

"And did your boy give you a description?"

"Just some old guy. But I, um, just wanted to call you and, um, ask you something. If that'd be okay."

"That's fine, but let's continue choosing our words carefully," Metzger said. "Never know who's listening."

"Uh, it's just . . . you're not giving up on me, right? 'Cause I still wanna keep trying."

"What are you talking about?"

"I was thinking that with the new guy coming in, you might, um . . . "

"That he's here to replace you?"

"It's just, after last time . . . I seriously thought I got something. I *swear* when I checked my messages, it sounded like—"

"You did hear something, Ryan. A credit card offer."

"I know, but I guess I was still fucked up so, it sounded kinda like me, like my voice. You said it would, when he—"

"*Careful.*"

"Sorry. I'm sorry. It's just . . . *fuck*, it's really hard," Ryan said. "I wanna hear it, but every time I try . . . " [*long pause*] "My arm still hurts."

"The body needs time to adjust to the idea something's gone missing."

"Sam's gotta help me shoot now. Can't even do *that* on my own, and it's all you need me to do, and listen for when—"

"Ryan, I'm not on a burner. In fact, you have my other number, why don't you call me on that?"

"I'm sorry, I'm sorry, but this will only take a sec. Okay, so I know I fucked up before. And *you* did what *you* said you'd do if I fucked up or lied. I own that. Next time, I'm gonna do it right, I'm gonna—"

"Where's Sam right now? At home, with you?"

[*sigh*] "Nah, he's fucking around someplace. Down at Connie's, maybe. Been obsessed with the laundry room lately too."

"Because it's warm down there," Metzger said. "Turn on your heat. It's ten below tonight."

"But the bill's gonna up."

"I'll worry about the bill. Turn on the heat for your kid."

"Um, about that. This isn't real easy to just come out and say, but . . . I don't mind looking after him, Gerry, he's a good kid and everything, but is this gonna be like a permanent arrangement?"

"Just be there for him, Ryan. When I was his age, I could've used someone I could depend on. You too, I imagine."

"Yeah. True. I could've."

"So be that for him."

"Okay. I will. I will." [*pause*] "So, uh, just to double-check, you aren't replacing me?"

"No. Listen, come up tomorrow around noon. Don't call me before."

"You're gonna have me try again? Because if you are, I swear I'm gonna try really hard, I *swear* I'm—"

Click.

Dwayne pulled the earbud free. The elevator doors hadn't moved; the grease-blackened sneaker was still holding them apart. Fluorescent light poured from the laundry room doorway. Dwayne approached, his heartbeat matching the rhythmic slams of the unbalanced dryer. The boy's father—who, perhaps, wasn't his father—had been the one to lose an arm for lying about *hearing somebody*, somebody that's supposed to sound like the person receiving the message? And who the hell is Connie? How many accomplices did Metzger have in the building, all sharing a roof? Junkies just do weird shit wouldn't hold up to these questions. What the hell is going on in this place?

Stepping into the suffocating balminess of the laundry room, Dwayne pocketed his flashlight. "Sam?" Maybe the kid, if handled correctly, would roll on his old man, who might, in turn, roll on Metzger. "Sam?" The single machine clanged and swayed—and when it buzzed, cycle complete, Dwayne damn near had a stroke. He chuckled, until a sharp, precise pain pricked the back of his arm.

He whirled, hearing something thin and metal *plink* as it broke. "Listen for him," a small voice said from the dark, close enough Dwayne could smell the milk and sugar on the boy's breath. Dwayne never saw him, only heard him skitter away and the elevator doors roll and thump together. Dwayne shouted for Sam to stop, and again only heard the echo of his own voice calling back—now slurring its words.

It's a sensation unlike any other, being submerged in abject terror while a chemical invades the blood, one that presented to Dwayne a euphoria the likes of which he had no comparison. Not even on his loneliest, most inebriated nights had he ever felt this disconnected from his aged physiology. Legs jellying under him, feet and hands tingling, he stumble-climbed the stairs, hearing his own panicked gibbering bounce off the cold cement walls as the world turned slippery.

On all fours, he clambered, squishing a dirty diaper under his palm, its warm contents shooting up his sleeve. Every forward throw of his right arm caused the stubbed needle to scrape painfully against the bones inside his elbow. He glanced back down the stairs. No one followed, but he felt watched and surrounded. Crowded. Unwholesomely inhabited.

From the dark, "*You* said then *you* said then *you* said then *you* said . . . "

Time broke. He staggered inside apartment 306, his keys crashing to the floor loud as a gunshot. Nothing on his phone's blinding screen made sense—and when it fell from his hand, it was eaten irretrievably by the shadows. He was afraid to feel around for it, thinking he might fall into the dark after it.

Someone laughed, close behind him. No, *he'd* made that noise. Why?

Crashing into the bathroom, he raised his arm to show his reflection the metal stub sticking out of it. He sliced his fingers pinching at the jagged tip. He couldn't get a hold on it, couldn't get it back out. A brief spark of lucid thinking—I'll need to get tested, if I live through this. Dan Wells, in the mirror, nodded in grim agreement. Disturbed, Dwayne retreated from the mirror, moving backward into the barren living room, Dan Wells on his side of the looking glass doing the same. But it seemed insincere. Play acting. In his eyes, "You caught me breaking character."

43

Fearing he might crash through the sliding glass door and go over the balcony railing to his doom, Dwayne kept his distance, even as Dan Wells reappeared in the smeary duct-taped glass to cruelly mimic him hugging the far wall. *That's just you, it's fine, you're fine. Slow your heart down. Deep breaths.*

Black lightning dashed before him. Dan Wells, the ghost in the sliding glass door, started clutching his head. The pink stain in the carpet rushed up at Dwayne's eyes. He heard the impact but didn't feel it. Darkness—

—was pierced, a peeled face shoving itself toward him, boiled reds, white cartilage stringing thunderbolt fractals across a ribbed, conical skull, greasy bone, wide-set eyes shivering and bulging from sunken sockets, milky orbs under vein-laced translucent membranes, lips pinned in an inflexible snarl, jutting equine teeth, the whole of the being shone as slickened, shuddering with fever and bottomless rage—*hear me*—Dwayne knew it could see him and knew its blistering hate was for no one else and though its jaw didn't shift, the entity communicated—*hear me*—and sent him running away into the deeper darkness of this void, the entity's glare needling his retreating back—*hear me*—a phone receiver materialized in his sweaty fist—*hear me*—black plastic shiny as a beetle's carapace, spiral wire connected to nothing—*speak for me*—having forgotten all words, he could only scream—

—as he flinched awake, something cold pressing against his face. He sat up and wiped the whiskey-scented crust from his cheek and ear. The bloodstain of 306's previous tenant had become an enflamed, lidless eye, with Dwayne's puddle of sick supplying the iris.

His throat hurt. He'd blacked out lying on his gun; the ribs of his left side felt bruised. Holding the wall for balance, he got to his feet and faced the sliding glass door. It was either still dark out or it was dark again, he wasn't sure.

His nausea recommended throwing up again, but he could only give the toilet bowl bitter yellow strings. A yearning stirred, much more potent than the workaday thirst that whipped him toward the bottle every night. His entire body, it felt, was grinding its teeth.

The minute Dwayne could dump off the scraps he'd amassed during this botched surveillance job, he'd give his exorcism from krokodil however long the detox center staff deemed necessary. *I will not leave here unable to say we never lost control—I, I never lost control.*

Struggling off his jacket, the broken needle snagged and tore at the sleeve's lining. His reflection grimaced when he showed it the mottled gray flesh surrounding the injection site. The bite of the krokodil.

With a pair of pliers from his toolbox, he pinched the end of the needle and pulled. He winced unnecessarily. For the first time in his life, he wanted pain. This wasn't good. Coming free with a sickening pop, the bent needle rattled about the sink and settled blood-slicked at the rusty drain. He couldn't spread the fingers of his right hand or make a complete fist. He went to his bottle of Maker's, took a swig, and poured some across his elbow. Only the swallow burned.

Unable to locate his phone, he woke up his laptop to get the time.

Sixteen hours had passed, and in that time the tap had logged zero incoming or outgoing calls. Shit. He clicked over to check what his cameras were currently seeing. No one was outside his own door, same as Metzger's three floors up. Dwayne scrubbed over the footage, saw himself mounting the cameras and lingering at Metzger's door to listen. That look of hunger, a man desperate to make an arrest. When Dwayne had moved off, the three men he'd dodged in the hallway had slipped inside Metzger's apartment, only opening the door as far as necessary, denying the camera so much as a peek of what had been going on within—like they knew they were being watched.

Sixteen hours ago, Dwayne had tripped into frame outside his own door and struggled with his keys, the broken needle in his elbow and his sweaty forehead shining under the hallway's bare bulb. He watched himself fall into the apartment, leave the door hanging wide open, and go wandering listlessly into the dark, passing through the space he currently occupied. He watched himself drop his phone, losing it under the refrigerator. The present Dwayne looked over the monitor. There the phone remained, held by dust and crumbs.

When he returned his eyes to the screen, he saw someone's turned back—someone who, fifteen hours and forty-five minutes ago, had stood at the open apartment door. A gaunt and hunched silhouette, left sleeve of their oversized T-shirt sagging from their shoulder, empty. For a moment, Ryan had stood nervously shifting his insubstantial weight before bringing a phone to his ear, its screen lighting the side of his head an icy blue, the cords in his stack-of-dimes neck twitching as he spoke to someone. Dwayne regretted not swiping cameras with microphones. This likely would've been helpful to overhear.

Past Metzger's one-armed flunky, Dwayne watched himself stagger backwards from the bathroom and startle at his reflection in the sliding glass door, fail to notice Ryan standing in the doorway, and finally collapse face-down on the stained carpet. The watchful junkie pocketed his phone, reached over the threshold, drew Dwayne's door shut, and made brief eye contact with the camera before moving back up the hall, leaving frame. 3:42 AM.

The jig was up. All Dwayne had to show for his efforts was the imminent trip to the ER to get a portion of his arm scraped of necrotized tissue. Amputation wasn't off the table, but he'd hold onto hope. At least he was alive. They'd had several opportunities to kill him, but had taken none of them. Maybe it was a warning, one Dwayne wouldn't fail to heed. You win, Metzger.

His head threatened to pop when he bent to retrieve his phone from under the refrigerator. He wiped the dust from its screen, considering how to word the white-flag call to Cleckley. He'd missed a call at 3:44 AM from UNKNOWN. They'd left a voicemail.

Though back in the safety of waking life, he felt the nightmare's hateful stare burn him again. Scalp tingling, he let fear turn him to look. The only thing watching him was the eye in the carpet, made of stains. The phone shook in his hand. Play voicemail 1/1?

8.

HOURS LATER, DWAYNE left the door hanging open as he exited apartment 306, only fleetingly registering the crying coming from behind the door to 305. Clutching his phone, Dwayne felt his body move itself up the hall. He reached to push open the stairwell door, stopping when an electronic chime sounded brightly behind him.

The sign reading OUT OF SERVICE was peeled free from the elevator doors as they rumbled apart. Cardboard boxes stood in columns within, some nearly reaching the elevator car's ceiling. From behind one stack, Leslie emerged and flinched, noticing Dwayne looking at him. He regarded Dwayne with an almost apologetic cast coming into his leathery face. Dwayne could only stare, slow-blinking, mind too afire to form words.

Leslie slowly lowered his focus, perhaps noticing the phone crushed in Dwayne's grasp. When the elevator doors started to close, he blocked them with one hand—and beckoned Dwayne aboard with the other. "There's room."

Leslie tapped the button marked 6. The doors rejoined, and their slow, shuddering ascent began. Most of the cardboard boxes were stamped with one pharmaceutical company's logo or another, and wore shipping labels for places that weren't Dunsany Arms. Behind one stack of boxes was a folding chair with a coloring book lying open on its seat. An incomplete butterfly with only one wing filled in with manic scribbles of black—coal, if Dwayne was right in remembering the trademarked hue. A metal pail stood near the chair, two inches of dark urine shivering at its bottom. The emergency switch had a piece of yellowed tape near it, marked DON'T TOUCH! The switch itself had pieces of hair and grime stuck to it. It'd been touched.

"We send everything downstairs when you all go charging up," Leslie said. He didn't sound proud. "And bring it up when you head down."

Dwayne said nothing. He was neither impressed by their ingenuity nor enraged. Aside from the single question he had for Metzger, Dwayne's mind was still and silent. Nothing else mattered now.

They slammed to a stop, sixth floor. Across the hall, framed by the elevator's parted doors, the doorway of apartment 603 stood open, allowing Dwayne sight inside, to Metzger's windows. The daylight hurt his eyes even though it was drowned behind heavy cloud cover. Gray above, gray below. He accepted his body's desire to get a better look, and did not fight as it stepped from the elevator to enter apartment 603. He passed equipment spread across tables, hoses and ribbed tubes stringing this way and that, suspended by twine. Plastic covered the walls, the floors, the ceiling, hemmed together with long bands of tape. The multitude of utility lights positioned everywhere denied any shadows to grow.

As he continued toward the window, Sam peeked from under a table and gave an unreadable look before apathetically making a finger-gun at him.

Dwayne passed a cot pushed against the wall. Upon it, Ryan lay pale, eyes closed, a needle sticking out of the bandaged stump where his right arm used to be. Riding his bony chest as it rose and fell, a phone. NO NEW VOICEMAILS.

Reaching the window, Dwayne's skull knocked against the thick glass. He looked out over the wasteland, his eyelashes brushing against Dan Wells'. He couldn't find the horizon—but from the grayness, a door opened and Metzger, translucent, came into view, walking on air. He passed from the glass, coming to stand at Dwayne's side.

Peeling his forehead from the window, Dwayne turned and watched Metzger pick up a syringe and a paper plate. Easing down the plunger, a drop of foggy liquid clung on the needle's tip before falling to blemish the plate with a *tap*. A cloudy hemisphere shaped itself, no bigger than a dime. Dan Wells wanted to press his tongue against the plate to absorb the dot of death—but Dwayne refused his double's lust for the void.

"That's how little I gave you," Metzger said.

Dwayne's lungs felt full of sawdust; his throat threatened to close. He struggled lifting his arm to shake his phone at Metzger. "How did you do this? What does that mean, what . . . I said, on there?"

Metzger set the paper plate aside but kept the needle in his other hand. He gently took the phone away. Dwayne covered his ears and watched Metzger listen to the voicemail. He felt certain the world would dissolve around him.

Metzger's face never changed. When he was done listening, he tossed the phone to Leslie. "Copy it and log it."

The building manager nodded, disappeared.

"What does it mean?" Dwayne said. "Why did I say that?"

Metzger turned away. "Sam. It's time to take your father home."

The boy climbed out from under the table. "He's done for the day?"

"That's right."

By the one hand his father had left to hold, the boy led him from the room.

Dwayne swiped at Metzger, but grasped nothing. "What did you do to me?"

The door closed. They were alone. "You've heard. So now, let's see what you can see." With the syringe, Metzger motioned past Dwayne. "Look."

Dwayne turned and let his forehead rejoin Dan Wells' again. Through his double he saw, far below, vague figures drift from the snow and fog. They wove meandering, crooked paths about the snow-buried factories and crumbling smokestacks, slow and sore, collecting into a line to raise their collapsing faces and milky eyes as one. They could see him.

"Who are all of those—?" Dwayne started as something bit him behind the ear, fear leaving him as bliss revisited.

"Listen for him again," Metzger said and, embracing Dwayne, eased him to the floor.

Enraptured, the world fell before Dwayne's eyes and, somewhere, a phone began to ring.

II

The Possum's Crossing

1.

DESPITE THE LATE HOUR, there was a line at the crossing Jack hadn't expected. He turned off his car's heat—even though it was supposedly going to drop to five below tonight, he didn't need it, his addled nerves were keeping him plenty warm. He watched as a minivan was directed to take an off-shooting path instead of being allowed to leave the States. The path led to a garage of sorts, where dogs were led up inside people's vehicles and mirror-poles were used to inspect the wheel wells. Men in tactical gear cradled assault rifles and stood by watching, missing nothing.

He couldn't slow down his heart. He turned on the radio to distract his racing mind, but it did little to help.

"Pull ahead and turn off your engine."

He did as told—his car let free a cracking backfire of vehicular indigestion, drawing the attention of border agents several booths down.

The uniform behind the glass partition glared down at him. They always do this, stare you down a second or two, measuring how you might fidget or avoid their eye. The trick is to look back at them, look impatient, but don't look *too* hard at them. No tough guy shit, just play it like a road-worn traveler eager to get home to the missus.

"One moment," the agent said.

"Take your time." Jack glanced away, noticing a few lanes over another agent walking a German shepherd—and slowly making his way toward his lane. Wonderful. A strange tingling in his left pouch now, and a creeping numbness began to spread as his pulse took an abrupt uptick—this was different from the standard jitters. Had one of the baggies popped a leak?

The glass partition scraped open, startling Jack. The agent leaned his upper half from his booth, really getting a good look at him—altogether ignoring the passport Jack was offering for him to take and inspect. "Where are you from, sir?"

Jack thumbed over his shoulder. "Erie," he said, quickly lowering his arm again.

The agent gave a slow, stony nod. "And what's the purpose of your visit to Canada, sir?"

"Visiting a friend up in Toronto."

"And how long will this visit be exactly, sir?"

Jack maintained eye contact with the agent, but could hear the German shepherd being walked closer, closer. "Back home on Monday."

"Any firearms in your vehicle or on your person tonight, sir?"

"No."

"Any illegal substances in your vehicle or on your person, sir?"

Jack was ready to lie—when the German shepherd supplied the truth for him.

* * *

While he sat in a small, windowless room, he thought about how when certain dogs bark, it sounds like they're saying *truth—truth*, as a demand. His thoughts were turning weird, he realized. It felt similar to how sometimes, even before a single sneeze, he knew a cold was coming on because his thoughts would start refusing to complete, wires deep inside getting crossed or cut. Focus.

He wanted to check his pouches to see if his suspicions were correct, that one of the baggies had in fact burst, but he didn't dare. Though the drab little space they'd shoved him into didn't appear to have any cameras, maybe there just weren't obvious ones. Maybe they were watching him now, waiting for him to fish the stash out of wherever he was hiding it, catch it on tape to save them the trouble of performing a strip search. Well, seeing how his options were currently quite limited, if this wasn't going to be a pleasant experience for him, it wasn't going to be pleasant for anyone. It was the least he could do.

It smelled like Connie's operating room in here. Fear sweat, disinfectant. Remembering how smell was the sense closest tied to memory, Jack considered if he closed his eyes, concentrated on the smell, and let the slow leak of drugs entering his system aid his transportation, if he could give himself a dream-vacation before the gavel bang. Though Connie's apartment was pretty low on Jack's list of favorite places in the world, it sure was better than here. Anywhere was better than here.

He recalled reading this thing one time that kind of blew his mind. There's supposedly this phenomenon that, in rare cases, can happen when a person misses somebody so much that their worry and sleeplessness is almost worthy of a trip to the hospital. The thing is, the person who has gone away is still alive, just absent. That part's important. Okay, so the supposed phenomenon goes: One day out of the blue, the individual who's awaiting their loved one's safe return will randomly get a knock on the door, right? And when they open it, okay, standing on their front step will be an eyelash-for-eyelash duplicate of their estranged loved one. Not a ghost or anything like that, but an actual living, breathing person. Flesh and blood, *exactly* like the person who's not supposed to be, you know, here. The double can talk, knows everything they should, has memories, they can give hugs, eat and drink, go to the bathroom, do everything that person who is being missed could do . . . except explain how they got there. And when that question is inevitably raised—because who *wouldn't* ask that?—the double will vanish like a bad special effect, self-editing themselves from time and space, *gone*. And once the doppelganger's host has managed to peel themselves off the ceiling and contact the person whose double had visited, and they describe to them this highly irregular and troubling event, more often than not the missed person will admit to having a dream about returning home, doing everything their double did, talking about the same exact things the double had talked about, all of it. So even though Jack didn't get the impression exactly, maybe Connie, despite her rather brusque attitude toward him, had secretly taken a shine to him and was wishing right at this moment that Jack would plop himself down in her make-do operating room again. All right, if not Connie, maybe someone else was hoping Jack was there with them. With luck, he wouldn't just have dreams about the visit, he'd self-edit himself from this smelly, windowless room and be *there* instead, wherever there might be. But he considered how both his mom and dad were gone and how his friends could more accurately be described as customers—and how many, even among them, would feasibly be able to recall his name without having to think too hard about it first. *Shit.* Maybe right now this was exactly where he belonged, things progressing exactly as intended.

An agent entered the room, closed and locked the door, and began pulling on gloves, never taking his eyes off Jack. "Stand up."

Jack stood.

"Strip."

Starting with his shoes, he noticed strange thoughts brewing on the peripheries. Mutterings in an impossible tongue, and horrible visions that were as abstract and visceral as they were thankfully brief. Once he was naked, he looked at the border agent again—and saw part of his head was dribbling off his skull, forming a puddle on the floor that shimmered like oil on water.

"Turn around," the melting agent hissed, "squat, and cough."

Jack squatted, coughed, but laid no eggs.

"Bend over. Spread 'em. I apologize in advance for having to do this dry. Government cutbacks."

He accepted the agent's invading, unlubricated finger without comment. He stared at the far wall, wishing some eye-catching artwork would materialize to distract him, but even with a powerful hallucinogen in his blood, the cinderblock remained unchanged.

Wincing, Jack felt the finger withdraw.

"You don't have to keep doing that, we're done with that part."

He stopped spreading himself open and stood upright again, shivering, feeling beyond naked—*skinned*. The agent smiled, his eyes bubbling out of his head, leaving streams of viscous black down his face. Jack looked away, assuming the ashamed drug mule.

Without a word of warning, the abstract agent throttled Jack's cock in a gloved fist, pinched its head to force the piss-hole to yawn, and shined in a penlight. He lit up, every vein visible, an obscene Christmas tree decoration.

While Jack suffered this new indignity, he wondered how much a guy could possibly smuggle inside their urethra. The ass, sure, he knew from experience that could serve as a worthwhile cargo hold, but the dick? And if you were willing to force-feed dope to your pecker and got caught, wouldn't that prove how dedicated you were to a habit and, at that point, couldn't they just let you keep your shit? In a just world, dicks would count as sovereign territories, like the inside of your mind. Of course, they'd probably come up with a way to stick a flashlight in there too before long.

The door closed, the bolt shot. He was alone again, his dick was no longer being strangled by the long, latex-gloved arm of the law. They hadn't said he could get dressed, but he pulled on his sweat-soaked clothes anyway. There might not have been anything to find of note inside the orifices they'd checked, but they would find the baggies soon enough. This would be prison time, and a good long stretch of it too. And Metzger would have some friends sitting in county waiting for him. Fact.

Twenty-three years and this night, this hour, this exact second, had been waiting ahead of him. As unfair as it seemed, at the same time: Yeah, this about fits. There was a lazy comfort in inevitability. He hadn't fucked up his own life, no, it was just meant to *be* fucked up and he'd merely been caught in its tow, along for the ride. Nobody's painful longing for his presence had magically edited him away from this room. He was here, inviolably *in* this. But he had one option still available to him.

Having never put much thought or genuine planning into any other major life crossroad, Jack didn't see much point in starting now. He lifted his left arm, punched his armpit with his opposite hand, and stood listening to the muffled crackle as the baggies within burst. A blast of poison skewered his brain. Having to act quickly now, he repeated the process on the opposite side and was chemically broadsided again. Letting himself drop to the floor, he smiled, ready for oblivion. When the predators with their plastic badges returned, they'd find their cornered prey wasn't just playing dead.

2.

"MAKES YOU THINK back on all those times you was in the shower or mowing the lawn or something and you swear you heard someone say your name," Ryan said to Dwayne from the dark enveloping them both. "They always sound so *clear*, don't they? Every time I've heard it, it's always the same voice. I've never heard her any other time, anywhere else. She don't sound like my big sister, any girlfriend I ever had, none of my female teachers, none of them. She's her own thing."

As quietly as possible, Dwayne touched at the open mouth of his holster—empty. His back and shoulders hurt. He tried to rise, but couldn't. He was on the floor of a stuffy, dark room and his eyes refused to adjust. The air was thin, used—carrying the singular smell of sleeping people, that strange aroma he'd first noticed after moving in with Sarah. He'd never shared a bed with anyone else before, or since. But the smell of sleep was too strong for only him and Ryan to have produced alone. Dwayne was trying to listen for the breathing of others when the younger man said:

"Now that I've heard some of the calls other people got, it makes me think, could she be over there too? No joke—and this is between me and you—it kinda makes me miss the times back in the day when things could be written off as just being 'all in my head.' I don't know about her anymore, man. Don't know if she's . . . *real*, I guess is the word. Heard her since I was little, I'm talking *little*. Going like, 'Ryan . . . ' with this nice voice, real nice. Like a singer or something. And she's got this funny little laugh too." He snorted. "Can't do it like she does, but that's sorta how it sounds."

It was a small space, wherever they were. Ryan's voice felt bottled— like they were buried alive together. Dwayne struggled to lift his arms, to feel over himself, finding a sticky bead of half-dried blood behind his right ear. Otherwise, he wasn't injured. Weak and horrendously dizzy, but not hurt.

How long had he been in here with Ryan talking at him? He feared the young man—over there in the dark, sounding like he was no farther than an arm's reach away—was holding a weapon, perhaps Dwayne's gun. Allowing the younger man to ramble, he considered how to get away, even though he couldn't ascertain where the door was, or if he'd even have the strength to stand to run toward it.

Ryan was saying, "I always hated how people say, 'Oh, it's just all in your head.' Like how *the fuck* is that better? Because that just means the bad shit didn't need to break in—and there's no getting away from it either. Can't tent your brain like it's got bed bugs. You can't evacuate you from you.

"I've been at this shit for two years," Ryan went on, "and not a voicemail. Not one. I wish I could go back to how I was before I knew what I was missing out on—that there was even anything *to* miss out on. I gave him my arm, man. I gave that, for this. Is this how dedication pays off? Who knows. Not me."

Ryan breathed heavily in the dark a while. "What's life when you only get to see what's real through a peephole? That's the last thing Jack said to me, night he blew his head off. Right here in 306."

306? Is that where we are?

"Ryan," Dwayne rasped, "you need to let me go. These are very dangerous people you've gotten involved with." Maybe he didn't say that aloud. Ryan didn't seem to hear him either way.

"Gerry tell you we was upstairs when Jack did it? Because we were. Me and Sam used to stay right above here. One night, I'm on the couch, right, and out of fucking *nowhere* here come somebody's brains flying up outta my floor. Brains and blood and teeth going all over me and all over my shit . . . and my kid's coloring books. Yeah. Good thing he was in bed and not lying right there in front of the TV, right? Fuck, man. The way shit can go, at any point. Especially here. Shit I seen, man.

"You think it's possible for somebody to think themselves crazy, Dan?" Ryan said. "You think that's possible? People can choke on their tongues and that doesn't sound like something that should be able to happen, but it does. Design flaw. Do you think somebody can think so much their mind just . . . *unravels*, up inside their head?"

As Ryan's excitement made his volume rise, a slow swish of cloth on skin—blankets, sheets, clothing—came from somewhere in the dark to Dwayne's left. And where there'd only been silence filling Ryan's infrequent pauses, the breathing of multiple people, not quite awake, rasped all around him. How many was impossible to determine. An elbow bumped his side; a young woman groaned, close to him, her body vocalizing fear while a nightmare chased her back to her flesh.

"I had a twin brother," Ryan said. "We both have this problem with our heart—he *had* a heart problem, I mean. The doctor said we should never have anything too full of sugar or anything with caffeine. No soda, no Cap'n Crunch, not even a stick of fucking gum. We shouldn't go out for sports, he said, or watch scary movies. Nothing that tends to get the blood up. From when we were three, we were told we'd have an oatmeal life. Bland as bland can be. That might actually explain a few things. If you want somebody to do something, tell them they can't.

"Anyway, it didn't matter how careful we were. Can't control the subject matter of your dreams. We were poor as shit, so me and him shared a bed up until we were both six, when he died. I thought someone had broken into the house. I heard somebody walking around in our room, taking their time about it. Like they didn't care if we knew they were there. I was too scared to look. I'll admit, I was hoping Josh would hear them and scream. I waited for him to do that, but it never happened. I listened to the person in our room just *stand there*, at the foot of the bed. Felt like fucking hours. I was afraid even if he didn't do nothing, my heart would give out anyway. I was scared more for our mom than anything. What if this piece of shit kills one of us and the other one dies of a fucking heart attack? And when he made his decision, I guess, he started going around to his side. And his steps just . . . stopped. I reached under the covers, to try and get ahold of my brother's hand, to shake him, wake him up. I had to be careful, only moving a little bit at a time because I was *sure* they were still standing next to the bed, looking at us. When I touched his arm, he . . . he was cold, like fucking *ice*. My mom ran in when I started screaming. There was nobody in the house, the police checked the doors and windows—they were all locked. But Josh was still dead. I was there to hear Death make a decision, I heard him *pick* one of us." Ryan paused. "I don't know why I told you that."

Though Dwayne hadn't heard him move, when Ryan spoke again, he sounded much closer. "I don't know if I wanted to crash, but after Josh died, I was tearing around on my bike and hit this, like, cement barrier thing. Never saw it coming." His breath was rancid. "I wasn't wearing a helmet and I went over the handlebars and I got con*cussed*, man. Stone cold *out,* nineteen days. Nineteen days doing nothing but dreaming." A long pause. "You a church-going kind of dude, Dan?"

Dwayne didn't respond.

"Leviticus has this part about leprosy. What somebody's supposed to do if somebody catches that shit and also what to do if the house, itself, ends up sick. Yeah. If the *house* catches the shit, which I didn't think was possible. So, the priest is supposed to go in and look at the walls and if he sees these red or green blotches that—and this part always tripped me out—that if they appear to be *deeper than the wall,* then that place is unclean and he's supposed to light that bitch up ASAP. Red and green blotches that look like they're *deeper* than the wall. Jesus. Just think about that. Might've been a mistranslation or something, but that used to freak my ass out bad. 'Course, that was before, back when I didn't know everything that I didn't know I shouldn't be trying to know.

"Around here, in this sick house? I have *seen* some shit. All this isn't nothing but a skin over something else, and grief and desperation have scratched it thin. And it's bleeding onto us. I mean, you've seen it. Now you'll get peeks all the time. But that's our job, I guess. We're pilgrims. Except our New World isn't across any ocean. It's already here. No need to look for any part of a wall that looks deeper than the wall, it's already as close as a thing can get. Already with us, in us, all in our head."

A cold fingertip pressed Dwayne's brow. He shirked back and tried swatting Ryan's hand away, only striking the dark and trapped, body-warmed air.

A light detonated the room of its darkness. Only he groaned; none of the sleepers made a sound. He squinted, seeing Leslie standing in the doorway, his hand on the light switch, looking in at Dwayne—and only Dwayne. The room was empty. He lay alone on the stained bedroom carpet in his filthy clothes. The sleepers as well as Ryan were gone—though the rankness of the latter's breath lingered, and Dwayne could still feel the burn of the unwanted touch, Ryan poking him on the forehead, seconds ago.

Throat packed with gluey phlegm, Dwayne said, "I'm an officer with the Pennsylvania State Police."

"Dwayne Alan Spare. Lieutenant, Narcotics. We know." Leslie rested his palm on the handle of the power drill holstered in his tool belt—which was also weighted with a hammer and a utility knife with a bright yellow handle. His large, callused hands were powdered white—he'd recently been at work on something, but Dwayne didn't expect it was routine property maintenance. "Spare. You related to Austin Osman Spare?"

Dwayne said nothing.

"Might help if you were. Anyway, need help getting to the can?"

Struggling to stand, Dwayne locked his knees and stood wavering, seasick and half-blind. "You're an accomplice."

"That might be true," Leslie said agreeably.

"You're helping Gerald Metzger." Every blink left tracers of Leslie looking at him, doubles bleeding doubles. "You're helping him do this to people."

"That might also be true. Let's get you to the can."

"Don't fucking touch me." Dwayne heard himself. Old and ill, afraid.

"Okay, all right." Leslie left the room, his heavy steps muffled by the worn hall carpet. "Get yourself there, then."

Alone, Dwayne remained in the cramped bedroom's far corner, struggling to keep his exhausted eyes open to the blinding light—though it may've only been a thirty-watt bulb burning above him. The closet door stood open, only the empty hanger dowel within and those M-shaped birds drawn in crayon. Cadet blue.

He hadn't been alone, when it'd still been dark in here. He'd *heard* other people, grunting drowsily and shifting around. He'd *smelled* them. He'd been *listening* to Ryan ramble. He'd been touched by him, poked him as if to gouge Dwayne's third eye.

He shuffled out into the kitchen, finding Leslie in a lawn chair, his lined face lit by the flickering glow of a portable TV standing on the counter. It was apartment 306. There was the eye-shaped stain on the living room floor; his vomit was gone, but it'd left its ghost. The place reeked of bleach. The view past the railing of his leaning balcony was the same, dark again. How much time had he lost this time? Everything he'd brought with him from home was gone, even his coffee maker. The front door's deadbolt was different—no, taken out and flipped around with the keyhole facing *into* the apartment instead of out. He tried the knob. It wouldn't turn. He wasn't trying to mask his noise. Leslie, not ten feet away, had to have heard him—but the building manager evidently wasn't interested enough to look away from his portable television. Tinny speakers droned sports scores. Dwayne's hands balled into fists as whispering suggestions swarmed him, prodding him and demanding that he ask Leslie for another hit. The word *need* fell short, but his imagination was happy to offer a visual aid. His circulatory system abandoning the rest of his body's dead weight to go crawling after chemical contentment as a red framework of arteries that looked like a hollow version of him animated pitifully by unending want.

No. Find a way out of this fucking place, get to a phone, call Cleckley, and tell him to send every available unit. While he very much wanted to do all of that, even remaining upright to look at the portable TV over Leslie's shoulder required concerted focus. Entire scenarios, all positive outcomes, would play out in a blink and each time he'd still be here, in this apartment, with this man, watching a grainy TV screen together.

The building manager produced a pack of unfiltered cigarettes from his shirt pocket, lit one, and dropped the pack onto the discolored linoleum floor next to his chair, near a travel mug that read #1 Grandpa. He was the kind of smoker who sucked in drags with quick, sharp gasps, the same way Dwayne's father smoked—all the way up until he fell asleep with one burning between his fingers.

Leslie didn't turn around. "Might as well get comfortable. He wants you to have a full day off between sessions. You can have the chair in a minute." Adding, "Reception's good up here. I can't get this channel downstairs."

"Unlock the door, Leslie."

The building manager looked back at Dwayne. Over the length of a sigh, "Park it somewhere, you're hanging around with us a while."

"You can't keep me here."

"Yours was one of the clearest we've had. Gerry wants you to see how much more you can hear. With a little guidance, you might help him finally crack this thing."

"Crack what thing? What is this?"

"Go and relax. He wants you well rested."

Dwayne couldn't be sure if it was the cigarette smoke, his overwhelming exhaustion, or recalling the nightmare that was trying to pull him to the floor, but he fought his vertigo, whatever its cause, and stood clutching the kitchen counter. His head was a heavy, unfeeling mound on his shoulders. "How did he make me say those things? It sounded like me, but . . . "

With an annoyed grunt, Leslie stood. "Maybe you should go ahead and take the chair. I got some other things I should be taking care of anyway."

"Just let me go home."

"Come take a load off, watch some TV. You'll be all right." A stony hand clamped Dwayne's forearm and, with care, led him toward the empty lawn chair. "Right over here, couple more steps, nice and easy. You seem like the kind of guy who likes his structure, just think of this as your new one."

Looking down at his dragging feet, Dwayne only now noticed he was missing a shoe. Next to him, Leslie's prominent gut drooped over his well-stocked work belt—the bright yellow handle of the utility knife catching Dwayne's eye. Certain he couldn't make his situation much worse, he tore the knife from Leslie's belt and rushed to thumb forward the blade.

Backhanding the knife, Leslie sent it clattering across the kitchen floor. He snatched Dwayne by the wrist and, with the same stony hand that'd so gently led toward a place to sit, threatened to dislocate his shoulder as the building manager slammed Dwayne's wrist down on the counter. Even the smallest movements chipped away at Dwayne's bottomed-out strength. He could only watch as Leslie pulled the cordless power drill from his belt, hovering the long metal spiral over the back of his hand. He gave the drill two pulls of the trigger, the machine's motor keening awfully. "This is the arm Sam jabbed you in, isn't it? *Isn't it?* Answer me. Or do you *want* another hole in you?"

"It's the same arm, it's the same arm."

Leslie set the power drill aside, tearing the claw hammer from his belt next. He weighed the tool by its hand-smoothed handle, studying Dwayne for a reaction he was too tired to produce. A moment passed where they stood staring at each other, with that regretful look surfacing once more in the building manager's eyes—but it didn't stop him from cracking Dwayne on the back of the wrist once, then twice.

It was like the pain was on a delay, taking detours from the injury to his brain, going around the damaged tissue at his elbow. When it connected, the pain was enormous. Leslie released him, watching as Dwayne stumbled, tangled himself in the legs of the lawn chair, and toppled into the living room.

"Still feels something, looks like," Leslie said from the kitchen doorway, the hammer still in his hand, blood on its head. He grunted as he bent down to collect the utility knife from the floor.

On the stained circle of carpet, Dwayne lay on his back under the patched shotgun crater, legs tangled in the lawn chair, clutching his arm to his chest. Through his pained growling and panting, he listened to the familiar music of Leslie hauling out his heavy ring of keys.

"Don't yell across the courtyard for help, because I keep a window open. I'll hear you. Don't try breaking open this door. Don't jump from the balcony, because whether or not you break your legs, I'll let my dog loose on you."

Tears ran from Dwayne's eyes. Aside from the hopelessness, which was considerable, it felt as if the hammer was still crushing his wrist, each throb reigniting the pain. His bladder released, a shock of warmth. He didn't care.

"I'm leaving you my travel mug. Get hydrated. Don't break it, it was a gift and I'm going to want it back," the building manager said. "Your next session's tomorrow. So watch a little TV, get some water in you, and get some rest."

The door thumped closed. Keys jingled, a bolt shot, and footsteps moved away.

Under him, Dwayne could feel when Leslie used the elevator—that nauseatingly subtle shake of the mechanisms threatening to pull the building in on itself. The tremor faded, and he was alone in the apartment, perhaps the entire floor—the music next door was gone. He'd never felt so far away from home.

3.

"BREATHE OUT . . . BREATHE IN . . . "

Jack opened his eyes and was blinded. Everything was blue: the hardwood floor he lay upon, the walls, the arched ceilings. The room was cold, and he was alone in it. Lush curtains stood drawn, though there wasn't much to see other than blue. A tarp had been hung outside the room, and the sun filtered through, painting Jack with a cobalt cast—his hands looked like those of a drowned man's.

He stood, feeling dope sick. He was in the clothes he'd fallen unconscious wearing—a sweat-damp T-shirt and jeans, and still barefoot. Head pounding, he searched his jeans pockets, finding no keys, wallet, or phone. His armpits itched. He pulled up his shirt and hooked a finger inside his left pouch and dredged out pieces of the ruptured baggies, coated with flecks of a waxy gray substance—impurities his body couldn't absorb.

The door across the room was closed. He paused to listen, then exited, finding himself at the top of a staircase. A chandelier hung, bagged in plastic. There were other doors about him, all closed, blades of blue light escaping from under each. He held his breath to listen, unable to even detect any sounds from outside the house either—no wind, no sounds of traffic, nothing. Maybe Metzger had somehow intervened, had a mole planted among the border agents, and had gotten Jack shipped here instead of county lock-up—wherever *here* was.

"Hello?"

Nothing.

Moving to the first door to his right, he knocked. He tried its fancy glass doorknob, but it wouldn't turn. He put his ear to the cold, lacquered wood. Silence. He tried the next door. An exhale of mildew-laced air rushed out at him. A claw-foot tub. The coldness of the bathroom's moldy tile stung the bottoms of his feet as he entered, finding shards of a broken mirror gathering at the sink's drain, but nothing more.

The staircase creaked and popped under him; every noise he made was thunder-loud. A central hall with lofty ceilings, massive front doors with black iron bracings, and a beautiful parquet floor. A rotary phone stood upon a finely-carved pedestal, its cradle empty—just the base with a dangling coil of black wire connected to nothing, and electrical tape keeping the cradle's pins depressed in the receiver's absence.

Jack tried the front doors. Locked. He banged his shoulder against them and kicked, but his slight frame couldn't so much as budge them.

Crossing into a library that only offered dust on its many shelves, he drew open the curtains and faced another wall of blue. He passed through a cavernous dining hall, bare feet slapping on the marble floor, and entered a long galley-style kitchen, a peninsula jutting from the marble countertop with antique stools in a neat row. Everything here, too, was washed over with blue. Outside the kitchen's windows was more of that unbroken span of the house's shroud, billowing as the breeze swept over it. He attempted to open one of the windows, and found they'd been nailed shut.

There weren't any glasses in the cupboards, so Jack curled his head under the kitchen tap and drank. The water tasted rusty and felt cold enough to crack teeth, but he wiped his chin, feeling a shade better—though his headache, and his confusion, held.

He pulled on the kitchen's back door, only rattling its glass panels. He could see through the narrow gap between the doors. The bolt retracted when he turned the knob, but something was keeping them pinned shut. Slamming a palm against the door in frustration, the bang echoed, faded. Perhaps this place belonged to one of Metzger's friends, a hideaway for hosting private and likely prolonged executions. Dread joined his dope sickness in churning his bowels. Though the house was vast, claustrophobia set in.

He swung one of the stools against the window and the glass shattered to the floor. Setting the stool aside, he saw the tent had swollen into the vacancy—a tongue pressing the space where a tooth used to be. Jack pushed at the bubble of rough blue material with two hands. It would only yield a little, dimpling shallowly under his palms. He carefully pinched a shard of the broken window, but the tent wouldn't pierce, and slashing at it didn't produce so much as a slit.

He stepped into the hallway, approaching the front doors again. He stopped, noticing a door standing closed under the stairs. On the wall next to it, two light bulbs had been installed, one green and one red, with only the latter currently aglow. He tried the door, which he assumed would lead down to the basement. Thinking maybe he'd find a storm door to escape through, he tried the knob—locked. Beyond it, he could hear a hum of machinery, the low droning of electricity, and soft scratching, like a piece of soft wood being dragged across another by a languid hand in small, thoughtful movements.

"Is someone in there?"

As if in reply, a door boomed upstairs. Jack whipped around, the triangle of broken glass fell from his fingers and shattered on the parquet floor.

"Hello?" In the echo, he heard the terror strangling his voice reedy.

He turned and looked up at the second-floor railing. Dust drifted on the blades of blue light. Silence. Behind him, the phone on the pedestal rang with a disharmonious clatter—the bells inside sounding damaged, over-rung. Heart hammering from the startle, he started to reach for a receiver that wasn't there. Jack could only stare as the phone rang up at him, pleading to be answered.

Leaving it, he climbed back upstairs, pausing between the phone's ear-splitting pulses to listen for other possible sounds, deeper inside the house. The moment his bare foot met with the landing, the phone stopped ringing. He turned and looked over the railing and there it sat—untouched, striped with electrical tape, silent.

He returned to the upstairs hallway. As he passed a closed door, he heard something being stretched, making a rubbery sound, then *snap*. A slow creak as it was drawn long again, *snap*. He looked at the light sneaking from under the door. Shadows passed, drawn long and gangly-limbed on the floor. He swallowed his fear and knocked.

Nothing.

The door was unlocked. He pushed it wide, finding an empty dentist's chair bolted to the hardwood in the center of the room and a dark-haired figure in black clothes sitting on a stool with their back to him, pulling on latex gloves. He could smell her coconut shampoo hanging on the dusty air. When she'd gotten her second glove on, she turned   no longer in her wheelchair.

"Hey, Jack." As before, the bottom half of her face was hidden by a surgical mask, but her sparking green eyes crinkled at the corners, perhaps smiling underneath it.

"Connie?"

"Constance, if you don't mind." She gestured at the chair.

He remained where he stood. "Why am I here?"

"Sorry if I didn't hear you before, I had my headphones in. So, shall we?" Again, she motioned for him to come take a seat. Jack shook his head.

She stood effortlessly, painlessly. The hardwood popped and moaned under her motorcycle boots. He withdrew, presenting empty hands. Her eyes crinkled again and she gave her small, sniffing laugh.

"Are you still wasted?" She leaned in close to him. "Look at your eyes. Could flip a quarter into one of your pupils and it wouldn't even touch the sides . . ."

"Stay away from me."

"Don't get pissy. We're friends."

"We are not friends."

"I've performed surgery on you," Constance said. "I've seen under your skin. I've felt the warmth of your blood on my hands. Name a deeper intimacy."

"Who got me out of the border station?"

"Dunno. I was just told to come here because you'd be here, so I came—and here you are."

"Told by who?"

"Gerry. Who else?"

Past her, next to the chair, a tray waited with various medical instruments arranged—many of which were bladed, keen edges flashing blue-stained light.

"Yeah, that stuff sure is intimidating looking," she said, "but we've got to get you healthy again. We didn't happen to rinse out our pouches when we woke up, did we?"

"No. And stop saying *we*. You weren't there."

"What's wrong? Don't enjoy a little butt stuff now and again? Fine, sourpuss, you're right, I wasn't there, but Gerry's counting on me getting you better, so that makes this current situation a *we* situation."

"Where's your wheelchair?" he said. "Or was that just for sympathy, the crippled girl who couldn't possibly be up to anything bad?"

"First, it's 'differently-abled,' asshole, and secondly, don't worry about that," she said. "You should be more concerned about the fact that if we don't get you cleaned up, you might be looking at double amputation," she said. "Can't imagine it'd be too easy whacking the weasel without arms."

"What will you need to do?"

"See what may've gotten infected and, worst-case scenario, remove any bad tissue."

"Whose house is this?"

"It's just a space. Chill. Please get in the chair. I don't need Gerry mad at me too."

"Why is the house covered?"

Her lightning-bolt eyebrows knitted. "Covered in what? *Please* tell me you didn't make a mess downstairs."

Jack thrust a finger at the windows. "The fumigation tent. You haven't noticed there's no way out?"

She turned and looked. Jack could see the blueness reflect in her eyes—but when she faced him again, she took him delicately by the wrist and said, "Hey, everything's going to be just *fine*."

He let her lead him to the chair. Turning him by the shoulders to face her, she pinched the hem of his T-shirt and lifted it over his head. He cooperated and raised his arms. Momentarily blindfolded as the shirt passed over his face, a memory flashed—of his mother undressing him to get him ready for a bath when he was very young. He'd find her in the same bathtub a few years later, pale and still, the water red, no note. He thought, sometimes, he'd been broken that day. Having never bothered to gather and examine the pieces, he'd walked on into adulthood willfully uneducated, only making money to burn it and turn around and scramble for more, never able to place trust in anyone—not with the same level of unrestraint he'd had with his mother, anyway—and as far as himself, he trusted that prick least of all, watching him shrug whenever enticement called, whether it be the promise of sex, money, or chemicals, he couldn't stop not caring, an addict for apathy.

Constance sat him down. "Lay back." She scooted her stool close and sat looking at him a moment, her eyes compassionate. "Going under the knife always makes you review a few things, doesn't it?"

He nodded, his eyes burning.

"Give them a couple months and they'll close on their own. Back to your old self in no time, however you choose to define him." She patted his shoulder. The intent may've been sincere, but the glove made the touch feel artificial. "Ready?"

Lifting his right arm, he turned his head away and allowed her to explore him.

"That's odd," she said.

"What's odd?"

"It's got teeth now."

"*What?*"

"I'm kidding. God, you're easy." A pinch of pain; her finger withdrew. "Looks good. Definitely could've been worse. Belladonna's nothing to fuck around with."

"How am I alive? It was a half-pound of pure extract."

"Must keep up with your vitamins."

Metzger rambling factoids about possums returned to him, their immunity to rabies and the venom of most snakes. Had this been planned?

Pulling down her mask, Constance let it dangle by its thin elastic strap, a narrow indentation stringing across her cheeks and the bridge of her nose like the scar of two half-faces stitched together, both untrustworthy. "How was it?"

"How was what?"

"The high. Keep up."

"I don't remember."

"Mm. Too bad."

"Is there someone in the basement?"

"Why?" She flashed her eyes. "Did you *hear* something?"

"You're not convincing me this place is haunted too."

She sniffed her little laugh. "Sorry."

"Are we alone?"

"Yes," she said, and he believed her.

"Did Gerry know I'd . . . "

"Did *you* know you were going to do that before you did it?"

"No."

"Then how could Gerry?"

"It was like they knew I was coming," he said.

"Nobody knew shit. The Narcotics pigs have been watching Gerry for years, that's no secret, but you probably wouldn't even qualify as a speck on their radar," she said. "Plus, if you *were* on their radar, why would they let you get popped at the border? With cops, it's all about the win, who gets to jerk it to the mug shot."

"There was a different guy at the drop," he said. "I'd never seen him before."

"It's kind of pointless discussing this now," she said. "Doesn't matter how, they got you and Gerry's out nine hundred thousand big ones."

Jack ran his hands down his face. "I'm fucked."

"Maybe. Maybe not."

"What do you mean?"

She peeled off her gloves inside out and reached for him. He laid a hand in hers, assuming that was what she wanted. The gloves' powder gave her fingers a papery, delicate quality. "Gerry appreciates what you did," she said. "Or tried to do."

Jack felt inclined to admit, "I didn't think I'd live."

"Well, you did. But, as things have turned out, not to receive one unexpected favor then turn around and ask for another, Gerry wants me to break some news to you."

Jack waited for more, Constance caressing his thumb with hers.

She said, "You weren't carrying what they said you'd be carrying."

"It wasn't belladonna?"

"No. Test product, a new mix. They had a guinea pig in mind, but it wasn't supposed to be you."

He pulled his hand from hers. "They would've killed me."

"Yeah, well, welcome to running drugs, Jack. Maybe get a job flipping burgers if you're so risk-adverse. But, since you did the very brave thing you did, Gerry's willing to forget about your little whoopsie-doodle at the border. If you do him this favor."

"Do him a fucking favor? If things had gone like he'd wanted, I'd be dead."

"That's not off the table."

"Fuck you."

Constance sighed. "You know as well as I do you're going to do this. Because, really, what option do you have? Consider Gerry the rock and this house your proverbial hard place."

"Did he tell you to kill me if I said no?"

"Nah. They'd give you a few weeks to get comfortable thinking bygones are bygones, then one random night you'd wake up to someone sawing your head off. After tugging out your teeth, they'd huck your noggin in the lake and bury the rest behind one of the many, many closed mills around town. Plenty of options, Erie's pretty much one big potential gravesite now."

"I'll run. Especially now that you've told me all that shit."

"And go where? You might've gotten away, but your passport sure as hell didn't. And maybe I was saying *all that shit* to run out the clock. Maybe when I was looking in your pocket, you failed to notice I administered you something. Maybe the possum's already well on its way to seeing Elvis."

Her tray of tools—a hypodermic needle, among them.

"*Maybe*," she said, "being the operative word there."

"What the fuck."

"I know, right? That would've been super shitty of me, wouldn't it? Brass tacks. Do Gerry this favor or have your head flung into the lake. I know which I'd go with."

"What . . . does he want me to do?"

"In the closet over there," she said, nodding sidelong, "there's a phone receiver. It goes to that old-school phone they've got downstairs, by the front door."

"It rang, before."

Constance blinked. "It did?"

"Who's trying to call here?"

"Forget about that. Gerry managed to intercept your burner after you got popped. When you take the call downstairs, I want you to do what they say, then call *your* burner's number the minute you're done doing it. You remember your number?"

"What're they going to ask me to—?"

"I can never remember my own number. I mean, how often does a person call themselves?" Her smile failed to reach her eyes. She paused, studying him, leaving something unsaid. "With me so far? I know you've had something of a rough go lately, but this is important."

"Can't Gerry call them himself?"

"No."

"What are they going to say?"

"Dunno. I've never been able to understand them."

Jack felt his face twist.

"I still like helping," she said. "That's why I'm here. To help connect people. You ever feel you were tailor-made for a job? That the minute you started doing it, it's like you *finally* found a hidden lever that ejected you from your old you?"

"I fall into shit," he mumbled, unsure where this sudden honesty had come from as he looked around this empty room, this house, where he'd wound up. "Things happen around me, to me."

"Maybe this'll be just what you need, then," Connie said. "If your tryout—for lack of a better word—goes smooth, Gerry's willing to take good care of you. Forget about keeping the landlord off your back. No more hustling for scraps. Free from the conveyer belt, you'll be a part of something. Something amazing." Pushing with her heels, she glided her stool back, offering him room to stand. Not unkindly, she said, "One phone call or your head bobbing in Lake Erie, getting pecked by seagulls. Isn't exactly a tough decision."

She was right. Jack stood, opened the closet doors, and saw lying lonely on a shelf a black plastic horn, with its spiral cord wrapped neatly around it. He was surprised to find it so warm, like someone had moments ago been clutching it and screaming into it for hours.

The phone started ringing downstairs. The echoes collided and mixed as they ricocheted about the empty house, creating one continuous and disputatious ringing that found him up here, sounding like it was coming at him from all sides.

Constance raised a pale hand, indicating the door. "Good luck."

Before exiting, Jack looked over his shoulder at the blue plastic covering the windows. "Can you really not see that?"

She didn't look at the window, only at him. Her lips paled as she pressed them together, and the blue light lent them its stain and made her look dead, all but the concern in her eyes that renewed now, more alive than before. "Listen closely, okay? Every word."

Downstairs, he approached the ringing phone, feeling sick and afraid and alone. Attaching the receiver, he brought it to his ear and peeled away the electrical tape from the cradle. The phone's bells silenced as two hard clicks sounded—one in his ear as a connection was made, and a second click as the basement door unlocked, the red bulb snapping dark as the green illuminated.

In his ear, a whisper. "Come downstairs."

4.

DWAYNE OPENED HIS EYES. Outside the sliding glass door, darkness again. Without a watch, phone, or laptop, he had no way to know the hour. Hissing at his crushed wrist, he got to his feet and limped to the door to the hallway. Locked. He yelled through it, deafening himself as he pleaded for help. Either nobody heard him or, if they had, they didn't care. He put his eye to the peephole. Taped to the door across the hall was a note, in what Dwayne knew to recognize by now as Leslie's handwriting:

Respect your neighbors, keep it down.

And above the door to 305, the micro-camera hadn't been removed. They'd taken his laptop; perhaps they were watching him right now.

He fought with the sliding glass door that kept wanting to jump off its track and went out onto the balcony, the cold cement stinging his sockless foot. Three stories wasn't too daunting a height until you were considering jumping from it. He didn't think the courtyard's snow drifts, while pillowy-looking enough, would do much to break his fall.

To either side, 306's balcony was divided from that of its neighbor by a cement privacy wall. Unwilling to trust the railing, he leaned out, only glimpsing next door's sliding glass door before his fear of falling pulled him back. To successfully jump across—and *not* slip grabbing the icy railing—seemed unlikely. No good.

Across the courtyard on the ground floor, a silhouette stared back at him from one of the windows. The only discernable feature was the eyes of Leslie's dog, brought to gleaming green discs by the courtyard's lights. The pit bull's ears pinned back, and it let loose one bark, a warning. Replying with a middle finger, Dwayne returned inside.

In the bathroom, the mirror was gone. The lid over the toilet tank, the shower curtain and its rod, had all been removed as well. In place of the mirror, a box was now bolted to the wall, clear Plexiglas. Inside, three flip-phones lay atop one another in a tidy column. He tried prying open the box's door, but couldn't. Failing to rip the whole thing off the wall, thinking he could get at the phones inside that way, Dwayne guessed Leslie must have used some very long screws. He'd try again later, once he had his strength back. If that ever happened.

Careful of his swollen wrist, he removed his gun harness and fashioned a sling for his arm. He wasn't sure, but it certainly felt broken. He couldn't turn his hand or close his fingers—they remained splayed and grotesquely puffy, the fingernails ready to come shooting off any moment. The hammer had left two overlapping bruises, a Venn diagram of deep contusions.

Using what little reflection the Plexiglas box offered, he turned his arm to check the site of the injection Sam had given him. The skin was gray, surrounding a blackened, sunken spot the size of a pinhead. Dan Wells, in the face of the plastic box, frowned. Dwayne folded his right ear forward, seeing the skin was gray there too, reaching up into his hair and down a couple inches along his neck, following veins in darkly-tinted fractals. If he survived this, he might lose the ear as well as the arm. A black surge of rage awoke in him.

The tower of burners within the box crumbled as footsteps thundered past him overhead. Dwayne exited the bathroom and stood listening as someone moved around apartment 406. Frantic and directionless, never remaining in one room for longer than a second before turning around and racing to another—like they were desperately looking for something, or trying to keep away from a pursuer that, unlike them, could move without making footsteps.

Tracking from below, head cocked to listen, Dwayne had a shout chambered in his throat, but since he couldn't be sure the person up in 406 wasn't a friend of Metzger's, he swallowed it. Ryan had mentioned living up there when Jack had shot himself—but Dwayne stopped, remembering he couldn't trust that story, even though it had felt so real.

A hard stomp made him twitch. The person above pounded a second time, with enough force 306's fluorescent halo went dead, dropping the apartment into darkness for a second before it flickered to life again. Another stomp. Then another.

White dust trickled from the ceiling, powdering into place a milky cataract to the eye-shaped stain in the carpet. Without any furniture to hide behind, Dwayne could only watch as the patch began to buckle a little more with each successive stomp. Cracks formed, and when the patch received one more blow, it broke free and thudded to the floor, loosing a swirling cloud of white particles. Dwayne remained clear of the hole, expecting gunfire or a stream of gasoline. But only silence poured down.

Cautiously, Dwayne stepped up under the hole, seeing only a circle of blackness filling the reopened void. He hadn't heard any footsteps moving away. Perhaps they were looking down at him now from the high shadows.

A fly buzzed down through, scribbling around Dwayne's head before weaving its way to the sliding glass door where it slammed itself against the glass again and again, its freedom denied.

"This isn't my apartment." A young man's voice, hoarse and whispering—from above. He spoke so softly the fly's small body rhythmically striking the glass nearly drowned him out.

Dwayne said, "Who are you?"

The darkness didn't respond, but Dwayne could hear his ragged breathing. He was staying near the hole, perhaps lying on the floor with his mouth inches from its rim, just out of sight.

"This isn't my apartment," he said. "I looked outside. It's too high up."

"If we work together, we can get out of—"

"Are you in my apartment?" he said abruptly, clear and angry. "Did you break into my home?"

"No. They locked me in."

"That's my fucking home!"

"We have to keep quiet, okay?" Dwayne turned away to look out through the sliding glass door—below, across the courtyard, the dog was gone from Leslie's window. The building manager might've heard them, and now he was on his way up. Dwayne whispered up at the hole, "I need you to find a phone. Please. Tell them Lieutenant Spare is being held against his will and they need to send someone, now."

Something small and red fell from above, landing in the shards of plaster and dust on the floor. A shotgun shell. The tough plastic petals were spread on the one end. The soot-stained cylinder was hollow, spent.

A realization bathed Dwayne in pins and needles. He backed away from the hole, starkly aware he had nowhere to run. This isn't real. I'm still asleep.

Above, a hinge moaned. Through the hole, he saw the living room wall lit by a perfect, sharp-edged rectangle—the door to the hall had been opened. A shadow slipped across the light, and 406's blackness was made complete again as a door slammed shut.

Rushing to his own front door, he saw only Leslie's sign across the hall. No one passed by, no shadows, no sounds. He put his ear to the door. Whooshing air shoving through the building's ducting, its lungs. Water and waste pounding in its copper and PVC circulatory system. Somewhere deep within Dunsany Arms, a metal door crashed open, then footfalls clamored through a stairwell, their pitchy echoes making it impossible to discern whether they were ascending or descending until a second door crashed, just up the hall.

The stomping steps approached, their destination clearly set. Dwayne drew back from the door. He flipped the light switch, making it so the only source of illumination was now the security lights coming in from the courtyard.

The steps drew closer, louder, and stopped.

Dwayne's ears rang, anticipating their knock. But none ever came.

The dim shaft of hallway light pouring in from under the door was unobstructed, no shadows of legs. He wanted to look through the peephole, but his feet felt rooted to the kitchen linoleum. He stood staring at the door, at the light trickling in along its bottom edge, at the motionless tarnished knob, at the narrow beam filtering in through the peephole. He had no means to keep them out—with Leslie's alterations to apartment 306, it now locked from the outside. His heart hammered, his bowels liquified. As thankful as he was for the adrenaline dulling the pain in his crushed wrist, he feared more, worse injuries might be imminent.

He couldn't be sure how long he stood looking at the door, waiting. The bulbous shadow of the fly still determinedly beating against the glass door, drawn enormous by the courtyard light, glided across Dwayne, the floor, the walls, its buzzing as loud as a chainsaw in the apartment's plunging silence.

His dread for what might be standing outside didn't lessen, but the visitor continued to not push their way in—if they were even still out there. Dwayne drew together enough nerve to approach the peephole.

At first, he only saw his neighbor's door, with the sign Leslie had put up, but his relief was premature. A lumpy black shape, dotted with shining wet red, hovered low within the peephole's constricted vantage. Whatever it was, it was too close to the peephole to make out clearly—but while blurry, he could tell it was moving ever so slightly, rising and falling, as if taking metered, hushed breaths. When it bobbed up again—taking a deeper breath—Dwayne noticed the black coloring was made up of individual strands—wiry dark hair, adhered together with clumps of red and pink. Someone was standing hunched close against his door, believing they had successfully hidden themselves.

In the pool of light he was standing in, his visitor had no shadow.

Dwayne backed away until his back touched the wall opposite the door. He turned and, as quietly as possible, moved up the short hallway to the bedroom. He didn't turn on the light, but closed the door and found it had no lock.

He moved to the far corner of the empty room, the farthest point in apartment 306 from its front door, and stood listening—it was as if the entirety of Dunsany Arms was holding its breath with him. He let his gaze drift to the open closet door and the crowd of shadows standing within.

Of all the things Leslie had removed from the apartment to make it a place free of improvised weapons, he'd forgotten one: the bedroom closet's hanger dowel. It took little effort wrenching it free, and though this could serve to protect him somewhat, Dwayne didn't feel anything close to safe.

He opened the bedroom door a crack and looked out. He wouldn't be able to tell if the head-shot visitor was still out there unless he went out and checked.

He wanted to believe this was another dream trip Metzger had sent him hurtling down into, that perhaps the second dose had been of a larger quantity and thus made this new dream more vivid and last a longer duration. He had no way of knowing. The exchange with Ryan, with Dwayne surrounded by what he'd been *sure* were dozens of sleeping people, hadn't been real. Maybe none of this was real. Maybe he was lying unconscious in the laundry room following his first introduction to Metzger's drug, or slumped against the wall in apartment 603, drooling on himself, now a permanent resident of Dreamland.

Remaining at the cracked bedroom door, he tucked the hanger dowel under his arm to take his bruised right wrist in his left hand. He squeezed and swallowed a scream. Genuine pain. This was happening. He was here, awake, *in this.*

A dry crash of debris falling into the apartment, out in the living room, where the hole was. Adrenaline made the new, self-inflicted hurt bolt numb.

With his usable hand, he held the dowel ready above his head and stepped from the bedroom. He paused a moment, looking at the front door—it was still closed. He advanced another step, moving along the wall that, once he turned the corner, would allow him full view of the living room. The eye-shaped stain in the carpet and the used shotgun shell were both snowed over completely with broken drywall dust. Above, poking down from the hole, the shape of a small head.

Dwayne nearly didn't notice. He choked on a gasp. Backlit by the courtyard's lights, their features were lost save for the wet shine of two unblinking eyes, trained on him. Dwayne could feel their malignant gaze, and even though they must've known he'd seen them, they didn't withdraw. The head remained suspended by its thin neck, looking at him a while longer, a thing half-born from the ceiling hole's shadows.

In years of pursuing suspects through dark backyards and cluttered alleyways, he'd learned something. Nothing is as still as right before it moves. The wet gleam of its two staring eyes stayed on him as the shape slowly withdrew back up into the ceiling and was gone.

With the casualness a body will adopt when the mind is threatening to rend itself in two, Dwayne turned on his heel and returned to the bedroom, closed the door behind him, and stood in the empty room staring at the far wall. He turned on the light, but it did little to blunt his fear. All at once he began to shake and hyperventilate, feeling he'd never catch his breath again. He could see each puff smoke ahead of him, producing small ghosts of his own. Struggling to make sense of *any* of this, he failed. Only dead ends; nothing could be settled as solidly understandable.

Though apparently alone in the apartment again, he now knew that could change at any moment from any number of entrances. Safety, he'd already learned before ever coming to Dunsany Arms, was just a made-up word, but here, even the *idea* of safety was anathema. In the absence of a lock, he sat with his back against the door. The bedroom window across from him was dark, a glistening layer of frost on the inside. Dawn, and what little sense of safety it might lend, could not come soon enough.

5.

JACK REMEMBERED HIS eyes were closed when he heard something thud to the floor. He'd found himself still standing in the living room, wondering if something had gone wrong. He was surrounded by a blindfold of dense white smoke. Then, like it'd started raining inside, he heard a steady pattering and looked up, finding its source: shattered drywall falling from the hole he'd just made in the ceiling. Someone lying at his feet, wearing familiar clothes. They lay on their back and, when the smoke thinned, he saw everything above their nose was blown off and a column of smoke climbed, unbroken, from their blackened, bloodied mouth—*his* mouth.

He remembered there'd been people screaming upstairs then, and footsteps rushing around. Time turned mercurial, and he remained where he found his own corpse, watching Leslie and Ryan move about his apartment as if in fast-forward, first wrapping his dead body in a rug and carrying it out, then using furniture dollies to remove Jack's handful of things he'd brought here with him when Gerry had "asked" him to move in. Jack yelled at them, demanding to know if they could hear him, but neither Ryan nor Leslie said anything. They completely ignored him even when Jack struck at them, unable to make any of his attacks connect, as if the furniture thieves were made of thin air. He could only watch as they carted out the last few boxes, and then followed them out into the hallway, noticing Ryan's boy Sam was there. The boy gave a sad look at Jack's door, raised a half-hearted finger-gun, and turned away to follow his father and Leslie toward the elevators. Feeling like he probably shouldn't wander too far away from his home, Jack returned inside his apartment—which was strangely easy to do; just thinking about being back in 306 and he was there, one place then the next, the self-edit immediate, painless, and not at all jarring. Small blessings.

Soon the apartment was dark and there was only Jack, alone, terrified about what might happen next. He stood at the sliding glass doors watching the sky, but no angels slid down on beams of golden light; neither did any aperture in the floor crack open to belch sulfurous smoke and reaching red hands. There was only the stain he'd made on the floor and the hole in the ceiling and the sun outside rising and falling as time pushed inviolably on, Jack feeling none of its crawl like he had before. The same as he felt nothing else, too, because to be dead, he learned, meant surrendering all feelings save for regret. He thought about the house covered with the blue tarp he'd visited, about the thing Connie—or Constance—had urged him to speak to down in the basement, but couldn't draw back any of what it'd said to him with any clarity, or even what it'd looked like. All he could remember was being scared.

He considered something he'd learned in high school science, how studying a thing will always change that thing. If applied to his current condition, did that mean if he continued trying to make sense of his existence as it now was—as a dead person—would his fumbling just crush the broken pieces more and more granular? Would he cause a self-atomization of the self, borne from frantic attempts to reassemble what could never be again? He thought about the weirdo who always stood on the second-floor landing mumbling to themselves. Perhaps they were a ghost's counter, a body that managed to still mumble after it'd been robbed of its vital essence. Jack didn't know which would be worse: to be half a person without a body or half a person without their consciousness. He'd taken being whole for granted. Nothing was immutable. He'd learned that in life. Things change all the time, and seldom for the better. And most changes come from within, usually small adjustments issued over time—and each, once set in motion, come to fruition imperceptivity slowly—but sometimes changes come in great heaving shifts where, in an instant, nothing's recognizable from how it was the second before. Blowing his own head off without a doubt fell into the latter category. That was, in hindsight, a rather brash decision he'd made. At the time, he'd hoped every theologian had gotten it wrong, that on the other side there'd only be a painless, silent nothingness. He certainly hadn't expected this. The only comparison he had was taking a very long road trip, the kind where making good time is so paramount you won't even stop for a rest room. And when you reach your destination, and step from your vehicle that's started to feel like a second skin, you have to remember how to move without pushing a pedal. Shucked from your shell of glass and metal, you're confronted by the notion you're suddenly so much more exposed to everything now. Beyond naked, beyond skinned—*bodiless.*

He tried clapping his hands, but he could produce no noise. He yelled but his dark, now-furniture-void apartment, even cavernous as it was, lent his voice no echo. He was still present here, in this room, existing by some definition and anchored by an unbreakable linkage he couldn't understand. Twice he'd attempted to throw himself into the abyss and twice he had slammed into the hard rim instead, damaged a little more each time, still stuck on this side of it, rejected. The first attempt in the border station had given him a crippling speech impediment, owlishly desynchronized blinks, a tough time remembering names, brain-crushing migraines that spat into his mind's eye atrociously violent hallucinations, and an increasing inability to think in a straight line about the simplest subjects without winding up snarled and lost in them, which usually resulted in entire afternoons disappearing. Further doses taken into his blood at Gerry's insistence would only dull Jack's pains for a handful of hours, which he did welcome, even if those moments of rest were all too short and piled with nightmares. Until the bleed-over into his waking life became a permanent condition. Constantly that *noise*, that *face*, those *eyes*, seen and heard everywhere. At the time, when he'd asked Leslie for help, Jack didn't think there was much that could exacerbate his situation. Again, at the time.

* * *

Without a coil of flesh, he was free from the demands that came with having one—which was both a blessing and a curse. Sure, he didn't need to worry about making rent or feeding himself. He'd never need to get a haircut again. But having no brain meant no dreams—a blessing—but no sleep either, a curse. Locked in constant awareness, to distract or calm himself he'd try concentrating on his parents' house, the bar he used to frequent up the street from his duplex, his ex-girlfriend's, hoping he might be able to transport himself to one of those places, like that thing he'd read about doppelgangers made manifest solely by a person's yearning for another's safe return. But the lowest point he could vanish to was the building's laundry room. The highest, the sixth-floor hallway. And it was there, curious to what Gerald Metzger might be up to right this moment, that Jack realized that although he was dead—and in theory past additional harm or further degradation—he was still afraid of the chemist. Unable to bring himself to peek inside apartment 603, he decided to mark it, for himself, as off-limits and continued vanishing and un-vanishing himself about the building, soon discovering he couldn't go past the front doors.

Though nothing appeared to be in his way—and no other solid object had stopped him before—he couldn't even step out into the parking lot. Standing in the lobby, looking past the glass doors—an inch or two in from which was where the barrier appeared to be—he could only watch the cars pass on Bergen Street in the distance, their taillights strobing through the dead trees. They might as well have been red comets in the sky. It took him longer than it probably should've to understand that what he was doing now was . . . haunting this place.

He watched the sun rise and watched it fall. He watched the traffic on Bergen Street thicken in the morning and again in the early evening, then thin to a trickle after it'd gone dark. None of the cars parked directly outside the building moved. He watched, never needing to blink once, as no one exited the building all day; neither did anyone park and come inside. Not a soul came or went . . . until he was about to give up to go watch something else.

A man in heavy snow boots, torn jeans, and a deteriorating flannel jacket, who coughed with every third step, passed through Jack and pushed his way outside, shoving wide the glass doors Jack couldn't so much as touch. The man, in his late middle years, crunched his way across the unplowed parking lot, stopped as if he'd heard someone call his name, and turned to look back up at the building. And that's when Jack recognized him. Standing in an orange circle of a lamppost, deep shadows filled the low spots in the delivery man's weathered and pockmarked face. He looked up at one of the windows, maybe the third or fourth floor, his face never changing—as if anticipating something that never happened. He then got in a car, used the wipers to clear the snow from the windshield, and drove off, his red taillights joining those streaming along out in the far dark, on his way to drop off another load of product, ruin another life, help the chemist make another ghost.

The delivery man would leave at what felt like, to Jack, the same exact time every night. During the day, Jack searched for the man's apartment, hoping to find him asleep, maybe give him a scare if Jack could manage to knock over one of the delivery man's belongings, hopefully something expensive or dear to him. But he could never find where the delivery man, before coughing his way down the hallway toward the front doors, would exist at any other time. Jack stood in the hallway, his back to the lobby, waiting, but then the delivery man would come down a different stairwell or take the other elevator Jack hadn't been watching. Sometimes Jack would be facing away from the building's front doors, but then hear them creak and turn around, seeing the delivery man trudging through the ankle-deep snow, having somehow gotten behind him, maybe holding his coughs until he was clear of the dead man—as if the delivery man had sensed someone was trying to sift a pattern from his nocturnal behaviors.

Remembering something he'd read online about the dead, long before he'd become one of them, Jack considered whether *he* was actually the one stuck in a pattern, because some hauntings, according to the article that had some really bad click-bait title, are like time-stains on a place. And the ghost isn't what's called a sentient haunting, but rather someone's miserable final moments running themselves out again and again and again. A sentient haunting, free from a loop, won't do the same things over and over, and is often aware they are well and truly dead. Could it be he was some mix of the two, cursed to be aware that he was stuck witnessing as the same things happened around him over and over again? But that didn't seem possible, because the delivery man slightly altered his route every single night. And Jack watched other people go about their lives—though, like when he was alive, those patterns, once they'd been ingrained, didn't vary that much. But small differences occurred. Have the day's first cigarette *before* brushing your teeth, belt the kids *after* school, for example.

What was stranger, Jack never saw the delivery man return, only leave. He may've gotten lost in his own thoughts, but it didn't seem likely he'd fail to notice the delivery man park his car and come back inside, walking right through him a second time. But as if he was blinking, despite not having need to do so anymore, in one instant the delivery man's car would be gone, the void in the snow slowly filling back in, and then the car would be there. Like it'd been edited into place, a splice in a film.

Maybe the delivery man doesn't exist. Maybe he's dead as I am. Maybe that dose I gave myself to work up the nerve before I blew my head off followed me here, and now I'm not only dead but permanently fucked up, stuck seeing and hearing shit forever while riding out this never-ending bender.

That was as good a guess as any.

The sun rose, the sun fell, and Jack watched the delivery man limp from the stairwell door, push his way outside, stop, look up at the building a moment, get in his car, clear the snow from the windshield with the wipers, and drive off.

And drive off.
And drive off.
And drive off.

∗ ∗ ∗

Being dead, but still hanging around by some definition—Jack couldn't bring himself to even think the word "ghost"—made him feel deceived. It wasn't like it was in the movies, or even those Charles Dickens stories he'd had to read in high school. It wasn't much different from when he'd been alive, really: he was constantly ignored. Except, when he was alive, he could make someone pay attention and listen to him, if he made it clear they could use him to make money, but now his value was less than zero. He couldn't get a straight job. He had nowhere to be, nothing needing doing. It should've been a relief, really, but it didn't take long for the monotony to set in. And if he couldn't get anyone's attention by talking to them, he didn't think they'd mind if he watched them. But it wasn't *really* watching, and it wasn't really like studying them, either. He tried telling himself he was some sort of phantom anthropologist, but frankly, it was theft. And what he stole was existence, "living" by accompanying the tenants without their consent as they went about their very human moments, doing things that people do when they trust and believe that they're alone, because they have no reason to not trust and believe that—a glance about the room, there was nothing near them but the air and light and silence. Animal things. Things that might be read as funny for those who still do them, but Jack honestly missed sitting on the rim of his bathtub while clipping his toenails or taking a good life-affirming shit or jerking off or the contented dread that follows finishing a cigarette and looking at the smoldering butt wondering how many more of these I will burn in my life before the doctor tells me I should start regretting having ever taken up the habit but feeling okay about it because, right now, I am not yet dying—not in that way, anyway. He watched them, and watched with envy. It was an invasion, watching them, and Jack knew this, but loneliness and monotony can shove a person toward odd behavior sometimes, even the dead. New habits were already slipping into new addictions. He wasn't a phantom anthropologist; he was a leering and envious bodiless voyeur. And what he'd cataloged was this:

Every day, the building was brimming with routines—a majority of which, when he was a visible, living entity of flesh and blood and thus busy with his own routines, Jack hadn't been allowed to witness. His stepdad had given him an ant farm as a kid, an opening salvo to convince Jack he had a new buddy, and though the relationship with Jack's mother only lasted until the end of that following summer, Jack kept the ants for years. He thought back on his hundreds of small pets that could all fit together in the palm of his hand while watching the cars flowing along the interstate. When one has been pulled out from under the pounding, erosive flow of time, the busy-work of those still trapped under its crush will begin to look like speedy, if rudderless, wanderings. How *urgent* everything seemed to be to them, the self-assigned importance everything has, always hurrying and rushing around, so much to do and so little time to do it in. Jack considered how much of his life he'd wasted standing in lines, walking junk mail he hadn't asked for to the trash, saying *yes* I'm serious you *do* have the wrong number. The three minutes here and the two hours there that, if allowed, will account for a bulk of a life.

But he had a familiarity with this world, unlike that of the ant farm. He knew what it was like to have hopes, to always feel like he was moving—or *being* moved—toward something, a desperate if hollow drive to obtain things or complete tasks, done and done. Relieved of the burden of purpose, he could observe those who still had one pursuing theirs— even as an unshakeable fear took form and demanded to know: What if one day as he watched, he realized he'd missed, while alive, something vital about the human experience he was no longer able to participate in? Something he'd like to amend, but was now wholly barred from?

There was never anything to see when he tried looking in mirrors but, as he was now, he saw himself—or the person he'd wasted—much clearer. He always hated the saying "twenty-twenty hindsight" because it felt like a self-defeating prophecy, that no matter how hard anybody tries we're all doomed to wind up looking back on a trail of fuck-ups. Maybe by misinterpreting that expression, he was forging his *own* self-defeating prophecy. He'd never traveled outside of the United States other than up to Toronto, and on those trips he was never without something illicit hidden on—or within—his person. Either because he'd been late, dope sick, or working one of his many dead-end jobs, he never got to say goodbye to his mother or his father or any of his grandparents. The list was endless, but he'd felt, at the time, he still had the rest of his life, there was always tomorrow, and some fortuitous night his fairy godmother would flutter in through his window and *prang* him with the give-a-shit wand. And from that moment on, things would be better, *he'd* be better. More present, better equipped, less prone to repeating the same mistakes.

One regret stung the deepest. He had never truly been in love with someone. There'd been connections, sure. Rough understandings he'd allowed people to *think* they had about him, and those he assumed he'd developed about others, but there'd always been a Jack Cotard standing behind another, peeking over the other's shoulder. And even safely hidden alone with itself, that Jack Cotard, the supposed "real" one, wasn't even that familiar with itself. Maybe there'd never been that much there *to* know. He never knew why he did anything. Like he'd told Connie, or Constance, things just happened around him, to him. Maybe the pointless little errands and the series of shitty part-time jobs weren't the only things guilty of sneaking off with crumbs of his time. He'd thrown a lot away. And then himself too, twice.

Was it possible for the dead to lose their minds? Though he didn't have a body anymore, would something akin to a chemical imbalance soon begin to itch him? Was this a permanent condition, or would he start to slowly fade at some point? If so, what would follow? And if this state was of the permanent sort, would he still be nailed to this spot after the building was eventually knocked down? Will I still be here to see the sun go dark and watch as the world shifts into a silent gray rock? Why aren't there others like me around? Can I just not see them? Or is this meant to be an explicitly solitary thing, to each dead their own infuriatingly lonesome plane? These concerns prompted him to remind himself, every time before he'd engage in another session of watching: You had your chance. This is what you wanted. You are where you led yourself.

* * *

Every morning, Ryan Waite would step from 437, the new apartment he shared with his son, and Jack would join Ryan on his ride in the elevator down to the first floor. There, Ryan would check his mailbox—which never had any mail in it, though he still checked it every day—and then he'd knock at the door marked MANAGER.

Leslie and Ryan would exchange small talk about the number of inches of snow they're due to get or whatever had been on TV the night before, and then Ryan would return upstairs where Sam, up now, would be seated on the floor with a bowl of cereal, his sandy hair pillow-matted, absorbed in his cartoons. At noon Ryan typically climbed upstairs to Metzger's apartment, knocked, and without opening up, Metzger would pass under the door a small baggie—and sometimes clean works, if Ryan had requested them. Giving himself to the dream, Ryan typically would rouse around two AM, glower at the lack of messages on his phone, pick at something he found in the fridge, shower, misaim some frustration at his kid, and go back to sleep for another ten hours, just in a different room.

Jack felt he'd already known Ryan's life. In the months leading up to what he'd done to himself, the routine was identical, except Jack hadn't had a four-foot roommate. But it still depressed him, nonetheless, to see another locked in such a wearisome cycle, perhaps even more so seeing it from an outsider's perspective. Ryan seemed to have as little worry for the slippage of time. There were no calendars, none of the clocks in apartment 437 were in agreement, and never did Jack see him set any alarm to wake himself. It didn't matter what day it was or what time it was within that day. All that mattered was revisiting the dream for as long as possible, as often as possible.

Could one's "true" reality be defined by which one they spend the most time in? If Ryan dreams for Metzger sixteen hours out of the day, occupying more time inside his head than the world that surrounded it, could what's popularly known as the waking world—for Ryan and anyone else who opted to spend their life that way—be labeled the dream?

Though Ryan's daily rituals were as depressing as they were tedious, Jack did enjoy watching Sam keep himself entertained while his father burned his days slowly killing himself. The boy was a walking fount of creativity that had no need for store-bought toys to make his own fun. When he wasn't filling a page in a coloring book, he'd spend hours building little people out of knobby twigs and rubber bands and snapped shoelaces. He'd murmur to himself, chin to chest, as he sat and detailed aloud the lives he'd invented for his stick people. Jack watched the boy use a gap in the courtyard's brickface as a cozy cave for his people, using brittle brown leaves for beds and acorn caps for dinnerware.

"Your name is Mister Stick and your name is Missus Stick and this is your son Little Stick. You all moved here together from the land of Evergreen after the Great Fire. And even though it's not like where you used to live, you still like it here a lot."

"Sam," Jack said, watching the boy tuck each of the Sticks into bed. "Can you hear me?"

The boy told his stick people, "This is where you belong now. It's where you always belonged. Even before, when you didn't know it yet."

"Sam," Jack said. "Do you know where they put my body?"

For Jack, there was no difference between thinking and a thing and saying it, but if a dead man mutters to himself and nobody has the ability to hear him, is he still producing a sound? He didn't know, but had to try. "I don't want to see it, but . . . just know what happened to it, where it ended up. That's all."

"Goodnight, Mister Stick and Missus Stick and Little Stick," Sam said, and raced away, passing through Jack to boom through the door and return inside, never aware he hadn't been alone a single minute the entire day.

At night, once the boy went to sleep—usually curled into a ball on the living room floor in a pool of flickering TV light—Jack would sit with the boy's father, looking at the vague red stain on his bandage stump, where Ryan's arm used to be. He knew that even if Ryan was awake, he wouldn't be able to hear him, but Jack still expressed his remorse, saying that if he hadn't done as Metzger said and used the machete on Ryan, they'd both be dead now.

Some days Jack would follow and watch Leslie while the building manager went about his routines. Standing at his elbow, he'd watch Leslie carefully arrange his tools in his toolbox, exit his lonely home on the first floor, and go around the building fixing leaking pipes and half-starting small projects here and there—before abandoning them either out of frustration or boredom. Half-tighten a handrail in the stairway, buff some of the scuffs out of the lobby floor, then move on to something else he'd also leave half-completed. There was a schedule within the building manager's head, but Jack could never get a grasp on it. Leslie neither kept a ledger, nor did he ever see him write anything down—though he knew the old man wasn't illiterate; his handwriting was all over the place, his various signs about this being broken or that being broken.

Jack would be present for one thing Leslie wrote, though, in blood.

He had assumed the occupancy in Dunsany Arms was low—maybe half of the units had a tenant, at a guess—but it was rare for Leslie to need to knock before entering an apartment to tinker with something. Following behind as his incorporeal assistant, Jack noticed many of the apartments, though empty of people, often still had furniture in them, or food in the refrigerator. Or clothes in the closet. Or shoes by the door. Evidently unbothered by this—and in no clear hurry to clean out the units—Leslie would address the issue that needed his attention, not give the unit a second look otherwise, check his watch, sigh, and lock the door behind himself. There weren't enough hours in the day, Jack read in the old man's face. Doing it all alone, he would never manage to outpace the building's determined decay.

Once, curious, Jack remained behind after Leslie had left an apartment and surveyed all that'd been abandoned within it. The movie posters on the wall curling up on themselves, helped by the trapped humidity in the room. The open box of instant rice on the counter, now empty courtesy of the building's vermin, its volunteer custodians. The two toothbrushes in the bathroom, sharing a holder. The jewelry box on the nightstand, filled with cheap, flashy junk that apparently still held a lot of importance to whoever had adorned themselves with the pieces, because they'd been stored with such organized care, reverent pewter and plastic diamonds. Last, and arguably the most painful, the dents in the pillows of two people who had, whenever they'd last slept here, dreamed very close together.

"Is anyone here?"

Apartment 305 remained silent around him.

What's the difference between a personal possession and a prop? Does a prop exist only when an object is collected and arranged with insincerity, taking up space only to suspend disbelief in an onlooker, Yes, I am alive, see this space that bears the evidence of a life lived? What about something that has no tangible shape, that cannot be held or be placed or arranged, that has less cache in the world than a shadow or an echo of an echo's echo? What level of presence can a thing be said to have that's incapable of harming so much as the air it passes through to search on and on for its place?

If a dead man weeps in a room filled with forgotten things and no one's around to hear him, does he make a sound?

* * *

On the second-floor landing, Jack stood behind the former children's author who, like any other time, was pressing their forehead to where the stairwell walls joined, telling their story:

"—she said then he said then they said to which *she* said then they said then *he* said—"

"What's your name?" Jack said.

"—she said then she said then they said then the boy said to which *she* said—"

The story without end echoed up and down the stairwell, overlapping and cutting back into itself, the endless narrative being fed continuously by its creator, who never paused for a breath, voice hoarse from unreeling this story for . . . well, as long as Jack had been around, in one form or another.

"How long have you lived in the building?"

"—said then he said then she said then he said—"

"What are these people's names? Were they people you knew?"

"—then he said then she said then—"

"Did you make them up?"

"—said that she had said then he said then he said—"

"What are they even talking about? Nobody ever actually *says* anything."

"—then she said then he said then the woman said then—"

"Is it just one long quote? A person quoting a person quoting a person?" Jack had to stop himself before he started doing it too. "Is that what it is?"

"—said then he said then she said then he said—"

"When did the story start?"

"—then they said that she'd said that *he* had said that they said he said she—"

"When does it end?"

"—then he said then he said then he said then *he* said then *he* said then *he* said then he said that he said that he'd said then *he* said then *he* said then *he* said then *he* said—"

* * *

In the corner of the building manager's living room was a large C-shaped machine Jack took to be a drill press at first, until he watched Leslie using it one day. He watched him select a toothless brass key from a box and, after tracing the shape of another key, one with teeth already cut into it, Leslie had set an intricate jig in the machine and begun cutting the blank key to make a duplicate. To either side of the machine, the carpet was dusted with brass shavings that glinted like a dusting of gold. Squinting with concentration, each movement of scarred, old hands precise, Leslie would sometimes take hours to clone a single key.

Though he was hard to read, it appeared Leslie got a fair amount of satisfaction out of this particular errand. Jack would sometimes catch him, while he worked, singing along to a song on the radio—what could be heard over the apartment-shaking whirring the machine made and the high-pitched shrieks of brass being cut.

Done, Leslie would then take his massive ring of keys, find the one he'd made the duplicate for—its teeth dulled from use—and replace it with the fresh sharp-toothed one, tossing the uselessly smooth key into the trash, where it clanged with a musical sound.

Jack leaned to look down inside the waste bin that was apparently reserved for only disposing of old keys—it was more than half-full, probably weighing a ton. The keys, etched on each head with the corresponding apartment, shone like coins. Shifting side to side to watch the glimmering discarded keys wink at him in turn, Jack felt an idea piece itself together. Though useless to him as he was now, unable to pick anything up, if he could manage to tell someone where some keys could be found, ones the building manager wasn't likely to notice the absence of . . .

* * *

When he chose to spend the day watching the building manager, Jack preferred to keep him company in the evening, when Leslie would sit at his kitchen table and methodically hand-roll the next day's cigarettes. It reminded Jack of spending the night at his grandmother's house. His grandfather had passed away only two years after Jack's mother had been born and so his grandmother, deciding to never remarry, spent most of the last half of her life alone. Jack knew she liked his company—there was always this big smile on her face when he showed up, the incredible warmth of which spoke to its genuineness—but after about the third day of his visit or so, when all the board games had been played and she'd asked him every question about school she could think of, like she'd forgotten he was there, her posture would take on a slightly deeper hunch and her papery hands moved a little slower—and how those things would be undone the moment Jack said anything, reminding her she wasn't alone. She'd clear her throat and blink a few times, reanimating before him, and look at him as if he'd just materialized into the chair across from her. But the deepened hunch and the slowness of her hands became worse, and permanent, after her daughter, Jack's mother, had joined Jack's grandfather. Even in her last handful of months, the hunch remained fixed and her hands glacially crept and crawled and her milky eyes would not brighten, even when he said anything to remind her she wasn't alone. She'd only look at him, chin quivering, sadness having bleached the very color from her eyes, and a slight look of pain was all that would surface. Perhaps she was thinking about when she'd inevitably lose him too. Even at a young age, he was proving himself to be no stranger to the law.

So maybe Jack saw the same loneliness in Leslie he was starting to see in himself. Aware there wasn't anything he could do to remedy it for either of them, he stood up from the old man's kitchen table and approached the framed photos on Leslie's walls, wondering who all the people in them were. They must've been important to Leslie, Jack figured, because it'd be strange to display pictures of strangers—unless Leslie's loneliness had, in fact, become that severe. Maybe so. Leslie hadn't had any visitors, not that Jack had seen. Working as a drug maker's right hand would probably make Thanksgiving an awkward affair.

If the photos on his wall were of people Leslie knew, he must've always been the camera man, because Jack noticed he didn't appear in a single one. None of them appeared to have been snapped inside Dunsany Arms, either. The backgrounds were all beaches or churches, lakes at sundown and snow-swept pastures, amusement parks and campsites.

Jack moved to the next photo and found himself looking into his own eyes. He remembered that night captured in the photograph fondly—his grandmother had taken it, she being the only one who'd made it out to watch him run. It felt like a lifetime ago—which, apparently, it was. Long before he'd had pockets cut into his skin, before he'd ever heard the name Gerald Metzger, before he'd started fucking around with drugs, his high school track team had gone to state. They'd suffered a bitter loss, but you'd never have guessed it, given the photo. That kid sure was *happy*.

"You goddamn moron," Jack said to himself. Himself then, himself now. Some things were permanent, it seemed.

All the other photos on Leslie's wall around Jack's suddenly made sense. These weren't keepsakes. Leslie wasn't holding on to people's things out of respect for how much value they'd had to the dead. They were mementos he'd found and turned into trophies, nailing them to his wall. Worse was how everyone was smiling in the photos the building manager had selected to keep. Ghosts before they were dead, unaware they would someday end up here, in this place, dreaming for Metzger.

Finding him washing his hands in the bathroom, Jack charged up behind Leslie and screamed at the back of his head every insult he could muster. Free from the limitation that came with lungs, his scream, theoretically, could go on forever. He gave Leslie a few hours' worth, following him about the apartment, blasting him with a sound he couldn't hear; but seeing how it elicited no response, Jack gave up, failing to see any point in continuing. He was only aggravating himself.

Leslie's dog, a black pit bull he'd addressed as Keelut, was consistently at his master's heel, as if magnetically tethered. Only once Leslie had settled either at the kitchen table to roll the next day's cigarettes or in his recliner in front of the TV, would the dog go to the window that looked out into the courtyard, standing with its front paws on the sill, watching the snow fall, sniffing at the small gap Leslie had allowed the window to stay open.

Once he'd understood this pattern, Jack followed the dog to watch the snow alongside him. A low growl grumbled in the dog's throat. Jack scanned the courtyard, but didn't see anyone out there—same as he'd never seen anyone in the courtyard, except for Sam—but when he glanced at Keelut to see where its attention was fixed, the dog was looking generally in his direction. As if Keelut couldn't get a precise fix on Jack, the dog's amber-colored eyes kept drifting to one side or the other, with its ears pinned back and curled lip showing the yellow of its fangs. Knowing he was past harm, Jack slowly reached a hand toward the dog, just to see what it'd do. Keelut snapped, the dog's teeth passing through Jack's ethereal fingers as if gnashing at smoke.

Leslie appeared in the bedroom doorway. With one stern look from its master, the dog turned away from the window and approached Leslie with its head bowed in apology. The building manager gave the dog a scratch behind the ear and scanned the room, his watery old eyes passing right over where Jack was currently standing in the corner. Lit by the courtyard's security lights, Leslie's troubled expression remained fixed on his well-lined face, running his eyes about the room for another, slower pass.

"Can you hear me, Leslie?" Jack said. "Can you hear me talking to you, you stupid old fuck?"

If he could, he gave no indication.

Jack took a step closer. In truth, he wanted to give the old bastard a scare. After receiving for Gerry so often, the noise in his head had been getting to be too much. Jack had come down here to Leslie, and asked for something that might help him sleep through the night, something strong—less like a sedative and more like an off-switch, his exact words. "I think I got something," Leslie had said. "I'll bring it up to you later on tonight." What Jack found on his kitchen table the next morning—Leslie evidently let himself in during the night—wasn't pills in a blister pack, but something that had brought about Jack's current condition with one pull of the trigger.

The fault wasn't entirely on Leslie. He hadn't coerced Jack to do what he did to himself, merely offered him his off-switch as requested. Jack still hated him all the same.

Like he'd done with Keelut, he slowly reached toward the old man. "Can you hear me?"

His fingers were an inch from the old man's shoulder when Leslie, under his breath, addressed the bedroom and all that might or might not be standing within it, seen and unseen. "I'm going to start working on it tonight. All right?"

With that, Leslie turned away to return to the kitchen, Keelut following close behind. Jack, stunned, stood in the doorway watching Leslie chop onions and reduce a long curl of sausage to greasy pink checkers.

"Leslie," Jack said. "What does that mean? Leslie?"

Wordless, the old man stirred the ingredients around the sizzling pan. He tossed a piece of the chopped sausage to his dog. Keelut swallowed the treat whole and resumed intently watching Leslie cook, eyes wide with intense focus.

"Can you hear me?" Jack said.

Only the dog turned an ear toward him—and only briefly, much more interested in the prospect of another treat than in a dead man's pathetic cries for acknowledgement.

Jack stepped deeper into the room. "Leslie. Can you *hear me*?"

With enough violence to make his dog flinch, Leslie slammed the wooden spoon down, shouted for Keelut to get the fuck out of his way, and thundered into the next room. Smacking the wood-paneled TV's power button, he returned to the kitchen, sent the steaming pan crashing into the sink, and bent to retrieve a large plastic tub from a lower cabinet. From the tap, he filled the tub halfway and created three floating mountains, pitching into the water fistfuls of white power from a paper bag. After stirring the mixture into a loose paste, Jack watched Leslie carefully walk the tub of watery dough out into the living room and set it with care on the floor in front of his recliner, never spilling a drop.

Taking a seat, Leslie rolled up his shirt sleeves to the elbows—paused a second to check his watch before removing it and carefully setting it aside—and began tearing into long strips the stack of newspapers he kept next to his moth-eaten chair. When he'd amassed a large bird nest of paper strips, he fetched from a drawer a rubber-foam hand. Jack thought it looked like a jewelry store display, a way to showcase rings on its crumbling outspread fingers. Running a paper strip through the paste until it was coated, Leslie carefully layered the pieces to construct around the mannequin hand a patchwork cocoon.

As he watched, Jack said, "You *can* hear me. Can't you?"

To that, the building manager released a long sigh through his nostrils and remained focused on his task of mummifying the mannequin hand.

"What did you do with my body?" Jack said. Only once he'd said it did he hear the desperation tingeing his question. "Where am I?"

Hands dripping with paste, Leslie stood and moved toward the kitchen. Out of habit more than anything, Jack side-stepped to clear a path for the old man and watched as he tugged open the freezer door. Inside, among a frost-coated carton of vanilla ice cream, a vented box of baking soda, and some shrink-wrapped steaks, Leslie pulled out a fist-sized gray mass inside a Ziploc bag. He tossed it into the microwave, the frozen object hitting the glass platter with a solid *thunk*. While the microwave, set to defrost, filled the room with its low drone, Leslie kept starting to fold his arms before remembering the wet plaster all over his hands.

"What is that?" Jack said.

Posture shooting straight, Leslie turned a slow circle, running his eyes over every surface and through every cubic inch of empty air around him. Jack didn't bother asking if Leslie could hear him. He was too preoccupied trying to make out what the gray lump in the microwave was, watching it turn, the bag around it swelling puffy with condensation. On its next rotation, he saw something had been written on the bag. In black marker, the letters making out JACK ran in thin lines as the bag quivered and ballooned around the glossy gray slab inside it.

"What did you do to me?"

Leslie opened the microwave and the bag crackled as it collapsed, sucking in on itself to form a sagging transparent skin around the hunk of whatever-that-was. Carefully pinching it by its corners, Leslie upturned the bag and dumped the softened, steaming wad onto a plate. Jack, horrified, peeked over Leslie's shoulder at the mass, seeing it change colors from gray to a dull pink when the air hit it. And it wasn't one solid piece of . . . *him*. The clumps separated from one another with a tacky peeling sound, creating a little steaming pile of pink curds in a spreading puddle of red.

Twice Leslie told his dog to go lie down, but each time Keelut would only retreat as far as the kitchen doorway, leaning his long neck into the room, his sniffing nose having caught the scent of something awfully appealing. Evidently far more interested than he'd been in the sausage, rivulets of drool stretched from the dog's jowls.

It's a feeling unlike any other, staring at the sizzling contents of a bag that had your name on it, wondering which part of you that might've come from. Without eyelids, Jack could only turn away. He hadn't noticed Leslie had left the room until the old man returned with the mannequin hand he'd mummified. Jack watched as Leslie placed it palm-up on his chipped faux-marble countertop, next to the steaming contents. Pressing the callused pad of his thumb into Jack's stolen viscera, once it was smeared to the knuckle with blood and some soft red pebbles Leslie drew a line down the wrappings covering the mannequin's palm. Then, daubing his thumb again to reload his digit, he drew another line, going the other way down the palm, that ended with a spiral. Then a circle around the lines and the spiral, closing them all in. Apparently that completed the symbol. Leslie bumped the faucet on with his elbow and began scrubbing the blood and plaster from his hands.

Feeling like he might atomize and lose even more of himself if he spent another second watching this, Jack tried to vanish himself back home, back up to 306. At least, if nothing else, he could be in a familiar space. But he remained in Leslie's kitchen, feeling rooted to the spot. He tried again, but couldn't so much as leave the room, let alone the building manager's apartment. Drawing together as much will as he could, he attempted to launch himself up through the ceiling—much like he'd already done, albeit in a much different way—but again, he was still in Leslie's kitchen. With his next attempt, something impacted with a hollow, fragile sound behind him. There the mannequin hand lay, palm-down on the stained linoleum floor, as if something had pulled it off the counter by an invisible line.

Leslie, evidently having heard it too, turned off the faucet and looked down at the hand as he worked a towel through his hands. Again, he ran his eyes about the room without turning his head, but gone was his look of paranoia. Now he wore a look of tempered fascination, maybe even cautiously hopeful that something he'd failed to do in the past had, this time, finally borne fruit.

"I'll have to work on it off-and-on this week. I've got a lot of things that need attention around the place," Leslie said, looking just left to where Jack now no longer had any choice but to stand. "Go ahead, try it out. See how it fits. You won't break anything. Make a fist."

Remembering when he still possessed a mortal coil, Jack pictured his old hands, back when he had them, making a fist—and watched the fingers of the hand on the floor slowly curl, closing around the symbol on its palm drawn in his blood.

* * *

The rain drummed hollowly on him as he looked up to the sky, seeing only a span of churning gray. The rain silenced and, as snow began to fall, each flake spun and tumbled and dissolved before at last alighting upon the courtyard's wet flagstones. Creaking and unsure, Jack's steps knocked with empty sounds as he approached the brickface. He had to feel around to find behind which brick the Sticks called home. Finding the right one, at about waist-height, Jack removed the brick and looked in on the massacre of little wooden people. They'd been shattered, their pieces lying all over their home, their woodgrain innards bright white, splintered heads and splintered legs. Their brittle brown blankets of dead leaves had been crushed, their acorn-cap dinnerware flattened and cracked. The boy, when he'd found his friends had been broken into toothpicks, would not be happy.

"Who are you?" said a small voice, sounding wary of the stranger but unable to dam back their curiosity.

Ungainly, each small movement executed with a sharp twitch, Jack managed to turn his mobile prison around to look at the boy. He'd been keeping himself covered when he went around the halls during the daytime, and would actively dodge the other tenants when he infrequently came across one. He'd been caught this time without any covering, the snow settling and sticking to his frame, colder than the wet ground.

Seeing him, the boy didn't run away. He didn't move. Wearing only a pair of dirty-kneed cotton pants and mismatched shoes—one far larger than the other—the boy's busy mouth was always working on something, whether chewing his lip or clearing the crust of snot from under his nose with clumsy passes of his tongue. He had some serious bed head going: his hay-blond hair was mashed up into a tuft on one side, so deeply that a bright dot of pale scalp showed.

"My name is Sam," the boy said in Jack's silence.

Though Keelut had been present for when Jack had taken his first new steps, the dog would only growl and snap at him, giving Leslie things to repair on his creation. Unlike the dog, Sam showed no apprehension.

"I'm Jack." Struggling with his stiff joints and a neck that seemed determined to keep his chin hooked over his shoulder, Jack turned to point at the gap in the brickface, where Mister Stick and his family used to live. "I think someone found your friends."

"What do you mean?" the boy said, not looking anywhere but at Jack.

"Someone broke your stick people."

"I did that. I didn't need them anymore, because Mister Leslie said I'd be having new friends moving in soon. He said they might be shy, so I'd have to be patient with them," the boy said. "Do you know how to play four-square?"

6.

THE HOMUNCULUS CRUNCHED through the broken shards of the door it'd kicked apart and lumbered into her apartment, leaving a trail of dark, wet footprints of liquid rot on her carpet. Though she'd had the nightmare countless times—and felt she remembered this fact, going through it again now—it was no less terrifying. Connie screamed and kept pulling at her chair's brakes, but they wouldn't release, her wheels wouldn't move. She was trapped as the living pile of dead, necrotized skin lurched another step closer, then another step. One stride away now, it lifted its arm agonizingly slowly and curled all its fingers but one, reaching out for her throat. She twisted and thrashed in her chair, but she couldn't overturn it, couldn't pitch herself forward out of its seat. It was like she'd fused to it, imprisoned by her means to get around. And she felt it, the slippery and rotten finger alight upon her throat and start to push, little by little, at first painlessly then, as her air was cut off and the finger kept pushing in, the hollow crack as her throat collapsed and—

A phone chimed. Connie, sweating and caught in her tangled blankets, fought the dead weight of her legs and rolled onto her side. She squinted her burning eyes into the dark, spotting a small blue square burning retina-meltingly bright, floating in the blackness a few feet ahead of her. Her arm was numb from sleeping on it. When she reached for the phone, she only knew she'd found it when her hand, in the dark, covered the floating square of blue light. Lying back, she hesitated to bring the screen close to her face. She dreaded seeing UNKNOWN flash on the caller ID, almost as much as seeing ONE NEW VOICEMAIL. She hadn't taken a dose before going to sleep, but according to Gerry, after a while long-term dreamers wouldn't need a dose to get a call. Line locked open permanently, they would always be available to receive day or night, even while fully awake. Like what had happened to Jack.

She didn't recognize the number. It was an Erie area code, but that was all she knew. Maybe some fluke had finally happened, some hole in the system had broken open. Maybe it was her parents calling, or the police, *anybody* who wasn't trapped in here. Her weak hope snuffed itself even before she'd hit ANSWER—she knew she wasn't that lucky.

"Hello?" she said, and held a breath.

"Connie. I didn't wake you, did I?"

She sat up, her heart abruptly thundering. Gerry must've gotten another burner. She had dozens of his lines—some dead, some still in use—programmed into all of her own burners, but didn't have this one.

"I'm awake," she said, and rushed to reach for the lamp next to the couch, nearly dislocating her shoulder in her scramble to do so. She wasn't afraid of the dark, but it always took on a different atmosphere when Gerry called: deeper, full of sharp things she couldn't see.

"That's not what I asked. Did I wake you?"

"I was asleep, but it's fine, it's okay," she said, running her bleary eyes around her apartment, making sure he wasn't, in fact, right here with her. The door to the hallway was intact; her nightmare hadn't pounded it apart, and Gerry hadn't broken in, either. "Is something wrong?"

A pregnant silence fell and lingered. "I need you to come upstairs. Leslie said the elevators should be clear. Thank you, Connie." *Click.*

Connie's throat hitched when she tried to swallow. This was unusual. She was rarely summoned upstairs. They slipped her week's doses under the door packed neatly in an envelope, a fresh set of works accompanying them every other time, the drop comfortably hands-off. On occasion they'd send her a mule to modify, or maybe carry in through her door some overworked dreamer in need of some mouth-to-mouth or to be put on a liquid diet for a week or so, but to be asked to join the goings-on upstairs was out of the ordinary. She was afraid Sam had gotten hurt somehow. Or Gerry had murdered someone and wanted Connie to check them over, make absolutely sure they were now among the ether. As much as she often hated these four walls, being forced to leave this prison that'd become quite familiar and comfortable was almost just as painful.

She leaned off the couch, braced herself on her wheelchair's armrest, and with a sideways hop transferred herself over. Manually placing her feet on the steel footrests, she released her wheels' brakes and moved into the kitchen for a glass of water. Her nervousness was still denying her to swallow comfortably. Her throat felt like it was full of sand.

Flipping on the kitchen light, Connie froze when she wheeled herself up to her sink, glass in hand. The plastic bladder she'd laid on the sink's rim to empty itself overnight was full again, swollen to full capacity with dark red merlot, the spigot back in its original position, closed. She didn't think she'd merely laid it next to the sink but forgotten to turn the spigot's little handle. Though she'd been up very late last night—glancing at the clock over the stove, she noticed that had been only three hours ago—she could remember lying on the couch, *listening* to the wine steadily drumming against the stainless-steel basin.

An unexpected anger woke in her, maybe some of which was directed at herself and her uncertainty. Had she not actually done what she thought she remembered doing, or was something else at work here? Had she changed her mind in the middle of the night and sleepwalked herself over into her wheelchair, come in here, and closed the valve on the bag of wine? No, that couldn't be it, because it was completely *full* now. She'd had a glass last night before deciding to dump the rest. To look at the bag now, it'd be impossible to get another glass-worth in there, unless someone had broken in and replaced the boxed wine. But why leave it exactly as she'd left the other one, outside of its box?

Connie knew Gerry was waiting for her to come upstairs, but she had to try something. Again, she opened up the bag's spigot all the way and watched the redness circle the drain. As she watched, her eyes drifted to the boxes of cereal along the counter, the half-loaf of white bread. The package of Oreos she'd offered to Jack after they'd completed cutting in his pockets. She could remember, vividly, watching him stand right over there, in her kitchen, joylessly eating the cookies, standing with his elbows up and out like he was frozen doing the chicken dance, a little flag of Japan in either of his shirt's armpits. He'd eaten five of them and chased them down with a glass of orange juice, no pleasure in any of it reading on his face.

Pulling out the crinkly corrugated holder from the package now, Connie looked at the three monochromatic cookies it still had to offer. She couldn't remember how many there'd been before she'd offered some to Jack. Sam always sneaked a few throughout the week. Connie sometimes treated herself to a couple after dinner, or for breakfast to kick off the day with a sugar rush.

Starting with ten cookies, if a friend eats five but you happen to be currently losing your hold on reality, how many will you have left? Please show your work.

She couldn't remember when she'd originally bought them. Work got ahead of her once in a while, sure, but while the means to do her job was delivered to her door, Gerry had said when she moved in that she'd be responsible for getting her own groceries. She should be able to remember, but even the name of the store she'd go to—for her groceries, or her boxed wine—eluded her. Connie tore open her refrigerator and gave the carton of orange juice a shake. More than half-full, by the feel of it. Crushing the remaining Oreos in her hand, she threw the broken-up bits into the sink with the wine and upended the carton of orange juice to add that too, creating a beige stew shot through with spinning fragments of Oreo black. She sat a moment looking at the mess she'd made, committing it to memory. This is how I left things before I went upstairs. I expect it to be the same when I get back.

Before exiting her apartment, she gathered her keys, her cigarettes, all three of her burners, and felt under her left leg to make sure her knife was still there. Last, her Tarot deck, the thing she never felt comfortable leaving her prison-but-not-a-prison without, even though she couldn't remember the last time she'd done so. She had her hand on the doorknob, but then removed it. Had to. She shuffled her cards, made a bridge, shuffled them again, silently repeating her question again and again, desperate for positive news. She snapped down one card, sucked in a deep breath, and flipped it over.

The Tower, upright. Shit. A great and heretofore impregnable spire is struck by a searing lance of light and crumbles utterly. The foundation that holds aloft every one of your high and guarded truths will soon buckle. Destruction, disease, destitution, and death should not be ruled out either. All that can be lost will be. And soon.

* * *

Doubting Gerry would accept her refusal to come upstairs because a deck of cards suggested doing so would be inadvisable, Connie rolled herself out into the hall, closed her door behind her, and sat listening a second. Her new neighbor was still quiet behind the door to apartment 306, but directly across the hall, someone was crying inside 305. Male; on the younger side, too, judging by the pitch of their brokenhearted sobs. Before the weepies might prove infectious, Connie wheeled herself down the hall. She tapped the elevator call button, but didn't hear any machinery stir. The floor indicator light was frozen on five, some asshole having jammed the thing up again, so now she'd have to go to the elevator on the far side of the building to get to Gerry's apartment for whatever he needed her for. It wasn't any big revelation to say to somebody who lived here that everything in Dunsany Arms was holding one position on the fucked-o-meter or another, but that didn't make it any less frustrating.

As she turned the corner to start toward the far side of the building, she thought about how they always had to stay vague on the phone, given what they did here, and if Gerry got off on using that same agreed-upon vagueness to keep his people on edge. She had no idea why he wanted her to come upstairs. She could only assume he liked it that way, and was counting on her worrying the whole way up. Even if the task he had for her *was* awful, maybe it wouldn't be as bad as the worst-case scenario he'd made her expect, manufacturing her malleability by inhuming some slippery slope thinking. Hell, *he* may've jammed the elevator closest to her apartment to gift her imagination a few extra minutes to whisper in her ear. It wouldn't have surprised her.

Once inside the other elevator, shoulders and forearms aching, she hit the button for the sixth floor. Feeling seasick from the manic, inconsistent glide of the car as it shuddered in its ascent, she held her chair's armrests for stability. The lights flickered, cycling through patterns fast and slow, and this, naturally, didn't aid her motion sickness in the least. Holding her wheels now instead of the armrests, Connie could at least keep herself from sickeningly swaying. Once moving smoothly again, she raked her fingers through her hair and paused when she realized she'd forgotten to change. She was still in her cotton pants and a baggy old T-shirt she'd had since vet school. Emblazoned with the logo for Void-Moist Coil, a Floridian sludge metal group with which she'd been helplessly obsessed once upon a time, the image of a nautilus inside an eye dripping with viscous black goo was scarcely visible anymore after the shirt had gone through a thousand spin cycles—and right now the shirt *stank*. The nightmare had yet again inspired her corporeal self to sweat through her clothes. She'd also spilled some orange juice on herself, evidently, because there were little flecks of pulp all over her that looked like smashed bug wings, and she still had crushed cookie packed up under her fingernails. Fuck it. Call me this late at night, you can't expect to not get a wreck showing up at your door.

She hoped that when she returned home, her sink's trap would be full of wine- and orange juice-soaked pieces of Oreo. Trying to recall, again, when she'd last gone to the store, she brought out the three burner phones from her sweatpants pocket, thumbing through each one's calendar. Since she discarded them with such regularity, she never bothered to key in anything but the ever-changing catalog of Gerry's currently active phone numbers. According to one of her burners it was currently 3:33 pm, November 19th. The next was convinced it was August 6th at 2:07 am. The third was absolutely sure today was the 28th of July, 7:09 pm. But it *is* February right now, isn't it? Maybe a couple days past Valentine's Day, or before. Somewhere in there. February, though. She was confident she had that much right.

Above the doors, the light for the fifth floor illuminated. Someone had called the elevator even though, as far as she knew, none of the units on the fifth floor were occupied. Rolling herself back from the doors, Connie set her chair's brakes and reached under her hip to retrieve her knife. Holding it in her lap, she watched the doors rumble apart—revealing nothing.

The hallway stretching out before her was the same as every one above and below it within Dunsany Arms. Narrow, poorly lit, stained floor, walls all marked up and scratched from countless past tenants being careless when they schlepped their hand-me-down furniture in or out. But unless there'd been a crossed wire, somebody had hit the call button, somebody who wasn't there now.

Her hand tightened around her knife. She wanted to be neighborly and call out, because maybe someone needed help, but the words died in her throat. It's four in the morning. Her mother used to say nothing good happens after midnight. Connie had seen that proven true more than once in *this* building, but something still urged her to wait. Though she wasn't fully on board with the concept of Fate with a big F, she got the sense some occurrence—big or small, insignificant or world-shattering—was on approach. Every door on either side of the silent, unoccupied fifth-floor hallway remained closed. The wind moaned, scouring hungrily for a crack to wriggle through so it could throttle blue the first warm thing it found. Thunder detonated close, directly over the building, making Connie reflexively duck. The elevator cables twanged; the car gently rocked. Flashes of blue-white snapped out from under every door down the hall ahead of her, lashing the shadows back. Her breaths quickened and smoked. It always struck her as unsettling when a snowstorm dragged thunder and lightning along with it. The combination seemed ominous, primordial. Card XVI, the Tower, everything dashed apart by a white-hot bolt. As much as she enjoyed the mental image of Dunsany Arms reduced to a smoldering pile, she had little interest in being inside an elevator when it—

Another crash of thunder shook her and made her duck again like an idiot. Annoyed with herself, chest burning from the startle, Connie leaned from her seat to peck the CLOSE DOORS button until they obeyed. Very close to her, a sharp metallic *clink* made her flinch again. She only caught a glimpse of her knife slipping through the gap before the doors thumped together. "Goddamn it," she said, forced to sit listening to her sole means of protection tumbling down the shaft in a sequence of resonating clangs. Was *that* what she meant to witness? If so, dick move, Fate. Dick move.

"Breathe in. Breathe out," she told herself, as she would one of her patients. "In, and out. In, out."

The elevator screeched and commenced its climb, with Connie unaccompanied by any new passengers, and now unarmed as well. When this place is put out of its misery someday, she thought, either by controlled detonation or lightning-flinging supernatural intercession, perhaps anthropologists of the future will find her knife down there— with its five-inch blade, pearl handle, and nickel accents—and put it on display in a museum or something. Exhibit: Folding knife, a common tool among young women as a means of self-defense against ravenous meth-heads and other assorted creeps full of bad ideas that were native, and in abundance, to the Rust Belt dystopia.

The elevator creaked to the sixth floor. As soon as the doors had parted wide enough for her chair, Connie wasted no time wheeling herself out.

She rolled down the hallway with one forward throw of her hands at a time. It was quiet up here tonight. Gerry had first dibs on every apartment up here, using them as either storage or places to put up his skinny, frightening friends. Evidence of bad lives lived badly, the spoor of their most recent bacchanal clotted her path: bloated trash bags hemorrhaging pink garbage juice, a cracked pocket mirror dusted whitely, a crushed burner phone, a soda bottle puffy with either putrefying chew spit or distilling urine or both, another discarded burner, a spangling mosaic of pulverized CDs that barraged Connie with hundreds of her double as her wheels crunched over their faces, a broken one-hitter, a condom lying like a shed snake skin, an empty canister of baby formula, a rusty hypodermic needle screwed to a broken stub of a syringe, a TV with a kicked-in screen, a dead rat speared onto a crochet needle and ringed by an arrangement of stuffed animal spectators, a *thoroughly* soiled pair of men's underpants, a scattershot of loose pills of miscellaneous colors and shapes, a lidless Mason jar with two inches of suspiciously innocent-looking clear liquid inside it standing atop a leather-bound husk of a Bible that'd been violently relieved of all its pages, and throughout were the rat pellets constantly crackling under Connie's rubber wheels like black grains of uncooked rice.

She couldn't look down her nose at the types of people Gerry seemed to attract, because she'd be looking down her nose at herself too. Still, what a fucking mess. It'd been (subjectively) clean the last time Connie had come up to the sixth floor. How did Leslie feel about Gerry's friends treating his building so poorly? He'd probably never said a goddamn thing, truth be told. Though he may have looked it, Leslie Rider was not a stupid man.

She passed the elevator she should've been able to take up here directly across from Gerry's door—and like he'd been waiting on the other side, eye pressed to the peephole, the door to 603 creaked open before Connie could free a hand from a wheel to knock.

Breathe in, breathe out.

✦ ✦ ✦

Filthy bare feet; a stained and baggy boiler suit zipped to his chin under an unraveling cord-knit sweater the sleeves of which, when his arms were at his sides, completely hid Gerry's dexterous, fatless hands and his splintering, untrimmed fingernails. A shallow dent circled the bottom half of his thin, angular face like he'd recently been wearing a muzzle—or, more likely, a respirator. His hair, a greasy mop the color of rotting straw, hung lank about his bony shoulders, framing bloodshot eyes. He seemed to seldom blink and his smile, like the one he was issuing now in Connie's direction, never seemed all that sincere—like his mind was always half-elsewhere, a dream manning the helm as the somnambulist went about its errands and drug-making, hands able to be trusted to go on autopilot after years of muscle memory had been fixed into them, repeated task after repeated task.

"I'm sorry for calling so late," Gerry said. "I wanted to wait until the sun had come up, at least, but I thought we should discuss this sooner rather than later." Though Gerry wasn't a particularly tall man, he could see over Connie's head, and as to the disaster area she'd been forced to struggle through to reach his door, he evidently didn't notice or had grown so accustomed to it that he no longer saw it. She wondered when *he'd* last left his apartment.

"What's the problem?" Connie said—carefully, politely.

Gerry stepped aside to allow Connie room to enter. "Come in."

Connie entered—and immediately swallowed down a cough. She didn't know why she'd been worried about stinking; her body odor couldn't hold a candle to the reek of Gerry's apartment. He'd evidently just finished a new batch. There were cookie sheets set about the room, each one powdered over from corner to corner with a glistening crust the color of pissed-on snow. The room, as always, was overly bright from the work lights positioned everywhere. It was like driving down a pitted dirt road, trying to get her chair to maneuver over the extension cords laid every which way over the plastic-covered carpet. Across from her, she noticed Gerry had painted over his windows—blocking away the view, the only thing that'd ever made coming up here remotely appealing to her.

Gerry closed the door and threw all six deadbolts. Maybe even from behind her, he could sense which way her eyes were trained. "For privacy reasons. Infrared cameras. I had Leslie shred up some aluminum foil so I could stir it into the paint. The police apparently can't peek through that."

At least it wasn't tinfoil hats. Connie turned her chair around in place, careful to not bump her elbow against any of the many uncapped jugs of chemicals crowding every available horizontal surface. "Should we be worried?"

Gerry took a moment before answering, his absent smile creasing his drawn, pale face again. "No, Connie. You don't need to be worried."

She glanced around her. They appeared to be alone. Or at least, if anyone was behind all of the closed doors visible to her from the living room, they weren't stirring. Though she loathed his friends, she liked being alone with Gerry even less. There was always a low-grade tension that filled the air around him, like he was a live wire, a loaded gun, a sleeping dog, harmless right up until the moment he wasn't.

On one of the many folding tables arranged about the space where comfortable chairs and a television should be, a room intended for families to spend time together, there was a pile of burner phones still in their clear plastic packages. The pile, each time she was summoned upstairs, never seemed to grow or shrink, as if Gerry always maintained a specific number of burners on hand, ready for new dreamers.

"So, what did you need my help with?"

The plastic made a peeling sound as his bare feet passed over it. He approached her and knelt in front of her. He seemed to consider laying his hands on her knees, but then didn't. She was normally quick to snap at anyone who touched her chair, who tried to push her around like she was a shopping cart, but she said nothing as Gerry held her armrests and looked into her eyes, leaving a silence to hang between them as he did so, the noxious buzzing of all the work lights filling it—which almost seemed to be radiating from him, his hidden gears turning away behind the curtain of his unshaven face, that empty smile unchanging as he processed.

"You have a new next-door neighbor," he said.

"I guess so. I heard him through the wall."

"He told Leslie his name is Daniel Owen Wells. Dan's going to be doing some dreaming for us."

"He looks like a cop." Connie was trying to make a joke, even managing to force a smile.

"That's probably because he is."

Cold filled Connie's stomach. "Are you serious?"

"I am. Also known as Dwayne Alan Spare. Dan's an undercover narcotics investigator with the Pennsylvania State Police."

"How do you know that?"

Gerry's smile sharpened knowingly. He still hadn't blinked.

"Sorry," Connie said. "But won't they send somebody after him if he doesn't show up when he's, you know, supposed to be done?"

"Don't worry about that either."

"Are the cops onto us? Do they know what we're doing here?"

"They know about us no more than anything else. Otherwise they would've acted. They don't tend to make those visits the sneaky kind, sending in one man. If they knew anything concrete, this place would've looked like Waco. Suspicions. Rumors. That's all they have. Things overheard, or fed to them by insignificant nobodies looking to angle deals, protection. Leslie can handle the tattletales, if that proves to be the case, but Mister Wells is a separate issue. And not worth the worry."

"Okay." Connie wasn't convinced, but calling Gerry a liar was about as smart as jumping off the roof believing she'd sprout wings on the way down. Don't think about that now. Why would you think about that now?

She wanted to ask Gerry to get to his point then, but couldn't manage to think of a non-pissy way to word it. She'd just have to let him get there on his own, and wait and wallow in her fear until he did so.

"Questions, a lot like wishes, should be assembled and sent out into the air very carefully. There *are* such things as stupid questions. And dangerous ones."

"I won't ask any more questions." She heard her voice shaking and swallowed, hoping the next thing she said didn't show her fear so readily.

"Ask them," Gerry said, "that's fine, but just be careful about it. That's all. I'll answer anything you want to know, but again, also like wishes, you might not like what result you end up with."

Connie asked nothing, said nothing. She could only maintain eye contact with him, knowing if she glanced away even once it might sow a seed of doubt about her in Gerry. She wanted to go home: not to her apartment downstairs, but to her parents' home. Crawl under the bed like she used to during bad thunderstorms and hug a stuffed bear close. But like how foggy it'd become trying to remember when she'd last left the building, when she'd last seen her parents was equally lost to her—or if she'd ever actually done things like hide under the bed during storms. If she one day wheeled herself into the bathroom and looked in her mirror and saw an old woman, with the in-between days having evaporated, she would be disheartened, but she wouldn't be surprised.

Though he hadn't touched her, now or at any time in the past, she always felt like she was covered in bugs in Gerry's presence. It was a feeling she never cared for, because it was almost too close a neighbor to the feeling when she *wanted* to be touched—the multitude of ways a body can betray its tenant was, she felt, an unforgiveable design flaw.

"We're going to push Dan through the door," Gerry said. "Would you be willing to wait for him on the other side of it, show him everything he'll need to know?"

"Yes," Connie said.

"That'll mean you'll need to dream again as well."

"I know."

From his sweater pocket, Gerry produced a bead of his product in a baggie the size of a postage stamp. Not even this would he pass to her directly. Instead, he placed it with care on her chair's armrest and quickly withdrew his hand. She pocketed the pale yellow pebble, her next ticket.

"Do you need clean works?"

"I'm all right. My current rig's holding up."

"Keeping it clean?"

"Disinfected after every use."

"How are you doing on supplies?"

"I always seem to have just enough."

"Good. How was the house, by the way, the last time you went?" Gerry said, adding, "That was with Jack, wasn't it?"

Connie nodded. She very much wanted to stop having to look in his eyes. In an unpleasant inversion of how the phrase was usually used, she felt herself being pulled into them. "The house was fine," she said. "I unhooked the phone like you asked, so he wouldn't freak out if he answered it before I could explain everything to him."

"I know. Jack had told me, before."

"Oh. Um, did he say I did all right, telling him what to do?"

"He said you were very kind, to the point, and you never let him grow suspicious he wasn't actually awake. Checked his pockets for infection and everything—which, nice touch. He also said you asked to be called Constance." His face read, Ain't that quaint?

Connie had no memory of that, but tried, and failed, to not let surprise show in her face.

"No need to feel guilty about it. We're all different in dreams," Gerry said. "Maybe truer, maybe falser. He still got the call and then made his own, as he was supposed to."

She had to ask. "Jack didn't suffer, did he?"

"Were you awake when he decided to leave us?"

Connie nodded gravely, remembering she'd thought someone had set off a grenade in 306. She'd been nodding off in front of the TV. Nobody had to tell her what he'd done to himself. Through the wall, she heard a thud follow the gunshot, and no sounds of any doors opening or closing. Nobody left because there'd been no one else with Jack over there—then, nobody whatsoever.

"It was immediate," Gerry finally said. "There wasn't any suffering."

Except Jack had suffered. For the weeks—or maybe longer, she couldn't remember exactly—that led up to the night of his suicide, she'd hear him next door crying and screaming, as if his apartment was filled with his worst enemies taking turns dragging sharp things across his skin. She'd see him pacing around the hallways, oblivious to the shit dribbling out of his pant legs, eyes blinking out of sync, muttering about mechanisms and switches and gears and wires and the green light and the red light and the dream, the dream, the dream. His hands shook so much Connie had to help him shoot up. It was a cooperative effort, but they'd ruined him, and she was just as much at fault as Gerry, if not more so, because while Gerry had given the task, she'd held Jack's hand for every step of its completion.

Connie snapped back into herself as Gerry said, "I'd like you to do the same for Mister Wells. I've made a few adjustments; it shouldn't burn him out as quick as Jack."

"I'll unhook the phone and put it in the cupboard in the sewing room, like before," Connie said, "and tell him everything he'll need to do."

"Good."

"At the switchboard house, with Jack," Connie started, before she'd fully thought out *why* she felt the need to tell Gerry this, "he said the house was under a tarp or something."

"The more closed-off will build safety nets for themselves. Do you remember the first time *you* went to the switchboard house and looked out a window?"

"Yes. I do."

"Wasn't exactly a welcoming vista, was it?"

"No. It wasn't."

"We have Dan scheduled for tomorrow. I'll call you before he's gotten his dose so you can have time to ready the house."

"Okay." Connie put her hands on her wheels, more than ready to leave this room, but Gerry didn't stand up or loosen the clutch he had on her armrests. Like in her recurring nightmare, as much as she wanted to move, she couldn't.

"You might not believe this when I tell you, Connie, but I want to be done with this as much as you do."

"I don't want to be done," she said, the lie bitter on the back of her tongue.

"My dream—in the aspiration sense—was to just do what I loved, what I felt I was getting very good at doing, forever. No interruptions. Whether it was my body's need to sleep, or to eat, or a need to stay up on paying rent, or waste time worrying about any intervention from the police . . . all I asked for was a system to always be watching over me, that no matter what missteps I might make, I would never lose and/or need to leave my home. To never need to stop *working*. Because it's all I wanted to do."

Either she was shaking or his hands, gripped to her chair, had started to tremble. "I'm sorry, Gerry, but I don't think I understand."

It was as if, even though he was looking right in her face, kneeling two feet away from her, none of her words had made it through to him, into him. "Like I said before," Gerry said, "be careful with wishes and questions. That's what I learned, the hard way. Exploring unorthodox channels asking for help, I shouldn't have been surprised that's exactly what I'd receive. Unorthodox channels can *only* offer unorthodox help. I called, I asked, I received. And, unfortunately, many others have had to learn my hard lesson along with me.

"Tonight," Gerry said, "I really feel like I'm back with me, back where I should be. Not watching from other eyes as some stranger stands in my bones going through motions that should be mine, making mistakes I'd never make. And that's what I want for all of us, everybody who's helped me to occupy their *own* bones again, to be behind their *own* eyes. And you're more valuable than anyone, Connie, because you're helping our dreamers connect. I really feel like you're here right now, so when I say this, I know I don't have to hold back. We've seen the center. We've been made aware it deserves our respect. It made it easy finding a way in, but it's changed behind us—a punishment that should've only been for me. And for bringing you into it, I apologize. And I apologize as well for not being able to help more."

Connie understood none of this. The dream, the maze, the switchboard house, all of it she'd written off as coincidentally shared hallucinations. To wake next to a dreamer after spending upwards of twenty hours unconscious and tell one another a story, build it as they remembered it, Connie took it to be like Gerry said. Dramatics, using the pliability of memory to tack things on that sounded right, things they'd "seen." She thought that was the unspoken agreement that they all shared here: You can get high as often as you like, but all you need to do is hand in the pay-as-you-go phone after you've vomited yourself awake. That it was for *fun*, that they were merely playing along with Gerry's bullshit—mazes, other planes of existence, how one night when overdosing he sailed on a dream to the switchboard house—because he was offering free highs, free room and board. Even if that meant living in a place that was falling in on itself and carried a well-earned infamy around Erie, there was a special kind of safety to be had, lying close to the dragon in its deep den. And she'd been under its wing for a long time, maybe even to the point that now the story (either from prolonged exposure to it or endless repetition of it to herself and others) had become fact. It required little concentration to hold the switchboard house in her mind as solidly as she could see the walls standing around her now. A place with no true doors, but bountiful with entrances nonetheless, access granted by a needle's tip for a key inserted, then turned, in the crook of an arm, between two toes, behind the ear, in the white of one's eye.

"I may've told you this before," Gerry said, "but the doctors said both me and my brother should try avoiding so much as arguing with each other. Brothers who weren't even allowed to argue! And nothing else that might get the blood up, either. Which I tested to the absolute limit because, if I'm being totally up front about it, I was told I shouldn't." His smile sharpened more, then nearly fell altogether, as if miming sudden sadness as he added, "Which, now that I can't, is exactly what makes you so special. How much you help them not only *in* the dream, but when they've come back out of it too. Like you did for me, when I had my little cardiac event last year."

She'd performed CPR on him. Hit him with about ten different things, slipping him out of death's hand by slickening him with a cocktail powerful enough to send anyone who didn't use as often as Gerry used to over the fucking moon. She'd tended to him that night like she cared for him. And at the time, panicked and afraid for a man whom any other time she feared, she had cared for him—if only for the keystone he operated as within this place that kept everyone from immediately murdering each other. Or maybe there was some latent admiration she had for him, the bigness of what he hoped to achieve, even if she still thought, at the time, that it was all make believe. Stories to give plot to our chemical journeys as we depth-charge the void, make them *mean* something other than us habitually shortening our lives. And when he took a breath, reborn again on her living room floor, the color rushing back into his face as he sat up to croak a thank you at her, Connie's relief was transubstantiated at once with regret.

"I'll never be able to thank you enough," Gerry said now, just as he had then.

A question that she knew likely fell into the dangerous grouping took form, diamond-hard, within her mind. One that she had to put breath behind, to send it out, to know. "What's in the basement of the switchboard house?"

Gerry's gaze flicked from her left eye, to her right, to her left. And either he'd stopped shaking or she had; the wandering tremor moving around in her wheelchair had stopped. "It's not uncommon to forget dreams, but I'd think you'd remember that."

"I don't." She no longer had the capacity for politeness. "What's down there?"

He took a long time to answer, and blinked for the first time since she'd arrived. "The way in. The way out."

＊ ＊ ＊

In the unreliable light of the elevator car, Connie held out her hands, fingers flat, studying how badly she was still shaking. She turned her hands over, palms up, hoping maybe to divine some hint from them, an insight as to what she should do next—if not cook the entire hit Gerry had given her and inject it into her temple. The hash marks on her fingers, between the first and second knuckle, were still there. The one little crease just below her pinkie on the edge of her palm, the one child she might have in her lifetime—an idea she'd never been that motivated about *ever* making true. Evidence of lives *not* lived. And then she noticed something that wasn't always ingrained into the sworls and swoops of her palm, something new. Her life line, running the edge of her thumb's heel, had previously joined with her head line, running horizontally across her palm. Now her life line curved sharply in on itself, cutting over her Venus mount, the fleshy ball of her thumb. And as she looked at it, hoping it was only a trick of the elevator car's stuttering light, it curved back on itself again, and again. Like a worm was under her skin, chasing its own tail, but only succeeding in making . . . a shape much like Void-Moist Coil's logo, a spiral, painlessly etching itself onto her hand.

Slowly, she placed her altered palm on her chair and faced forward, looking at the poorly-defined, smudged reflection the scratched steel doors offered. Reduced to swaths of color, her black hair, a smeary suggestion of the purple lightning bolts on her brow. She wouldn't look at her palm again, not until she'd had some sleep. Maybe she'd gotten a contact high in Gerry's apartment, breathing those fumes. That's all it was. A micro-trip. That's all it was. Breathe in, breathe out. In, out.

Back on the third floor, she passed the crying still going on behind the door of apartment 305, and then listened briefly at the door across from it, her new neighbor's door, Dan Wells. Hearing nothing, she re-entered her own home. Door closed, light on, she steeled herself in the kitchen doorway, afraid to look, afraid to confirm whether or not the ruined cookies, orange juice, and boxed wine in her sink had obeyed her and remained the mess of which she'd left them. She could sleep off the weirdness going on with her palm. She could ignore that problem until then, but not this one.

She moved her left wheel forward, her right one back, turning herself in place, and sighed at what she saw in her sink, because it didn't surprise her. But the man standing in the far corner of her living room, chalky white skin almost self-illuminating in its paleness, did surprise her. Her hand flew under her leg, where she used to keep her knife that was no longer there because it was down in the goddamn basement, at the bottom of the elevator shaft. The ashen man stepped forward, making sounds like his clothes had been soaked, then frozen while he wore them, cracking and popping. With tight, small steps, as if his legs were bound at the ankles, he shuffled painfully forward into the kitchen light. Connie's shadow was caught by his skin, as pale as a projector screen. It wasn't her nightly visitor, the homunculus made flesh, but a man made of paper and plaster. She felt she knew his voice, but he was hollow-sounding, like he was speaking to her from inside a sealed casket thrown down a well.

"Connie. It's me."

7.

WITH NOTHING TO busy his eyes, the frosted-over window became a screen upon which Dwayne revisited—and individually questioned—every decision that had led him to this point.

Would he become a name on a missing persons poster and known only after that, as the status continued to not change, nothing more? Just non-specifically absent, the dematerialized man? Would he eventually be marked irretrievable, swallowed by the oblivion he himself had voluntarily leaped into head-first? And what about after he was no longer useful to Metzger? Would Dwayne join the spirits and haunt whoever next was forced to fill 306's vacancy? He wanted to blame Cleckley for agreeing to let him do this, but it'd been no one's idea but his own. He questioned why, since he'd stopped sending text updates, help hadn't been dispatched. Soon, the topic feeling inevitable, he dreaded to think that if his body was never found—and thus closure never provided—if he'd become for his daughter an unresolved obstacle she'd never be able to move past. He hadn't thought to consider that, drawing up his proposal. He'd only seen Metzger.

An obsessive nature had always been with him, since early childhood. He wasn't so beyond self-reflection that he was ignorant to its origin, his tendency to quickly form habits—both beneficial and not—like how he couldn't lie down if his shoes in the downstairs closet were touching. He knew.

Before he'd even begun school, Dwayne's mother had taken him to a church with her in the middle of the week. Which was unusual, but he was happy to sit in the pew alongside her in the peaceful, cavernous space, doodling with cheap crayons that'd made a soft *pop* every time he lifted them from the paper as his mother knelt and whispered, head bowed. Looking at the side of her face, he saw her making expressions he'd never seen her produce, ones he had no words for at the time. She wasn't smiling, he knew that much. While she knelt and whispered, he drew her a picture of a group of birds in flight. When he presented her with the drawing once they were back in the car, she put her hand to her mouth and her eyes filled with tears—which scared him. He tried apologizing, thinking maybe she'd misinterpreted the simple M-shaped renditions of seagulls, inspired by the ones he regularly watched glide over Lake Erie, as something else, something that hurt her. But she thanked him and hugged him close. He could feel her heart beating.

His mother didn't tell him until years later—the day after his father was found charred and half the house burnt down—that she had been planning to kill both herself and her son that afternoon, and she'd taken him to church. She had asked God for a sign she shouldn't carry it through and her son's picture of the birds, to her, served as that sign. God had worked through him, she said. Being a time in which admitting anything might be wrong was expressly un-American, when his mother finally got a CAT scan, the tumor had already grown inoperably large. Engorged with potent inspiration, it dispatched constant visitors to her, mostly benevolent imps at first, but things would shift dramatically when night fell. Replacing her dancing cherubs, ashen-faced creatures would lunge at her face as she lay in bed, gnashing small barbed teeth, "like a shark's," as she'd described them, and a black dog—that was only visible from the corner of her eye— would promise her, every night at three AM, that when she'd died he would be there to watch, and only then would she see his true face. That was early on. In the final months, those nighttime visitors became analogous to the daytime ones. She refused to say much about her new midnight company, fearing that even when the sun was out they could still hear her. She only slipped once, saying they were escapees from "the red prison," before turning away from her son to address the empty chair next to her hospital bed: "Jacob, look what you're doing, you're getting ash everywhere."

Dwayne got the call at work. He knew before he even looked at the number. The hospital staff advised not seeing her. He'd regret not listening to them. Hands locked around squeezed fistfuls of the bedsheet, she lay with eyes wide, fixed on an empty corner of the room. The black dog seemed to have kept its promise. Thus, how she had ascribed meaning to her son drawing seagulls all those years before meant, to Dwayne, nothing more than a boy saving his own life and that of his mother by sheer ignorant chance. Really, she could've just as easily chosen to interpret the M-shaped birds—flying away, flying near?—as an indication that yes, they should both be whisked off by the angels. Because of this, what he felt was one of the more important moments of his life, Dwayne believed that small, seemingly innocuous actions underneath, unseen, turned massive switches and the universe, in kind, rearranged itself to accommodate, giving pieces that might not have been there otherwise tracks to glide along until another rearranging came and dropped the path out from under them. Maybe he'd requested to come here and pursue Metzger because something inside had whispered that the time he'd bought with poorly-drawn seagulls was now coming to an end.

It seemed fitting. One small act had derailed one outcome, and from the wreckage of things-that-did-not-happen he'd sifted free decades that maybe weren't supposed to be lived by him. His life did feel stolen at times, or perhaps even an unimaginative fake. He'd joined the force because his father and grandfather had. Maybe he'd followed in their steps too precisely. He'd developed into another wary, sullen alcoholic, a cliché of their profession if there ever was one, but maybe that's all the Spare line was capable of producing. He'd managed to con a brilliant, vivacious woman into thinking it'd be a worthwhile venture to be his wife, and then he'd watched her tell herself for twelve years that she hadn't made a bad decision. While things had been good early on—mostly because they felt they'd were expected to, if he was being honest—they'd dragged another innocent from a comfortable non-existence to participate in this miserable mess that, in Dwayne's experience, only supplied constant evidence that nothing could improve, that things just got worse in different ways at different speeds. And now, after having gotten away with his heist of stolen time for so long, it didn't matter if he'd started putting serious thought into returning it voluntarily; its revocation was on fast approach. Conscious or unconscious, deliberate or non-deliberate, a track had been made to crash into place that cut off all others to route him toward nothingness where he'd belonged for so long, debt repaid. Crayon on construction paper and Cleckley agreeing to let Dwayne come here alone had been binding contracts both.

As far as wanting to catch Metzger, a man gets tired of only having himself to hate. Any cop will talk a big game about loving the law, or that it's about serving their community, but get a couple beers in them, and they'll show you a want to hurt was their only engine. Dwayne had himself convinced that because he'd narrowed his prejudices to one that might actually be useful keeping around, it somehow made him better. But good people, especially good cops, don't actually exist. Goodness can only be quantified by how convincingly one covers their ugly. Underneath, he was the same. It didn't truly matter to him, before, what the alleged chemist was up to or who he was hurting. He was merely something Dwayne could be allowed to hunt, collect a salary to remain obsessed over, a faceless target to aim his anger at. That had changed. Dwayne now knew Gerald Metzger was far from just a chemist, and his lonely tower was far from just an apartment building.

In Dwayne's left ear, appallingly lucid, "Dan Wells, pleased to meet you."

He pinched shut his eyes, dreading the hallucination would say more—but that, apparently, was all Dan Wells had to impart.

He realized he'd often been thinking about the voicemail since he'd heard it. It had replaced the scream *and* the name. It was disturbing hearing yourself sounding so afraid, your voice rendered to that of a stranger by fear. What Dwayne had specifically told himself—or what the skinless abomination had puppeteered him and *made* him say—was starting to fade. The more he tried to recall them, the faster the phrases fell apart, losing a word here and a word there until he could only dredge back that he'd said *something* as the memory dissolved to echoes of his confused, terrified screaming. Forgetting didn't bring him any comfort. If anything, losing what he'd learned rekindled his want for another hit, to crush the words back into coherent shape again. He found it hard to deny that some latently self-destructive side of himself, after having its psyche cracked by Metzger, now lusted after a full, irreversible shattering. It didn't want glimpses and fragments. No, it wanted him to become a vessel in which to house a luminous truth, even at the cost of having that knowledge become all that stood within a self-made ruin.

Let it fade.

Without his noticing, the frost on the bedroom window was glistening with red dawn light. Morning had come.

His body ached from sitting in the same place all night, and an acute hunger was upon him—one that wasn't interested in food. He'd felt the gnawing within him start to slowly revisit him late into the night, but had managed to ignore it, even as he began to sweat despite the cold. He couldn't allow the want to be fulfilled. Dan Wells wouldn't get what he wanted.

With the hanger dowel lifted, ready to bludgeon, Dwayne opened the bedroom door and looked out. The apartment seemed to have been replaced with another. Equally empty and squalid, the sunlight had banished the shadows—though, he was sure, the place was far from purified.

Keeping his distance from the front door, he turned his head to listen for what also might have waited out the night. He put his eye to the peephole—and wrenched back, initially shocked until he looked again.

At first glance, the adult-sized dummy sitting in the folding chair outside his door was convincing enough, until Dwayne noticed its eyes— two black dots in wide white circles, as if done by a child—were painted onto a lopsided papier-mâché lump for a head. The legs, old dungarees, looked unnaturally swollen, overstuffed. It was missing an arm, the sleeve of its T-shirt hanging empty. Is that thing supposed to look like Ryan?

Grumbling a curse, Dwayne started to turn away and stepped on the corner of a file folder poking in from under his door.

Smeary photos. Their color cartridge looked like it'd failed them. The house in the photos was engulfed by pink fire. He knew the house, knew the address by heart, knew what it felt like to spend Thanksgiving with the family that lived there. He moved to the next photo. Two charred skeletons lying in a bed that'd been reduced to a blackened frame, gray ribbons of smoke curling from their empty eye sockets. Captain David Cleckley and Doctor Suzanne Cleckley, burned to nothing.

And a sheet torn from a coloring book. Down the side of the picture of a butterfly, every panel of its wings filled with frenzied scribbles of black, the careful hand of an adult:

didnt you think it was odd
he was
fine
being the only one
who
knew
youd be
coming to this place ???

Dwayne contributed another fist-shaped dent of his own to the wall. He tore at his hair and kicked each of the lower kitchen cabinets in. He thrashed and swore and swiped at the air. He slipped, hit the floor hard, and lay raggedly breathing, coughing. All that talk about worrying who in the department might be in Metzger's pocket with someone who *had been*, the entire fucking time. Cleckley. Why?

Above him, the jagged hole in the ceiling had lost its inkiness. The sun revealed there was another apartment above this one—not just an abyss that used 306 as a drain.

He approached the sliding glass door, seeing that most of the other apartments had their blinds closed, and no electric light was discernible inside those with their window coverings open. But no people. He had seen some fellow tenants, however long ago that had been. He'd seen their shapes, heard them arguing, felt their bass-heavy music rattle in his chest. But now, stillness and silence had replaced them. Either everyone in Dunsany Arms worked the early shift, or they'd all decided to skip on their rent and flee, a calculated midnight exodus. Dwayne wondered if Metzger was done hiding, if he'd let his fellow tenants know what they'd been unknowingly living so close to for so long.

Nonetheless, he continued scanning one window to the next, desperate to see another soul, but only noticed one other living thing. Leslie's dog was at its window again, forepaws on the sill. Fogging the glass with its breaths, the dog gave him a long look before raising its focus to an apartment above 306. Dwayne watched the dog studying something he couldn't see, wondering if there were others similarly imprisoned here, doing the same thing he was a few floors higher—mulling the idea of jumping, fighting down the want to scream for help even if it meant their lives. Or maybe the dog was looking at those who'd visited last night. Maybe other dead toured the building in aimless circles, visiting their stolen places of peace. Losing interest, the dog dropped back from the windowsill, and the thin curtain swung back into place.

While Dunsany Arms remained mute, Dwayne noticed that outside its walls the city, too, was quiet. Gone was its ever-present hum. No car horns, no sirens. The sky was empty of any aircraft. Strange, since the airport was only a handful of miles up the highway. But the only sound that hit his ears was a soft wind insistently guiding the cold to this place.

Bracing himself on the cement privacy barrier, he leaned his upper half over the railing to see around it. 304's blinds were closed beyond their sliding glass door, and the glass wasn't fogged. Nobody was home, no one he could quietly get the attention of and ask them to call the police. He moved to the opposite privacy barrier and leaned out. The other neighbor's balcony was likewise unoccupied—no furniture, no grill, no footprints in its accumulated snow—but the plastic vertical blinds moved, someone inside apartment 308 stepping back out of sight.

Hoarse, Dwayne tried, as quietly as his fear would allow, "I need help. I know you saw me. Please."

As the blinds settled, each long plastic blade swinging pendulum-like and at various speeds, he was only allowed choppy, fleeting looks of something shiny and metal, numerous thin metal lines splaying out from a center point. Spokes of a wheel. Shadows obscured their face, but the person in the wheelchair had to have seen him.

When the blinds settled back into an unbroken wall, they didn't stir again. Dwayne reached the hanger dowel across the gap and clanged on their balcony railing. It elicited no response: the person in the wheelchair either didn't care or had no interest in getting involved.

Pulling himself back over to his side, Dwayne looked across at Leslie's window below. The dog had its forepaws perched on the sill again, burning holes into him with its ears pinned back, lip curling. Fearing a bark was imminent, Dwayne stepped back inside and dragged shut the door. The toes of his bare foot were blue. He sat rubbing the feeling back into his foot; the anger he felt toward his neighbor and their total disregard for his predicament made his jaw clench.

Avoiding the dusty debris under the hole, he entered the bathroom and put his ear to the wall next to the Plexiglas box with the phones inside. He listened at another spot, even climbing inside the shower to listen there. He knocked, heard nothing, knocked harder, but on the other side of the wall the person in the wheelchair neither spoke nor stirred.

He sat on the rim of the moldering bathtub, shaking his head at himself. He'd hoped, dumbly, that he'd be the exception, a special case, that luck would somehow spirit him away from this place.

Only being able to use one arm, in combination with the tight confines of the bathroom, prevented him from winding up much of a swing, and striking the Plexiglas box with the dowel only sent the three burner phones within bouncing and clattering. The screws holding the box in place remained driven deep. The box had no back to it, Dwayne noticed, so if he could pull it forward somehow, he might be able to squeeze in a hand and get at the phones.

From the living room debris, he picked out a piece of wood that'd broken into a wedge shape. He worked it up between the Plexiglas box and the bathroom wall and, tapping patiently with the dowel, backed one screw out. Once he'd pulled the box clear from the wall a couple of inches, he contorted himself to hook two fingers up inside, and withdrew one of the burners.

The phone's screen lit up, flashing LOW BATTERY. Hopefully the others, if he couldn't get hold of anyone with this one, had a better charge to them.

As he dialed the precinct, he was giddy with relief—freedom wasn't far away now. He brought the phone to his ear and listened . . . to nothing. It wasn't dialing. It had died in his hand. He flung the phone aside and fished out the last two. The next wouldn't turn on and the last—eleven percent charge—allowed him to dial the precinct again.

A shrill note drilled into his ear. "Additional minutes can be purchased from most major retailers or through the ConnectPlus website. For more information—"

He hung up and used the burner's spongy little buttons to dial 911, hoping that maybe calls to emergency services didn't count against the burner's deficit of minutes. Dwayne waited, considering his own deficit of minutes. This had to work.

"Additional minutes can be purchased—"

He fought the urge to smash the phone on the floor and pocketed it, as well as the other two others that had also failed him, and hobbled across to the door to the hallway.

He caromed the hanger dowel against the deadbolt's faceplate, only managing to pack the keyhole with splinters. He had more room to swing here, and the doorknob snapped off with his first attempt. He speared the hanger dowel in, pushing the mechanism through to the other side, only producing a second, lower-set peephole. Putting his mouth to the opening, his screams weren't answered.

He looked through the void where the doorknob used to be and noticed the glass eye of the mini-camera watching him, imagining Gerald Metzger smiling as he watched Dwayne's efforts at escaping degrading into the pitiful. The dummy in the chair stared at him with its painted eyes, mocking him.

On his knees, splinters stinging his cheek, Dwayne could see the deadbolt's switch above, on the opposite side of the door. His fingers were nowhere near long enough.

Someone was in the corridor. He'd glimpsed their shoulder, a white shirt sleeve. He couldn't be sure, but their face appeared to be bandaged. Dwayne shouted for them, saying he'd seen them, but they quickly stepped back without making a sound. Putting his mouth to the hole again, Dwayne yelled and begged, saying all he needed them to do was turn the deadbolt, until he could only produce raspy screeches. He heard a door up the hall open, then close. The indifferent watcher never returned.

8.

BODY STIFF AND UNFEELING and cracking with every small movement, Jack didn't knock before stepping into apartment 308. Per protocol, the surgeon's door was to never be locked. If he ever found it any other way, the chemist was to be informed immediately.

Her empty wheelchair stood facing her TV that, like any other time he visited, was on. She lay on the sofa, her head propped by a pillow, eyes closed. She wasn't asleep; he could tell by her breathing. He decided not to say anything regardless. Let her rest, she works so hard. He looked at her legs. Whittled to twigs by atrophy and pale as a stone, she lay having posed them herself, crossed at the ankle.

Jack stood watching her TV a moment: the game show host with the beaming white idiot smile, the pointless games and the canned audience noise. The neighbor was pounding on the wall, screaming like a trapped, starving animal. Without opening her eyes, Connie picked up the remote and bumped the volume a couple notches higher. A hard slam from the other side and a picture fell. Jack obliged to pick it up, though it was difficult for him to bend, things popping and cracking inside him. A photo of a smiling couple flanking a young woman who'd just graduated from high school, by the look of it.

"Something you need, scarecrow?" she said without looking at him, her voice dead. She had purple rings around her eyes, her blinks slow. "I'd think it'd be obvious we're fresh out of brains around here."

He set the photo frame on the end table next to her, propped up by a cheap cardboard stand. She looked at it, then lifted her eyes to Jack's face, regarding both only briefly. She never looked at him long, but he didn't blame her. He was aware of how he looked now. She'd helped make him this way. How much had she deceived those people in the photo, all three?

Jack said, "Hear about Ryan?"

She nodded, solemn. "Leslie called a little bit ago. You?"

127

"I was the one who found him."

Connie sighed. "Yeah, well."

"In front of 306, someone put his stand-in there, sitting in a chair."

"That explains all his screaming." She shook her head. "Assholes."

"How's Sam holding up?"

She shrugged. "Haven't seen him."

When she reached for her cigarettes, he noticed the cluster of track marks dotting the inside of her milk-pale arm. More than usual—she'd been working hard lately.

Smoke lit, first drag sucked, she nodded toward the TV. "That lady on the far right, Amber , makes it onto the Showcase Showdown." Connie exhaled through her nose, two jets of gray. "She wins a trip to Hawaii. I mean, good for her. Going by that accent, I assume she's from Minnesota."

Jack already knew this. It was the same episode of *The Price is Right* that'd been on when he'd first visited here. Neck crackling, he forced his head to turn, looking at the spot on the sofa where Sam had been sitting, now occupied by Connie's thin pale legs. Turning in place with slow, measured movements, he peered through the open door of her makeshift OR—the Goya print, the goat and his sycophants. Connie had tricked him into believing this place was haunted. Define irony.

He had fond memories of hanging out like this with his fellow dropouts, watching TV and getting stoned while the rest of the world punched a clock. How many from that old crew might still be alive? He couldn't recall many of their names anymore, only the shared, glassy-eyed joy they'd had as they articulated every detail of the bright futures they'd all surely have, while they took turns casting the means to pursue them onto the pyre. Laughing and dancing and fucking as time curled and blackened. Even if those years had been carelessly wasted, he would do anything to go back to them now. To restore that dreamy, naïve certainty that something good *had* to be waiting ahead for him. There was only a sooty smear inside Jack now. He'd been promised something amazing. This wasn't it.

"The paternity test confirms that guy's not actually the father," Connie said the moment she'd changed the channel. "Twist, he's *not* stoked about the news." She changed the channel. "That guy and that guy there are the same person." She changed the channel. "The amnesiac billionaire has a secret twin who's evil, of course." She changed the channel. "Turns out, the astronauts were trapped in a pocket universe." She changed the channel. "Everybody on the boat was dead the whole time." She changed the channel. "They're all hallucinations of a painter who lost his mind because the paint he'd been using for decades was slowly poisoning him. The Goya estate may have a court case." She changed the channel. "They overhype a blender, order now and get a free salad spinner, their gift to you."

Connie flung the remote onto her coffee table, where it skidded to a stop near a handful of burner phones, their screens all dark. Jack watched her hook her hands behind either knee and drag herself sitting upright, crushing the cigarette filter in her clenching teeth, a zigzagging vein pushing out on her temple. He didn't offer to help her, knowing better, and besides, he liked watching her struggle. Shoving her legs off the sofa, the dead limbs' momentum turned the rest of her on the sofa cushion, now facing him.

"Why are you here?" she said. "Need someone to hand you tissues? Did you and Ryan become BFFs when I wasn't paying attention? Was this before or after Gerry had you cut off his arm?"

Yes, he did think about killing her right then.

"Get over it," Connie said. "Ryan's not the first, and he sure as shit won't be the last."

He watched as she shuffled her cards, snapping three face-down on the coffee table.

"My advice," she said. "Think of everybody you meet here like they're goldfish, the walking ephemeral. And who knows, he might be back. Certainly can't get rid of you. I might start calling you Herpes."

She'd changed. Some of her brightness was gone, crushed out. He could scarcely blame her, but it didn't hurt any less to see.

"I'm worried about Sam," Jack said. "We should find him, see if he's all right."

"Be my guest." She flicked ashes in his direction. "That's what action figures are for, aren't they? Provide comfort and distraction, be a lonely boy's buddy?"

She flipped over the three cards in quick succession, left to right. He didn't get a chance to see what they had to say, but the look on her face didn't bode well. She sighed, cut the deck, put the three offending cards in, shoved them all back in their box, and flung it across the room. Elbows on her small, knobby knees, she squinted into the palm of her right hand, as if trying to make out some microscopic print. He watched her turn her hand toward the light of her lamp. And then he saw it too, only just catching a glance, the spiral in the grooves of her hand, a lifeline swirling in on itself. It was remarkably similar to the symbol staining his own palm, in blood that had since gone brown and flaking.

He found himself reaching out to her, to touch her cheek. He had to know if she was like him, albeit a much better-constructed . . .

Wrenching back from the touch before it could connect, Connie balled a fist on her strange mark and burned him with her ice-blue eyes. "Don't touch me. Don't *ever* touch me."

"I'm sorry."

"Christ. I hate how easy it is to forget you're in the room. Go somewhere. Go do something." Returning her attention to the TV, she murmured, "None of them find a way out of the cave."

The cop was still beating on the wall, his volume sharply rising as he started saying his own name over and over like he was trying to convince himself that's what it still was. Unwilling to suffer it a second longer, something cracked inside Jack as he bent to sweep together in ungainly hands the burner phones from her coffee table. He walked them into her kitchen, pausing when he saw what he thought at first glance was a cow stomach lying in her sink—until he'd noticed the ripped-open box on the counter and understood what the swollen red mass actually was—Connie had, yet again, removed the bladder from a box of wine. Though she gave the impression in conversation that she had accepted what was going on, apparently she still felt it was necessary to test the hypothesis in her idle nights. Had she been counting her attempts? How many tries would this make? Here, the definition of insanity—trying the same thing over and over, expecting different results—was up for debate. Maybe that should be the definition of determination instead.

After setting her burners in the freezer, he double-checked to make sure the door had closed and the rubber gasket had sealed, secure, soundproof. He hobbled back out into the living room.

Connie had ground out her cigarette and was looking at him, her lightning-bolt eyebrows meeting together. "What are you doing?"

9.

Listening at the wall in one place, Dwayne dragged his ear down a few feet and listened again. Voices, very faint. He slapped an open hand against the peeling paint, nearly hard enough that he almost broke his *other* wrist.

"I need you to call the police." Once he'd started, the pleas wouldn't stop tumbling from his mouth. "If you can hear me, my name is Lieutenant Dwayne Spare. Tell them I need immediate assistance. Dwayne Spare. Apartment 306. Please."

Silence.

He punched in another hole and tore the shards of sheetrock away. He reached the pink batting of insulation, the wall's subdermal layer, and tore that out too. Feeling around inside, fingers grazing the next layer of drywall, he speared the hanger rod through, but his neighbor's wall didn't come apart as easily as his. He ignored the protests of his injuries. The wall didn't give; he only managed to sink shallow round dents with the dowel.

Pacing the carpet, he circled the apartment in an endless loop. Think.

Noticing his lips and tongue were dry to the point of cracking, he snatched Leslie's travel mug—***1 GRANDPA—from the counter, but couldn't pry off the lid one-handed. He filled it under the kitchen tap through the mug's little spout, noticing it was crusted with what Leslie's mouth had left behind. Maybe he had yet to wash it since receiving it from his grandchildren.

The tap water smelled like a fish tank long overdue for a cleaning, but three big swallows and Dwayne's headache slightly loosened. A bad aftertaste hit him. Bitter. Slightly metallic.

He looked at himself in the dead gray screen of the portable TV. Dan Wells stared back, the bent shape of the glass transmogrifying him into a skeletal, long-limbed wraith. A possible future.

Placing the only other thing Leslie had left for him under the hole in the ceiling, Dwayne stood unsteadily on the lawn chair as he fed the dowel up through and set it across the hole above, then pulled with every ounce of his waning strength. His feet left the seat of the chair, toppling it, but he couldn't haul himself any higher. While he wasn't like many of his brothers on the force who'd let themselves go as they approached retirement, Dwayne wasn't a model of health either. He cursed every time he passed the precinct gym in favor of getting home to his recliner and his whisky. Come on, old man. Pull.

His fingers threatened to snap off as he growled and strained, only managing to hoist himself enough so that he could *peek* into apartment 406 before his hand slipped and he dropped, crunching the broken debris under him. A new pain flared. Something had punctured his bare foot. He rushed to sit, looking at the half-inch of rusty nail spiked into his heel.

Approaching footsteps, out in the hall. And they weren't alone. Something with a scattered, rapid gait accompanied them—on four legs.

Dwayne pulled the nail from his foot, reset the lawn chair, stepped onto its seat again, and reached for the dowel suspended across the opening above. Outside the door, he could hear the excited panting of the building manager's dog.

Jumping and pulling at the same time, Dwayne dragged himself high enough to plant his injured arm's elbow on the floor above, pawing with his other hand to grab a twist of the carpeting. He dragged himself up inside 406's living room just as he heard the bolt to the door below snap unlocked. Dwayne lay flat on the floor, listening to the dog charge into apartment 306, nails tearing at the carpet as he barreled around, nose working.

Heavy steps approached, stopping directly below the hole. "Son of a bitch."

Remaining still, Dwayne looked around himself. 406 was identical to 306, with the only differences being how the mystery stains and the dents in the walls were arranged.

Blandly, Leslie said, "You up there?"

Dwayne didn't answer.

"Meet your new buddy out in the hall? Me and Ryan's boy put that one together. Good for setting up in windows, makes it look like the building's got less vacancy than she does. By your third year here you won't look that different. Blend right in."

Dwayne gave no comment.

"Find the surprise in that cup I left you to borrow?"

Terror charged Dwayne's bloodstream.

"Didn't think it was odd the lid was stuck on with epoxy? Water probably tasted a little funny too, didn't it?"

As if the drug was waiting for the building manager's words before it'd activate, geometric shapes now started to coalesce and wheel above Dwayne, diving at his eyes.

"If you let me know you're up there, right now, I won't tell Gerry about this." A moment. "You up there?"

Remaining as still as possible, Dwayne turned his head to look across 406's floor. The door to the hallway wasn't modified like 306's. It didn't mean Leslie wouldn't have a key to this apartment, but Dwayne could leave before he got up here. But he had to wait until the right moment. Right now, the building manager seemed to think their prisoner had escaped hours ago.

Jingling keys, rattling links of a dog's choker collar. Fading, "Come on, boy. Use that nose. Find him, Keelut."

When he heard the door shut below, Dwayne shot to his feet and pushed through the things he knew weren't really impeding him—more red triangles expanding on the air, concentric rings—and limped toward the exit, leaving a dotted line across the floor from his bleeding heel. While the high had yet to crescendo, it was well on its way. The shapes were new. Metzger must have expanded his ingredients list. Find a place to hide and ride this out.

Dwayne stepped out into the fourth-floor hall. No one was around, the corridor stretched empty in either direction, silent as a tomb—until he heard the stairwell door downstairs creak open. He limped to the door directly across. Locked. The next, locked.

Behind him, up the hall, a jangling dog collar, labored panting.

He limped to the hallway's corner, slipped around, and listened as the building manager threw open the door to 406, calling out Dwayne's name—muffled; he'd gone inside the apartment. But the dog's rapid breathing didn't quiet. It had remained in the hall, perhaps aware the quarry wouldn't be where the building manager thought. Dwayne looked down at the floor and the pool of blood forming under his left foot, scenting him. He pushed off from the wall and hobbled to check the next door, then the next. Locked, locked. He could hear the dog's nose following his trail, interrupting its own sniffing with low growls, following the trail Dwayne was helpfully leaving.

Dwayne grabbed the next doorknob, to apartment 416, and it turned.

* * *

Inside, he quietly eased the door shut behind him and locked it. For the next half-moment, he was safe. 416 was unlike the other units he'd seen in Dunsany Arms—it had furniture, for one. A person sat at the kitchen table, so still Dwayne didn't notice them at first. Looking at them closer, it made sense why they'd neither moved nor spoken when the intruder had entered their home: the unpainted face of the papier-mâché head saw nothing. Another one of Leslie's off-putting art projects.

Despite how starkly inhuman it appeared under closer scrutiny, Dwayne couldn't help but feel watched by it. He thought about the other people he'd spied across the courtyard his first night here, how many shapes he'd seen positioned on couches before TVs or standing idly in their kitchens, too far away to be taken as anything but actual living people.

416's bathroom floor was layered with forsaken dirty clothes. He took a neatly-folded hand towel from the counter and wrapped his bleeding foot. From the kitchen, a gentle whisper: "He said then he said."

The former author. Stepping from the bathroom, he looked across 416 at the dummy seated at the kitchen table, its back to him, as still as the inanimate thing it was.

His thudding heart was pushing the drug deeper into the folds of his brain, and the worst was yet to come. But when scratching came at the hallway door, he had to trust that some of what he was hearing was real. Keys rattled. "You find him, boy? Is he in there?"

Dwayne tore open the sliding glass door and rolled it shut behind him. He swung one leg up and over the railing, then the other, sitting perched four stories above the courtyard. Out of the corner of his eye, he saw the papier-mâché occupant inside had turned around in its chair and was now looking at him with sightless holes for eyes—just as Leslie and his dog entered the apartment.

Dwayne threw himself across the gap between the balconies, scrambling with his only available arm to clutch 418's railing. Climbing over, he stood behind the privacy barrier, listening to Leslie and his dog move around inside apartment 416 before rolling open its balcony door. No more than six feet away, Dwayne made himself as small as possible, listening as Leslie caught his breath, slips of the man's steam curling past the privacy barrier. Leslie's shadow spilled across the cement before Dwayne—standing in profile, looking down into the courtyard, perhaps checking to see if his prisoner had, in fact, jumped.

The shadow remained, joined now by that of its dog—nose sniffing, searching. It didn't need to see him to know he was still nearby.

Shivering, Dwayne covered his mouth, silently pleading for the old man and his dog to go away.

An electronic chime, and Leslie said, "Yeah, he did, but we're looking for him. By the look of it, he busted that patch I put up and climbed into the unit over his. Yeah, he used the cup." Pause. "Somewhere in the fourth floor's east corner, I think. Shit, sorry, I thought you meant where's the cop. Right now, I'm on the balcony of unit 416."

The building manager's shadow didn't recede. Dwayne listened to him curse under his breath. The overhang of the balcony above appeared to be fanged with keenly-pointed icicles. One snapped off as a door rolled open not four feet over Dwayne's head. Someone approached the railing. The building manager's shadow turned—and looked up.

Metzger's disembodied voice said, "How much did you put in the coffee mug?"

"Hundred and seventy-five milligrams in a tea bag taped inside, like you said."

The wind moaned and lashed at Dwayne. His knees knocked together; he ground his teeth to keep them from chattering. He pressed his hand harder over his mouth, trapping a cough that wanted free.

The building manager's shadow: "His burners needed more minutes put on. That's why I was going up, so I could—"

"If we miss a transmission, that'll be on you."

"We'll find him."

"Seen Sam around?"

"No."

"Has Ryan's body been taken care of?"

"Not yet," Leslie's shadow said. "I was planning on doing that this morning. Then all this shit had to happen."

"Sam should be there. Ryan was a good man."

"Yeah, Ryan was all right." The building manager didn't sound particularly torn up. "Crying shame."

Metzger's voice: "If I caved in your head and locked your corpse in one of the vacant units with Keelut, how long do you think it'd take before he started eating you?"

Leslie's shadow said, "You don't have to say sick shit like that to me, Gerry. I'm aware this isn't good."

A moment. "Find his gun?"

Leslie sighed, and a wisp of steam curled around the corner, ahead of Dwayne. "No."

"So there's a loose firearm roaming around the building? A child lives here."

"I know."

"Start at Connie's, then check the laundry room. Ryan mentioned Sam likes it down there. Regarding Dan, if his receivers don't turn up, he'll have to give me an oral account of his dreams. Actually, bring him up either way. He and I apparently need to get some things straight."

"All right." Leslie's shadow remained, looking up. "You okay, Gerry? Jesus, careful of that railing . . . "

Metzger, sounding lethargic, "I don't know if it's him, but someone's pushing off. You don't hear that?"

"I'm . . . no, I'm sorry, I don't."

"Close your eyes and *listen*. They're about to peak. Oh, here it comes."

Dwayne didn't hear the building manager's reply. A crawling sensation splashed across every inch of him, bristling and stinging. By their own accord, his eyes moved to look out into the open space above the courtyard.

A pinprick of darkness winked into existence, expanding with heavy, silent throbs. Screams pounded him in a twist of agonized noise. The swirling blackness bled color—tendon-yellows and gristle-pinks—as the being vomited itself piecemeal into this world. The ripping tempest of void-regurgitated viscera snapped together, forming a boulder of amorphous anatomy. It split open with a nauseating tear, allowing steel-gray teeth to lever up and stand towering in its massive, shivering jaw. Above the mouth, one cavity, then a second, split wetly and wide, revealing a shriveled whitish lump within each. The vein-laced orbs squelched as they swelled until both cloudy eyes had bloated to fill their sockets and together, with a startling and ghastly unity, the living storm of blood and cruelty, complete, emptied the whole of its wrathful regard upon its prey standing vulnerable on the high balcony, so small.

Heat lapped across his face, flash-boiling him in his clothes. It's not real, it's not real, it's not real. Dwayne closed his eyes on the hallucination and trembled, nearly pushing his own teeth down his throat, damming his screams with his palm.

The searing heat, so real, threatened to bring Dwayne's skin to bubbling. He opened his eyes to the peeled face hovering before him and felt himself get ripped off his feet, piercing with his head the milky cataract lidding the entity's eye. He slid bodily into the darkness of its pupil, never touching the sides until he'd been engulfed and the fleshy walls had cinched tight behind him, dropping him into a humid darkness. The living passageway gaped wide ahead, allowing him to drop before catching him again, squeezing him again. He flailed and scratched, but couldn't find any purchase in the slickened tube to slow his descent as he was swallowed into deeper heat and further unbreaking darkness. The spongy, membranous walls cinched tighter, pressing their moist heat against his face, trying to work their way into his mouth, up his nostrils, push his eyes back in his head to gain access within his skull. His arms snapped flat, pinned at his sides, and his ankles were forced together, bones grinding.

His screams didn't sound like his alone—he was being joined in his blind shrieking by another voice, one he recognized. Trapped with him, lower, a man was trying to scream without a jaw. The ribbed walls around him shredded as innumerable hands grabbed him, forcing him along faster, the five-fingered papillae clawing and pushing, shoving him onward to meet the source of the broken screams—screams that were becoming clearer, closer, perhaps the jawless man ascending to meet him halfway.

III
Dwell and Despair

1.

SOMETHING WAS GOING ON. An implacable, panicked energy seemed to be filling the building. Jack was afraid the sudden excitement was about him, that someone had found out his plans before he'd had a chance to put them into action. It took no effort for Jack to let his body go still, but it took a much more concerted effort to make it move. He hoped he'd be overlooked as just another object cluttering up the hall. Leaning as tightly as he could against a closed door, he watched as Leslie went charging down the hall the other way, his ring of keys bouncing and jangling on the old man's hip. Keelut, as always, was close at his master's heel, and both vanished around the far corner. They were looking for someone.

Jack waited until he heard the elevator doors close before leaving his hiding spot to follow. Joints creaking, moving only in short, constricted shuffles, he maneuvered as quickly as he could manage down the hall and peeked around the corner to see which way Leslie had gone. The elevator's floor indicator light moved from three to six. Going up, which was exactly what Jack wanted Leslie to be doing, moving *away* from the place Jack wanted to go. Carefully turning himself around, he entered the stairwell, and with one hand clutching a handrail to either side, he cautiously and painstakingly eased himself down one step at a time, pausing occasionally to regain his balance and manage his speed. If his mobile prison happened to slip and shatter apart as it crashed down the steps, he doubted Leslie would be quick to set aside his other work to help Jack undo the predicament he'd put himself in.

He passed the former author in their usual place on the second-floor landing, who was too preoccupied with telling their story—"said he said that she said then he said he she said"—to notice the paper man slip past behind them. Reaching the first floor, Jack pushed his way through the heavy steel door. Up the hall a short distance, he saw someone step around the corner at the far end, wearing the same clothes they always wore. The delivery man, departing to make another drop somewhere. As much as Jack wanted to go chasing after him, maybe strangle him until he stopped moving, he had to focus.

The door marked MANAGER was locked. Jack figured it would be, but he had to try the obvious entrance first. First setback established, he'd have to find another way, and soon. Moving slowly to avoid losing his balance and falling over, he got himself turned to face the other way and palmed aside the door to the courtyard. It was snowing again, the sky a world-spanning blanket of roiling gray shades. Since Leslie only kept a narrow shoveled and salted path going through the courtyard's center, access to the windows of the apartments on the ground floor wouldn't be easy for Jack. He clambered up and over the snow dune and lost his balance when he reached its summit—gliding down the other side, he heard something crack within his mobile prison when it smacked against the brickface. He lost a finger and the tip of his thumb. It could've been worse, he told himself, and pulled himself to his feet.

When Jack had been inside another prison—apartment 306, across the courtyard and up two levels from Leslie's home—the building manager had said that he always left one window open, to make it easier for Keelut to hear if Jack was trying to escape. Leslie hadn't been lying: one of his widows was open a couple inches. Sliding it the rest of the way, Jack ungracefully climbed inside. He passed the wall of strangers' photos, including his own, and entered the living room, moving directly to the dented pail standing in the corner. Bending down to sift through the old worn-out keys proved too difficult, so Jack picked up the bucket and walked the heavy thing to Leslie's kitchen table. Pausing to listen for anyone approaching the building manager's door, Jack heard nothing, and upended the bucket. He padded his numb, nigh inflexible hands around the keys, sifting through them, turning some over, reading apartment number after apartment number—hurry up, find it—but none were etched with the specific apartment number he was looking for.

If Jack could die, Gerald Metzger could too. Wait for the right night, catch him dreaming, and ensure he remained mired in it forever.

Jack's hands froze when, out of the corner of his vision, he saw the curtains that covered the window through which he'd entered flare, air being sucked back into the apartment. Without having made a sound, someone had entered. Behind him, a door creaked closed. Jack remained as he was, his back to whoever had just walked in. This didn't look good, standing hunched over Leslie's kitchen table with the keys spread all over the checkerboard tablecloth. He scrambled to assemble a lie. He was merely trying to help find . . . whoever it was they were looking for. He was looking for key copies so he could search the locked apartments, cover more ground. Jack would wait until they spoke first before turning around, buy himself a couple extra seconds.

Wracked with sadness, Sam's small voice said, "Jack, where's Mister Leslie?"

Wet feet squeaking on the chipped linoleum floor as he turned his mobile prison about, Jack faced Sam, seeing the boy was wearing an oversized jacket that swallowed him and hung nearly to the floor. The hood was up, laying a shadow that hid most of the boy's face, but Jack could see the wet shine of tears in the boy's eyes. His lips were a livid red, and a tributary of snot-crust ran from his nose around his mouth, and down to his chin.

"I don't know. Sam, I'm sorry about . . . " He couldn't bear to say it. Having lost both parents, Jack knew exactly the agony the boy was in. He could read it in his face.

"You heard about Dad?"

"I . . . "

"How do you know what happened to Dad?"

"I came to your apartment early this morning," Jack said. "Mister Metzger asked me to bring down what your dad would need to dream today, and—"

"Why didn't you come find me and tell me?"

"I didn't know where you were."

"I was in the laundry room. I'm there all the time. You found me there when we played hide and seek yesterday."

"It was the next place I was going to look. It's a big building, Sam. I wanted to tell you, but—"

"Mister Leslie already did," Sam said. "*He* found me because he didn't stop looking to . . . mess around with stupid keys."

"I'm sorry, Sam. I know you probably would've preferred to have heard about your dad from me, but I couldn't find you, and I had something very important I needed to take care of right away."

"More important than telling me Dad choked to death on his throw up?"

Jack had no response to that. The boy was right. It pained him wanting to change subjects—what was the *only* subject to Sam right now, and would arguably be the most important subject to him his entire childhood, because today would color everything, Jack knew, again from experience. This place that was likely already swollen with bad memories had just gotten another shoved in. But Jack felt he *had* to change subjects. Though it was insensitive to do so, he was far too close to getting what he came here for to lose the opportunity now.

"Sam, can you help me find something? I can't see very well."

The boy ran the length of his sleeve under his nose and stood chewing his lip, considering. With a small sigh, he crossed the kitchen and hopped up onto the seat of one of Leslie's kitchen chairs, bringing himself to the same height as Jack. "What are you looking for?"

"A key."

"But which one? There's a lot."

"The one that has the numbers six zero three on it."

The boy turned on the chair to face Jack. It was strange no longer needing to look down to see into the boy's eyes—eyes, partly shadowed by the jacket's hood, that reminded him of someone else now that he and the boy were standing at the same height. But he couldn't place it, even as a mild fear clutched him—as if it still knew, ahead of him, even if he hadn't quite caught up to it yet.

"Six zero three," Sam said, chewing his lip. "That's Mister Metzger's apartment."

"That's right," Jack said, forcing his tone even, nothing unusual. "Can you help me find that one?"

Jack turned away and returned to sorting through the keys, sweeping his hand through them hoping the metallic hiss they made as they glided over each other would appeal to the boy's curiosity, inspire him to help—but the boy remained standing on the chair, staring at the side of Jack's head. He could feel Sam's eyes on him, more curious about Jack.

"Why do you want a key to Mister Metzger's house?"

"Because Mister Leslie asked me to look in his key bucket for it."

"But Mister Leslie never lets anybody touch his copies, not even the old ones," Sam said, and glanced around them—the old man's dishes standing in their drying rack, the boxes of his fiber-rich cereal on the counter, the oven mitt made to look like a happy pig, Keelut's water bowl and food bowl. "I've never been in his apartment when Mister Leslie isn't home. Do we have permission to be here?"

"It's fine. He said it was okay. Please help me find the key, Sam."

The boy didn't. "Jack, why would Mister Leslie ask you to do this when Mister Spare's missing?"

The handful of keys slipped through Jack's stalled fingers, tingling as they rejoined the others upon the tablecloth. "Mister Spare's missing?"

"Uh-huh."

"When?"

"I don't know. He got out of your old room somehow. I don't know how he could've, Mister Leslie made it so it locks from the outside now, but I guess he must've figured out a way to." The boy hopped down from the chair, his bare feet clapping against the floor. "I'm gonna go help look. Finding Mister Spare 'fore he hurts himself is more important than wasting time looking at dumb keys."

"Wait. If you see Mister Leslie, don't tell him I was in here, okay?"

The boy turned back around. "How come? You said he gave you permission."

Something rang in the boy's voice. Like he was aware that if he could hide behind a young face and keep wording things in a child's indelicate way, the true cleverness he secretly harbored would remain unnoticed. That, or it was true how Connie had described Sam. Not dead, not a ghost, just weird as shit.

"He did give me permission," Jack said, "it's just . . . I want to surprise him. I'm going to act like I couldn't find the key, then say 'Just kidding!' and hold out to him, like this." To show him what he meant, Jack picked up one of the keys and proudly raised it pinched between his damaged thumb and forefinger, like he'd just done a magic trick.

The boy looked at the key, and how Jack was lying about surprising Mister Leslie with it, appearing neither impressed nor convinced. Nodding at what Jack was holding, the boy's voice was flat. "You found it."

Jack looked at it, held by the stumped, broken thumb and finger, *306* scratched deeply into the key's brass head. Again, Jack glimpsed the curtains billowing out of the corner of his vision. A door hinge creaked. The boy had gone.

2.

Unable to bite, the jawless man scarped his teeth across Dwayne's forehead, his neck, his shoulder, his hands as the jawless man's prey tried pushing him away. Winding his own hands around Dwayne's throat and squeezing with incredible strength, when the last of Dwayne's air had gone dead in his lungs he was abruptly alone, released. It felt like the assault had lasted years, the man with no bottom jaw screaming at him in the cloyingly humid dark and trying, and failing, to kill him again and again. He lay now gasping on a field of white dust, a cold wind blowing across him. His imprint remained when he stood up from it. A red fog polluted the horizon, dimming the low-hanging sun to a feeble smudge that, to Dwayne's adjusting eyes, was still painfully bright.

About him squatted silent ruins. Half-walls with no glass in their windows, doorways that only gave passage to nowhere. Cement arches and columns lay cracked, revealing the rusty rebar within that had failed to keep them upright. He knew this place, but he'd seen it from a higher vantage before. He turned, looking at a hollowed-out Dunsany Arms, now another ruin. Nothing remained standing near it, either—the interstate, the city skyline, all gone, only a plain of white that stretched to join with the overcast sky, the world lidded under bone-white.

Counting floors, he looked up at Gerald Metzger's window, now a gouged-out void high on the building's face. He recalled his last visit to this dream-place and seeing the line of gaunt, empty-eyed victims standing down here, where he was now. His ears ached, desperate to pick up any sound other than the wind, but he heard nothing.

His pockets were empty. The three burner phones he'd stolen hadn't joined him here, though his arm remained tangled in the sling he'd made of his shoulder-holster, the two hammerhead-shaped bruises on his wrist still eclipsing each other, purple and black, the puncture wound on his left heel clotted with white powder and a flaking crust of dried blood.

He looked down at the impression his body had left in the dust. Shallow wells—left, right, left—moved away from his indent, the tracks of whoever had brought him here. Small feet.

Though Dwayne knew this wasn't a real place, he felt sick with panic when he couldn't wake himself. Squeezing his bruised wrist hurt just as much as before, while conscious. The wind blew, and the edges of the footprints softened, being erased. If he was going to follow them to where they led before they vanished, he had to get moving. He trudged, his body numb and the cold worming into his bones, and mounted a low hill of the white powder. He paused at the crumbling summit, seeing the footprints dotting across another plain toward a large, boxy structure in the distance—one that appeared to be entirely shrouded in some dark blue material.

He had time to study it as he approached it. The blue material shifted oddly. It wasn't being moved by the wind—there was none—but it still expanded and contracted. He followed alongside the line of footprints, watching the blue material snap tight with the house's inhales, giving him an imprecise bas-relief of the structure: the dormered windows, the arched front doors—which appeared to be open past the blue tarpaulin, given how the material sucked in deeper there before snapping back out as the house-swaddling tarpaulin expanded again.

Staked in rows across the gray waste, telephone poles leaned at wind-tipped angles with drooping black cables suspended from one to the next. Each line of telephone poles ended at the house, leading the cables, swinging in the wind, to pass through the blue by various holes in the material. Every direction he turned in, the suspended lines were being directed to the house, reminding him of a nexus point for nerves, a synapse.

The footprints ended here. Dwayne stood at the edge of the wrinkled indentation where the tarp pulled in the deepest, the cavity sucking tight into the open front door. It made him think about at a crime scene he'd once asked to come take a look at. A man lay with his features smeared by the plastic bag pulled tight over his face, the wrinkled, sucked-in cavity of his open mouth, frozen mid-gawp, never getting that breath he so desperately needed.

He felt he needed to go inside the house, but couldn't force himself to take a step closer. Looking at the tented house and the way it seemed to breathe, his throat dried and his head swam, the same feeling as when a vicious flu strain takes ravenous root in the guts. Something his physiology understood before his brain did was trying to warn him, an animalistic response.

As if it'd been waiting for such an unease to arise in him before it'd break the rhythm of its breaths, the tent covering the house burst to expand, reaching farther out than it had before and striking Dwayne before he could think to jump back. Blinded in blue, when the plastic tore itself from around him, he collapsed onto a surface harder than the white dust, his knees knocking hollowly on the hardwood floor and splinters biting into the one palm he could throw out to catch himself.

He stood, now in a dimly lit foyer. The house's double doors lay on the parquet floor, broken from their hinges. The unpierced tarpaulin remained, swelling the cavity impassably. He'd been eaten, sustenance absorbed by a cell.

He could see the house's layout opening in his mind—even the blue-stained light pouring in through each window, coloring the spaces in the dust where furniture no longer stood—though he couldn't specifically recall visiting this nowhere place before, with its walls hewn from calcified dreams. But within that deep familiarity, no pearl of comfort had been allowed to form. I've been in this house before and nothing good has ever happened in it.

Someone had dug into the walls, leaving rents that exposed a mass of insulated cables buried within, some as thick as Dwayne's wrist, others as fine as a spider's silver thread. Severed wires dangled, rubber insulation torn, revealing tufts of exposed raw copper hairs. He didn't remember the place looking so ravaged. What had they been looking for?

The two light bulbs outside the door under the stairs. Looking at the one currently lit red, a heavy feeling of disgust settled over him, but he wasn't sure why. He listened at the door, hearing a low thrum, like when you stand under a power line on a windless night. He clutched the doorknob and was surprised to find it warm and slightly clammy, like it'd only left someone's hand seconds ago. He was relieved when it wouldn't turn.

An old-fashioned phone stood on a nearby wood pedestal, the dangling spiral cord connected to a receiver lying off the cradle, dusted in broken pieces of plaster. He reluctantly listened at the earpiece. Someone was on the line. He could hear them breathing.

"Hello?" he said.

Sounding like the tide, they breathed in and breathed out.

"I need help," Dwayne said. "Hello? *Hello?*"

"We're sorry, all lines are currently in use," he heard a woman say twice, both from the receiver in his shaking hand and through the thin echo coming from upstairs. "Please try again at another time."

Dwayne dropped the receiver and used the handrail to haul his beaten body up the stairs, passing more holes in the walls, ripped wires and broken plaster scattered every few feet. It reminded him of how copper thieves go to construction sites and dig into the walls, but none of these wires were missing—it was like they'd only been taking the drywall. Among the debris, he noticed a phone cord trailing along the baseboard. It wasn't severed. He followed it to where it slipped under a closed door—beyond which, he already knew, would be the study.

He didn't knock. A dentist's chair had been bolted directly into the hardwood at the room's center, its curved seat positioned to face away from the door.

The cord drew a serpentine path toward the chair. Twisting it around his hand, he gave it a sharp pull and a phone was yanked from the chair and crashed to the floor, bells clanging a discordant note. The person in the chair gave no comment.

Before he could glimpse her face, the woman pulled a white sheet over her head. As confused as he was afraid, he watched as each time she exhaled, the sheet lifted in front of her face and then fell back again.

Aided by the tarp-tinted light, he could make out a suggestion of her heart-shaped face, her dark hair, her lively eyes looking up at him, the subtle smile curling her full lips, acting as if she truly believed she couldn't be seen.

Dwayne said, "How do I wake up?"

In the house's awful silence, whenever she blinked he could hear her eyelashes brush against the sheet.

"I need to get out of the apartment building before they fucking kill me. If you can wake me up, then do it."

"As I am, I can't answer anything," she said. "I can only take your message and pass it on when I'm at the switchboard again. I'll try to get back to you soon as I can. May all your connections with Mtahsab Belsharh be clear."

"What is Mtahsab Belsharh?"

"As I am, I can't answer anything. I can only take your message and—"

"Please, tell me what I have to do. What does Gerald Metzger want from me?"

"As I am, I can't—"

Enough. Dwayne took the sheet by its frayed edge and ripped it away. The mannequin torso in the chair had a lumpy papier-mâché head affixed to its neck by a thick band of time-yellowed packing tape.

There'd been someone under the sheet. He'd heard her eyelashes brushing the rough cloth. There *had* been someone there.

Bearing the signs of Leslie's previous craftwork that Dwayne had seen, this dummy had a sharply-angled lightning bolt jagging over either sightless eye in purple paint.

He shoved the mannequin from the chair. It crashed to the floor, where the head came detached and rolled, coming to rest face-up with its stapled-on wig settling into a splayed black halo. Inside its hollow neck was the reverse side of the newspaper that'd been carefully torn into uniform strips to give the head its shape and something else, a gnarled and kinked black cord.

He knelt and began drawing out the cord, feeling the weight of something that'd been tucked deeply within.

The wiretap device he'd stolen from the evidence lockup. Finally, last to emerge from the neck hole and still connected to the device, a dangling set of headphones. Faintly, without them anywhere near his ears yet, and with the device connected to nothing, nonetheless he could hear people—

3.

—A LITTLE BOY was saying, "Are you okay?"

"Yeah. Think I might have a migraine coming on." It was same voice of the young woman Dwayne thought he'd been talking to seconds ago.

"Connie, how come his eyes are moving like that?"

"There must be a lot to look at in his dream." A swell of static momentarily drowned her out. "—move too when you dream."

"They do?"

"Yep."

"That's weird."

"Sam, what's that you got in your pocket?"

"I wasn't playing with myself."

"I didn't suggest you were."

"Dad said not to do that in front of people 'cause a pervert might take it as an invitation. Do you remember Mister Pohl, who used to live in two-twenty-five?"

"Unfortunately, yes."

"I heard he molested his own son."

"I heard that too."

"Do you think that's why his son just tells his story to the wall in the stairwell all day now? Do you know what *molest* means? Dad said it's when—"

"How about we talk about something else, something nicer?"

[*static*] "—miss Dad a lot."

"I know you do, kiddo."

"Did you know my dad?"

"No, but it feels like I did, from all the stories you told me."

[*static*] "—came over again last night and we played."

"Oh yeah? Did you two have fun?"

"We spied on him. I think we scared him really bad."

"Sounds like you and Jack enjoyed yourselves."

"Connie?"

"Yeah?"

"Are Mister Spare's fingers gonna fall off?"

"I don't think so, he should be okay. It's very fortunate that you found him when you did."

"Mister Leslie's looking for him. I heard him yelling downstairs. Should we go tell?"

"Let's not bother Mister Leslie. Think of it like hide and seek."

"Okay."

"How about you tell me more about how you and Jack spied on Mister Spare? You two better not have drilled another hole in a wall. You remember how mad Mister Leslie got that other time."

"Nah, we didn't need to, 'cause there was already a hole from when Jack shot himself. Mister Leslie fixed it with the stuff he uses to make his paper people. Jack told me to kick it down, and when I did we could see right down into 306. And we *were* having fun till Jack started saying Mister Spare stole his home from him and ruined everything."

"Sometimes it's hard adjusting to big changes. Kind of like how you're getting used to not having your dad around right now. Speaking of which, do you like the present Mister Leslie gave you?"

"I guess . . ."

"What do you mean, you guess? Mister Leslie worked really hard on that for you."

"It's stupid-looking. The face isn't done."

"Well, he wanted you to have something as soon as possible, to keep you company. Did you thank him?"

"Yeah. I helped him get it dressed. I put Dad's favorite shirt on it. Mister Leslie made it so it's only got one arm, like Dad."

"That was considerate of him."

"I said we could put Dad's real arm on it, 'cause I saw where Mister Metzger threw it, but Mister Leslie said no because it'd attract bugs. There's already enough of them living here rent-free, he said."

"Sam, do you mind if I ask you something?"

"Dad hasn't made it say anything yet."

[*static*] "—don't have to talk about this, if you don't want."

"It's okay. I listen every night, but he still hasn't yet. Mister Leslie put it on the couch so we can sit together and watch TV at night. Sometimes

I'll mute it 'cause I'd think I heard Dad say something, but it's always just somebody on TV."

[*static*] "—needs a little time, Sam, to find his way."

"Jack's has this big hole in its head, right here."

"You know why Mister Leslie made it that way, right?"

"Yeah, because Jack was a bitch-ass pussy."

"Sam."

"That's what Dad said. He said only bitch-ass pussies kill themselves. Is that—" [*static*] "—bad thing to say?"

"It sort of is, yeah. What if you were coloring a picture and spilled something on it? Wouldn't it be frustrating not being able to undo your mistake?"

"I'd just start coloring a new picture. Or tear the messed-up part off."

"You could do either of those things, yes, but you still shouldn't say things like that. I tried hurting myself, and I'm very lucky it didn't work. If it had, you and me never would've met each other."

"But wouldn't we never know no different?"

"Yes, but don't you think things are better the way they worked out?"

"I guess."

"There you go with guessing again. You mean to tell me you wouldn't be sad if we hadn't met? Turd."

"Sorry. I would've been, yeah. I still wish you would've met Dad, though."

"Me too."

"We all lived in the same building for so long, and you two never even saw each other once."

"We just kept different schedules." [*long pause*] "Sam, listen. I hate to say this, but you probably shouldn't get your hopes up too high about hearing from him."

"I know."

"He struggled trying to receive for Mister Metzger. And when that happens, it usually means when the person's gone, we don't hear from them again. Jack is special like that."

"I know."

"I mean, don't give up listening for your dad. You never know."

"I won't."

"Good."

"Connie?"

"Yeah?"

"Why'd you wanna hurt yourself?"

"Well, I was really sad."

"How'd you, um . . . ?"

"I asked for a sign that I shouldn't, and when I didn't get one I opened my bedroom window and jumped out."

"You *did?*"

"Yes."

"Here?"

"Hm?"

"Were you living here?"

"No, this was at my parents' place, long before I moved here."

"How high up were you?"

"We lived on the eighth floor."

"Didn't that hurt?"

"I don't remember. I woke up in the hospital after being asleep for nineteen days in a row, and the doctor said I'd never be able to walk, ever again. It was a very stupid thing I did, and I regret it every single day."

"Did you have any dreams while you were sleeping?"

"Some. I remember I could hear somebody talking, but I couldn't see them."

"What were they saying?"

"It was a little boy, and he sounded afraid and lonely."

"Did he sound like me?"

"Kind of. He told me he fell off his bike and now he didn't know where he was, but I couldn't help him because he couldn't hear me that well either. I still think about him a lot."

"But he wasn't real."

"True, but for a little over two weeks he was the only friend I had."

"Connie?"

"Yeah?"

"You do dreams for Mister Metzger too, right? Like my dad . . . used to?"

"Yep, that's right."

"Do you ever 'member those ones?"

"Not really."

"Jack says he remembers. He said one time he did a *big* dream where he was in this big house."

"Well, some lucky people can remember their dreams really clearly."

"Jack said you were there and he talked to you."

"Is that right?"

"And there was a—" [*static*] "—in the basement."

"I see."

"Connie, how come you keep looking out the window, looking at the clock, then looking at Mister Spare?"

"Just wondering about something."

"Wondering about what?"

"Nothing. Don't worry about it."

"You're not still sad, are you, Connie?"

"I'm not going anywhere."

"But . . . you're not sad anymore, right?"

"No, Sam. I'm not sad anymore."

"Jack says now it's like he's watching a movie wearing someone else's glasses he can't take off and—" [*static*] "—screaming inside his head sometimes, 'cept they don't sound like how he screams."

"Has Jack ever told you what else he remembers?"

"One time we were playing and he told me Mister Metzger helped him when he got in deep trouble and got really sick, so Mister Metzger had Jack move into apartment 306 to start doing dreams, but he ended up having too many. He said it started making him feel bad so he asked Mister Leslie for something to help with it, and when Jack woke up the next morning there was a shotgun on his kitchen table. Can we watch the movie now?"

"In a sec. Now, it might not feel good to think about but—" [static] "—you to try for me, all right? This is important."

"Okay . . . "

"When was the last time you left our building, Sam?"

"Dad said if I didn't bother anybody he wouldn't make me start going to a school, 'cause what I learn here is all I'll need to know, helping Mister Metzger."

"Sure, but when was the last time you left?"

"You mean like the parking lot?"

"Even farther away than that. Can you remember the last time?"

"Dad and me walked to the Shell station for my birthday. Does that count?"

"That absolutely counts. When was that?"

"October the thirty-first. I thought you knew when my birthday is."

"I must've forgotten. I would think I'd remember something as cool as your birthday being on Halloween. I'm jealous."

"We made crazy drinks mixing all the pops in really big cups. Then Dad got two packs of Camels and he let me ride on his shoulders on the way back. But then Dad tripped and I dropped my pop on his head."

"Whoops! I bet that was cold and sticky!"

"A lot got on me too, but Dad was like, 'Think that's funny? I'd cave your fucking head in right now if we weren't in fucking public, you stupid piece of shit,' even though I swore I didn't do it on purpose. *He* tripped, not me, but he didn't care. I didn't even get to drink *half* my crazy drink yet. He said I could lick it up off the sidewalk—" [*static*] "—didn't taste like pop anymore, just dirt. Mister Leslie had to let me in when I got home 'cause Dad didn't wait up for me and wasn't answering the buzzer. Dad was on the couch trying to dream for Mister Metzger, so I couldn't ask him where the remote was so I couldn't change it to *Tiny Toons*, so I just watched a show about how cocaine is made, then I ate leftover mashed potatoes and went to sleep. I gotten woken up 'cause the TV room exploded when Jack shot himself downstairs."

"Jesus."

"What's that mean? Dad used to say that."

"Nothing, just a curse word. Well, at least that birthday started out pretty good, huh?"

"Did you know they used to put cocaine in Coke back when people thought pop was medicine?"

"Yep. I think maybe you told me that."

"I learned a lot from that show."

"Sounds like it. You know, I used to watch *Tiny Toons* when I was your age."

"That show's funny."

"I would've figured you'd think it's old."

"No. I like it. But I think I like the show about how cocaine is made more. I might not just wanna *help* Mister Metzger when I'm a grown-up."

"No?"

"Nuh-uh. I wanna *do* what he does. I wanna take over his territory and steal away all his customers and money."

"Um, that's great, Sam. I might recommend not telling him that, though."

"Yeah. He might get mad. And it'd be kinda dumb revealing my plans before I have the means to put them into action. I'd need to do it with precision, and fast."

"So, Jack did *what he did* on your birthday, last year?"

"Mm-hm. He told me the other day that if he'd known, he would've picked a different day. Why are you asking me so many weird questions? I thought we were gonna watch a movie."

"I'm trying to figure something out. How about the time you left the building before your birthday? Can you remember that?"

"You shouldn't worry, Connie. I like it inside."

"When did you and—" [*static*] "—Dad move in, again?"

"Dad told me he moved in the day after his twenty-second birthday. Did you know Mister Metzger has been living here his entire life? He's never lived no other place else ever."

"I've heard."

"Mister Metzger has lived in apartment 201, 239, 304, 416, 518, and now he lives in 603. Wouldn't it be funny if he lived up on the roof next?"

"That would be funny. Sam, were you in the picture when your dad moved in?"

"What picture?"

"What I mean is, were you born before or after your dad started living here? Do you remember helping him pack up your toys? What about riding in the moving truck with him?"

"Connie, can we—" [*static*] "—movie now?"

[*static*] "—the movie in a minute. Where does your—" [*static*]

"I don't know. Every time I ask—" [*static*] "—would get mad at me, so I stopped."

"Have you ever seen any—" [*static*] "—of your mom in your dad's stuff?"

"Nuh-uh. If we aren't gonna watch a movie tonight, I should go home. I know I probably won't hear anything but I—" [*static*] "—listen for him anyway, in case he tries. Why—" [*static*] "—me all this stuff for anyway?"

"What about when I moved in? Do you remember that? You were living here before I was, I know that much, so how long have I been here?"

"Why're you yelling at me?"

"I'm sorry, I don't mean to yell, but I really need you to think for me. When you and I met that day in the lobby, can you remember what I was doing?"

"Getting your mail?"

"That's right. Was it snowing out then like it is now?"

"I can't remember."

"Can—" [*static*] "—last time it *wasn't* snowing outside?"

"That kinda hurts, Connie."

"You know all those scratches on my bathroom wall?"

"Yeah . . . ?"

"I make one of those every night."

"Why?"

"I'm counting. And you know what I realized? It's snowing now the same as it's *been* snowing for the last—" [*static*] "—days, even though it never seems to get any deeper outside. And don't try telling me the sun's melting it. We haven't had anything *but* clouds in nearly as long."

"You're scaring me."

"For the last time, get your hand out of your pocket."

"Sorry."

"What do you have?"

"Nothing."

"And whose coat is that, even? It's enormous."

"I found it in the laundry room. I like it."

"Well, that explains all my missing hoodies. Sam, listen. You *had* to have noticed things are weird around here. I mean, right? Don't things seem weird?"

"Weird how?"

"Weird like nothing but the same shit runs on TV over and over. And why don't any of the news channels come in? Why hasn't the internet—" [*static*] "—in months? Why don't I get mail anymore, not even goddamn bills? I get why they need to jam up the elevator all the time, but why is it every time I even *think* about leaving, either Gerry sends someone for me to work on or *you* show up demanding I drop what I'm doing and watch a movie with you? Does he ask you to do that?"

"Does who ask me?"

"Mister Metzger. Does he tell you to do that, to distract me?"

"Nuh-uh. I just like watching movies here with you."

"So you can regurgitate every word your white trash father *ever* said, and the number of every apartment Gerry's rented in this dump, but noticing anything's strange about this place has completely eluded you?"

"Why're you squeezing my arm so hard?"

"Because I want you to tell me what's really going on."

"But I don't know. I swear. Why won't—" [*static*] "—believe me?"

"Tell me. Sam, tell me. Fucking tell me, right now."

"I don't know, I don't know, I don't know, *I don't know!*"

"Shh, we need to use our inside voices, okay? Mister Leslie and Mister Spare are playing hide and seek, remember?"

"I don't *care*. Let *go*."

"Okay, okay, I'm sorry, I'm sorry."

"My arm's all red. Lookit."

"Let me see."

"Kissing boo-boos is baby shit. Still hurts."

"Sam, do you want to keep this little arm of yours?"

"What do you mean . . . ?"

"Or would you like to be just like your dad? Sam, where did you get that?"

"I found it."

"Give that to me, right now."

"No. Why did you say that to me, Connie? I thought—" [*static*] "—best friends."

"We *are* best friends, Sam. We are. I'm sorry, that was an awful thing for me to say to you, but please give that to me before you hurt yourself."

"I won't hurt myself. I'm not weak like you and Jack."

"Sam, I—" [*static*] "—say mean things to you, but I feel like I'm losing my—" [*static*] "—sure I probably just miscounted at some point, but since you're the only—" [*static*] "—trust—" [*static*] "—promise that whatever you say—" [*static*] "—stop asking *because* I trust you so much, okay? Does that make sense? *Please* give me the gun and tell me why things are like this in this—"

4.

DWAYNE WOKE TO ringing ears, a water-stained ceiling above him, blankets pulled up to his chin. A door slammed. The air was laden with the unmistakable odor of spent gunpowder. Someone was gurgling, choking in pain. His eyes focused, seeing a yellow-eyed goat sitting ringed by a crowd of women offering up small children. Then he saw another young woman, as if in the foreground's foreground, reaching for him, terror filling her eyes.

She reached with one hand, the other clutching her throat, blood spurting between her fingers. Her mouth moved, producing no sound. Dark blood ran down her front, cascaded off her legs, and clung to the chrome spokes of her chair's wheels.

The room spun. He stumbled and crawled to her. She was already pale, eyes glassy, eyelids drooping. He felt the shocking warmth of her blood on his hands trying to help her keep pressure on her wound.

"Where's your phone?" he said. "We need help."

She drowsily shook her head, welling eyes closing and opening slowly. Weakly, she nodded to her coffee table.

A pile of burner phones lay there, six in all, next to a candle melted to a puddle. Three he recognized as the ones he'd taken from the Plexiglas box in 306. The screen of one other burner was alight, a call timer still going—twenty minutes five seconds, twenty minutes six seconds.

Wetly, she whispered, "How much did. You hear?"

"Everything."

She managed a smile, her teeth pink. "It worked."

He picked up the still-active burner and brought it to his ear, picturing himself standing in that room in the switchboard house, listening to himself listening to himself, waiting for the other to break the silence.

"Hello?" Dwayne said.

Dan Wells, with matching timidity: "Hello?" *Click.*

Chilled, Dwayne dialed 911. NO SERVICE. He walked the phone around the woman's living room. NO SERVICE. NO SERVICE.

"Don't bother. I've. Tried hundreds. Of times. Hundreds. Of phones."

He glanced about the room. Medical tools on trays, boxes of latex gloves, and through an open doorway was a dentist's chair, identical to the one from his dream.

He knelt next to her. "Tell me what to do."

She lifted a hand and touched his cheek, smearing it with warm blood. Listlessly, she pushed, turning his head away, toward the window. "Outside."

He remained helping her hold her throat. Again, she weakly pushed at him. "Hurry, *look* . . . "

He approached the window, using his sleeve to clear away the fog. Her corner apartment didn't look over the courtyard or the gray wastes, but the building's slow-drowned parking lot. A dozen cars, including the one he'd taken from the impound, their shapes all rounded under a foot of glistening white, uniform.

"Watch," she gurgled. "Watch . . . "

"What? What do you want me to see?"

A figure emerged, moving out toward the parked cars. They wore a flannel jacket, the hood of their sweatshirt up, breaths steaming over their shoulder. Though he couldn't see their face, their body language seemed familiar to him. The man started to reach for the door handle of Dwayne's car, but abruptly pulled away, as if becoming aware someone was watching him. Under a lamp post's flickering orange light, the man drew back his hood, and Dwayne looked into his own eyes.

The man wearing his face remained still, squinting past the falling snow, staring up at Dwayne unreadably. He tucked a hand into his jacket pocket, glanced around, and lifted an object wrapped in a shopping bag and secured with bands of duct tape, allowing Dwayne a peek of what he had with him and was perhaps intending to take somewhere. Letting the object drop back into the depths of his flannel jacket, Dan Wells gave Dwayne Spare a cold nod, got into the battered old Mercury, used the wipers to clear the windshield, and advanced from the parking space.

Numb, Dwayne watched the car move away until he could only see its taillights. When they turned onto Bergen Street, those too fell from view, leaving him only darkness and his reflection in the window staring back at him.

"It's always. You. And you. Always look. Up here. Now I. Know why. You're catching. Up to him."

Returning to her side, he knelt again in her blood. She tried to swallow, making hollow clicks from her open mouth. Her eyes would roll back each time she sleepily blinked and then lazily correct, looking at him, then the painting on her wall, then the door, as if taking in everything one last time, a final inventory of these things and the space that had held them and her, her life, her home, her prison. The blood was cooling and growing sticky between their palms. Her grip softened. He asked her gently, "How do I leave?"

"You'll. Never actually. Go anywhere."

"That wasn't me outside."

"Not yet," she said. "But at least. You'll be. Alive. I've seen what's. In the basement."

The dusty wheelchair he found, the night he set up the wiretap, a lifetime ago. Another basement appeared in his mind, a door he knew shouldn't be opened, a burning red light.

"What was that place, that tented house?"

She showed her pink teeth again. "Jack saw it. That way. Too. It was his. Idea to use. It, to get. To you. Only way. To go unheard. Here."

"Is Sam part of this?"

A string of red between her lips broke as she opened her mouth; the fear in her eyes deepened. "Don't trust. Him."

"What is he?"

"Nothing. Good."

"Tell me how I can get out of the building. I'll bring back help."

She sniffed an incredulous laugh. "Like you. Actually give. A fuck, pig."

"Connie, keep your eyes open. I swear, I'll send someone."

"We just didn't. Didn't want. To be confused. Alone anymore. I'm. Sorry, I. Hope you. Respond well to. Routine." She sniffed a laugh, coughed, spraying red. "It's not a. Perfect system. They leave. Things. By accident. Ignore them. They'll just. Make things. Harder."

He took her hand in both of his. "Does Metzger know how to leave?"

"Chase him and. You'll just. Sink faster. This place is a. Machine that eats. Life and. Time with. The only thing that. Come back. Out is. Product. So it can attract. More and bring more within. Itself, then. Make more. On and. On." Breaths shallowing, pallor white, she looked through him. "I just. I just want to go. Home, I. I miss. Miss them. I miss."

Slipping from her neck, her hand fell away, exposing the perfectly round bullet hole that only dribbled a thin red stream now. Pupils dilating, her absent gaze remained fixed on a framed photo across the room, a smiling couple with a beaming young woman standing between them, taller than both, wearing a mortarboard and a cadet-blue graduation gown.

Dwayne felt under her jaw, then closed her eyelids for her. He pulled the blanket from the couch, the one she'd covered him with, and draped it over her, familiar to him again this way, as she was in the switchboard house.

Her one hand dangled, limp and dripping. As if cut into her palm there with a keen blade steered by a sure hand was a spiral, worked in with the lines and creases already there, now highlighted by the blood that'd settled into its shape. The spiral met with itself in its center, hooked over and connected, complete.

Picking up each of the other burners, none had a charge. Dwayne tore apart the dead woman's apartment around her, looking for a charger or a phone card, anything that'd let him make contact with the outside world. Apologizing, he searched her pockets—she was still warm, as if only asleep—but only found a cigarette lighter and a hair pin. Looking through the peephole, the hallway was still and silent. Passing the dead woman again, something sharp nipped the ball of his bare heel. A brass jacket.

The boy has your gun.

5.

"PLEASE HOLD." A crash, then another. The door across from Connie cracked, buckled. She screamed and clawed at her wheelchair's brakes, but they wouldn't come undone. She couldn't move, couldn't escape. One of her burners on her coffee table rang, answered itself, and turned on speakerphone. "Please hold," Connie's voice said to Connie. The door fell in, the tower of gray flesh squelching over the broken pieces, absorbing them into itself. "Please hold." It spotted her, despite its lack of eyes, and started to approach, lumbering, scraps of gray flesh peeling off, swatting wetly to the floor. It reached a finger at her, pointing accusingly. Closer, it touched her throat, then pushed, piercing it, closing off her air, and she thrashed, gurgled, drowning in her own blood. "Please hold," she said to herself from her phone. "Please hold." A crash, then another. The door across from Connie cracked, buckled. She screamed and clawed at her wheelchair's brakes, but they wouldn't come undone. She couldn't move, couldn't escape. One of her burners on her coffee table rang, answered itself, and turned on speakerphone. "Please hold," Connie's voice said to Connie. The door fell in, the tower of gray flesh squelching over the broken pieces, absorbing them into itself. "Please hold." It spotted her, despite its lack of eyes, and started to approach, lumbering, scraps of gray flesh peeling off, swatting wetly to the floor. It reached a finger at her, pointing accusingly. Closer, it touched her throat, then pushed, piercing it, closing off her air, and she thrashed, gurgled, drowning in her own blood. "Please hold," she said to herself from her phone. "Please hold."

✦ ✦ ✦

When he turned on the light in her bathroom, he was shocked to see how much of her blood he was wearing. On his chin, a crimson comma from when she'd touched his cheek to turn his head, to go watch himself leave.

Pink water swirled the drain. Clearing the blood from his wrist, he found it still discolored, the skin tight around the bruises the building manager had given him. His fingertips were all blue and spotted black in places; some had no feeling to them anymore, the same as the toes of his one bare foot. How long had he been lying on that balcony before they found him? Any longer and he may not have woken up.

He showed his reflection the injection site on the back of his arm, the one from Sam. He pinched the mottled gray skin. It easily ripped. Underneath, slimy with yellow pus, the skin was an inflamed pink clustered with raised waxy speckles. He coughed at the smell of his own decay and noticed, in the mirror, blood on his bottom lip, bright red. Blood he'd coughed up. Pneumonia, at best.

He almost hadn't noticed the hash marks cut inconspicuously among the wallpaper's pattern of purple flowers in groups of five. She'd been counting the days for years.

He turned on the tap, filled a palm, but let it run through his fingers. While the water looked clean enough, he couldn't bring himself to trust it.

In her refrigerator, he found an unopened carton of orange juice. He turned it over in his hands, inspecting all its sides for punctures. Finding none, he drank deeply, feeling a charge of sugar shoot into his head. When was the last time he'd taken anything into his body that wasn't Metzger's poison? How long had he been here?

Pushing aside the plastic curtain that divided her living quarters from the makeshift operating room, Dwayne looked at the many tools lying half-submerged in pans of red water. He only found clamps and tweezers. Nothing with a blade. He tried a drawer, but it wouldn't come open, though he heard metal objects rattle within. He opened a closet, hoping to find some tool to pry open the drawer. He moved aside all of her black clothes and several pairs of leather boots, finding a toolbox buried in the back, *maintenance* stenciled on its lid, and from it he lifted out a pipe wrench. Before using it on the locked drawer, he paused, noticing on the wrench's handle more stenciled letters, mostly rubbed and chipped away. *D. Wells.*

They leave things.

Three knocks, the door to the hallway. Quietly, Dwayne moved out into the living room and listened to the young man whose voice he didn't recognize, calling out for Connie. The peephole was dark. Two shadows reaching in from under the door impatiently shifting their weight. "Is Sam in there with you? Connie?"

The doorknob rattled.

"Connie? Why is this locked?"

Dwayne looked over at the dead young woman sitting silent in her wheelchair, covered by a blanket. If her visitor has a key, they'll let themselves in. When they check the dead body, even if that isn't your name on the wrench, it'll work all the same.

Silence a moment, then the visitor knocked three more times before they gave up and moved off. Dwayne listened to them continue up the hall, counted to five, and as quietly as possible turned the deadbolt and peeked out. The corridor was veiled with a thin grayness, and he smelled smoke. Already several doors down, the young man—a mop of jetty hair, oversized T-shirt and jeans, thin—walked with an ungainly gait, perhaps stiff from the cold, carrying a machete in his left hand.

Kicking off his remaining shoe, Dwayne slipped from Connie's apartment and followed the young man. When he reached the hallway's corner and fell from sight, Dwayne rushed to make up the distance. Around the corner, the young man had stopped, and Dwayne nearly ran into his back. Against the wall leaned the machete—blade smeared black, edge chipped, well used.

Over his shoulder, Dwayne saw the blue light of the young man's phone as his oddly textured hands—peeling and sunburnt, liberally dusted with what may've been talc—dexterously composed a text: *Her door's locked. What did you do to her?*

They were standing in front of apartment 306, Dwayne noticed. Beyond the young man was the folding chair where, however long ago it had been, Leslie had stationed his paper person sentry. Now, it was empty.

The young man never got to send off his text. A hollow *crack* echoed down the hall. Phone clattering at his sneakered feet, the young man crumpled forward, the wrench buried in his head. The handle ripped from Dwayne's hands as the man hit the floor with a weightless rustle, like a bag of dead leaves. Around the wrench handle—*D. Wells*—jutting from his split skull, not a drop of blood ran. He had staples tangled in his hair. No, staples holding *on* his hair. Dwayne rolled the corpse over by the shoulder. It weighed next to nothing. Looking up at him with a ragged hole that accounted for the upper portion of its face, its only feature was a hooking frown in black paint. Inside, newspaper torn in neat strips, and the iron teeth of the wrench he'd driven through its reverse side.

It'd been moving. He'd seen it walking, on its own.

JACK was scrawled across the thing's shirt, crooked and childlike. IS

A PATHETIC COWARD seemed to have been added recently, still wet, the letters bleeding long black lines. Under both sleeves, red paint had been applied to the armpits of the shirt, two frowning faces.

Connie had said it'd been Jack's idea to use the switchboard house, to let Dwayne overhear. Was this Jack? Was he occupying this thing, a puppet made for a ghost?

Snatching the phone from the floor—and backing away from the motionless paper man, his skin bristling at the wrongness and impossibility of such a thing—Dwayne scrolled through the previous exchanges the paper man had had with Leslie. They were still searching for both himself and Sam, Leslie berating Jack for not being able to find the little boy even though, Leslie said, "You two are always giggling and carrying on together, you know where the little shit would hide." In the last text, Leslie was ordering Jack to check in at Connie's apartment again and force an answer out of her.

Dwayne dialed 911. He had to try. NO SIGNAL. He walked a few steps, tried 911 again, got the same result, then tried Sarah's number in Cleveland. NO SIGNAL.

Past the door to apartment 305, crying came again in the same hitching, full-bodied sobs, even though RIP in red spray paint remained, marking their home. Dwayne's mini-camera was gone, leaving only a bare spot in the paint where it'd been ripped down.

Feeling eyes on him, he turned. The peephole to apartment 306 was dark. Electric light at the base of the door glowed out, broken by two thin shadows. The keyhole to the deadbolt was facing outward again, as it had been when Dwayne had moved in. As if knowing they'd been detected, the peephole winked bright again, no longer obstructed, and the two thin shadows cleared themselves with a silent sidestep. Dwayne picked up Jack's machete, feeling the lingering warmth in its rubber handle from its previous owner.

306's bolt snapped, and the door creaked open. The door frame filled with gray and smoke soundlessly erupted into the hallway, engulfing Dwayne and the motionless paper man on the floor. The haze reduced everything around him to indistinct shapes. He entered 306, the smoke thickening, clawing at his throat and eyes. From the sliding glass door— standing wide, allowing the cold wind and the smoke to enter freely—a flickering orange glow penetrated the suffocating murk. He could see the windows of the apartments across the courtyard, their dark panes flickering and reflecting the drifting embers. He listened for whoever had opened the door for him, hearing only the roar of the smoke's source outside. Whatever was being burned, it seemed a great pile of it had been thrown on at once.

The hole in the ceiling was gone—like it had never needed patching at all, the nicotine stains uninterrupted. Under him, the discolored portion of the carpet, the eye Jack and Dwayne had made together with their stains, was gone as well.

He stepped out onto the balcony, heat lapping across his face, smoke burning his eyes. The courtyard's snow had melted into a perfect circle around the fire, furniture and apartment doors throwing a column of black smoke into the night sky, embers climbing in competition against the falling snow. There was no one attending the fire. When the heap settled, a burst of sparks gushed at him, and Dwayne stepped back into the apartment.

A single soft step on the carpet behind him. Dwayne spun, bringing up the machete. The blade bit into the forearm the man raised to shield his face—the only arm he had. He looked at Dwayne with black-paint pupils dotted into smeared-on whites. Sam had said he didn't like the gift Mister Leslie had given him because the face wasn't finished. It seemed it had been completed since.

The blaze outside lit up the newsprint that was giving his head its shape, a walking mass of words. From the ragged gash, hoarse and afraid, it said, "You're not burning me. I haven't said goodbye yet."

While the machete was still embedded, Dwayne's hold on it loosened. A living nightmare was standing before him and speaking to him with the voice of a dead man.

"He isn't mine," it said, "but I should still say goodbye, tell him everything's going to be okay. He should hear that from me."

"He killed Connie."

A sigh rattled from the smile-shape cut in its face.

"Ryan, who does he belong to?"

"I figured somebody overdosed and left him, somebody Gerry knew," the paper man said. "I didn't think I should ask. I just did what he said and looked after him. I tried my best." Adding, quieter, "I don't think I was supposed to be a father. Caught myself treating him like my dad did me. This fucking place."

Dwayne pulled the machete blade free from the paper man's arm.

Tilting its head, the puppet watched with painted-on eyes as a crack jagged down the length of its forearm, three of its fingers dropping off. Dust collected on the floor and was dashed away when the next frigid, smoky gale ripped through the apartment.

Somewhere across the building, a gunshot cracked.

"*Sam.*" Staggering and spidery, the paper man charged toward the door to the hallway, broke off its remaining arm while crashing against the jamb, and vanished armless into the dark and smoke, screaming his adopted son's name. He was gone before the echo of the gunfire had died.

Dwayne watched the fingers of the abandoned limb twitch once and curl, still, empty of its ghost, as past it a second paper man emerged, *Jack is a pathetic coward* written across its front. Moving as if every action was uncomfortable and unsure, the paper man—wrench in its right hand, fingers of its left blood-stained—carefully stepped over the forsaken limb in the doorway.

"Did you do that to Connie?" Jack's paper man said. It raised its hand, blood running down its arm and dribbling off its elbow. "Did you do that to her?"

"Sam did." Dwayne lowered the machete, its blade dusted with what Ryan had left behind. "He has my gun."

At that, the paper man lifted its chin, angling the hole in its face toward the ceiling, the portion directly above Dwayne. Dwayne had already noticed the hole in the ceiling was gone, so only watched Jack look for it. The doorway behind him was visible through the holes in his head, one of which Dwayne had given him while the larger replicated the hole he'd given himself, a reminder he'd have to wear.

"You're friends. You can talk to him."

"How many times do you think we've done this?" Jack's paper man said. "Exactly this, what we're doing right now?"

Choked by fear and smoke, Dwayne struggled to swallow, but had no answer. It felt like the first time, but he could no longer be certain about much of anything. He thought about small cuts in purple flower wallpaper, numbering in the hundreds, the thousands.

Another gunshot, somewhere deep inside the building. That, too, the paper man didn't seem to hear.

"It *feels* I'm trying to avoid making the same mistakes," it said. The wrench slipped from its hand, thumped to the floor. "Do you think we've ever tried this?"

The paper man tucked a hand into the neck of its shirt. Dwayne watched the bumps of its knuckles raise the red frown painted into its armpit as it felt around, pulling free a key pinched between paper thumb and forefinger. Dwayne accepted it into his palm, turned it toward the firelight. *603* had been crudely carved into the key's head, and the teeth were smooth from use.

The paper man aimed the hole in its face at the machete Dwayne was holding. "If you see Ryan, could you tell him I'm sorry? I'll try to say no next time." With jerking steps, the paper man lurched its way toward the open balcony door. It climbed over the railing and stood a moment, holding on with one brittle white hand. The firelight streamed through its head as it turned to look back at Dwayne. "Maybe third try's the charm."

The paper man dropped into the smoke and swirling embers and crashed upon the burning pile of furniture. The fire accepted his dry, hollow body, and he was gone in a near-instant. Embers spun into the sky, hung a moment, then turned dark, fire spent, and fell again.

6.

DWAYNE ENTERED THE stairwell, finding more of the lights were now out, a haze of smoke around those that still flickered. Navigating around mattresses, piles of clothing, and furniture clogging the stairwell, he stopped every few steps to listen. Nothing. He emerged on the sixth floor, finding every door on either side of the corridor standing open. Each unit had been cleared out, some even stripped of their carpet. More mattresses and end tables and dressers made easy passage impossible. He struggled over a bookcase and continued on, stepping in something slick hidden by the dark and warm under his bare foot. He leaned to move his shadow out of the way so he could see and found that among trash bags and soiled blankets and a broken lamp lay a large black dog on its side—fangs red, eyes open. Leaving only a husk, Keelut had been cut from throat to tail, no trace of the dog's innards, like something had escaped from inside it, shrugged it off, no longer seeing any need to wear the costume. Continuing, Dwayne's hand tightened around the machete, and he thought about another hallway, albeit one that'd been much more well-lit than this one, the air filled with an industrial cleaner smell and the endless beeping of machines instead of smoke and silence. His mother's room was the quietest, though by the look that was frozen upon her face, the silence had seemed incongruous. He hadn't been there to hold her hand, to tell her to look at only him, to ignore the thing that had come, as promised, to show her its true face on the day of her death.

He turned the corner and apartment 603 fell into sight, the only door he'd passed that was closed. He put his ear against it. Purring machines, and a crackle of someone crossing plastic drop cloth in languid strides, a wandering sleepwalker.

The key slid into its familiar keyhole and turned. Every table was overturned, machines puttering on the floor, gray puddles collecting in the hills and valleys of the drop cloth covering the floor amid shards of broken glass. A noxious vapor snatched the oxygen away when Dwayne tried to take a breath. Pulling his shirt up over his nose and mouth, he entered, his unprotected eyes stinging. He'd heard someone walking around just on the other side of the door, but there was no one inside apartment 603. The bedroom contained empty cots arranged in a circle around a shoebox heaped with burner phones and dead candles. The kitchen, barren of appliances, appeared to be used as another storage area—plastic containers packed with baggies of white powder, each as thick as a thumb, ready for dissemination. Since his last visit the windows had been covered on the inside with white paint. He opened the last door, the second bedroom, and the air was hot and smelled like burning dust and plastic on the verge of melting.

Threatening to crush the folding tables they were heaped upon were several computer towers humming together, chittering as they struggled to process the things they'd been ordered to contemplate. Dwayne could relate. Among the piled dead electronics was Dwayne's laptop—it looked like someone had craned its screen back too far and snapped the hinge. A mass of wires fed into a clear bin heaped with burner phones, with all of them connected to one of the towers, the lines sloppily spliced with electrical tape. On the first monitor, sound waves were being copied from a source, a burner presumably, and then run through a colorful three-dimensional graph. Though he couldn't recall a single time he'd ever used the phrase, it came into Dwayne's head as soon as he looked at the *audio spectrograms* being rendered. On the next monitor, past the cataract of some severe burn-in, one after another, portions of the spectrograms were being automatically highlighted, zoomed in on, and a prompt would appear, PRINT?, that answered itself nearly as quickly as it appeared. Teetering on the edge of the crowded table, a dot-matrix printer crunchily shoved out another image it'd screeched into form on a piece of paper. The page was spat out, adding itself to the growing mass on the floor. Each bore a black-and-white image; some depicted one constellation or another, one appeared to be an unlabeled flow chart, and another was a grainy picture of a flower with five petals, which Dwayne recognized from his research as belladonna. One was filled with series of numbers and letters. A picture of a quaint home on a quiet street. A child's drawing of a butterfly. A recipe for making your own papier-mâché at home using everyday household products. Most of the printouts seemed to have been rejected, crushed into knots and cast aside to clutter the floor, while others—evidently interpreted as holding some sacred meaning—had been tacked or taped to the walls in clean columns, most scribbled over with frantic, illegible notes and ravings, things underlined or crossed out so aggressively the page had ripped. Above the columns of nonsense, smeared onto the wall with a finger in what appeared to be grease: I WILL UNDO THIS.

Leaving the suffocating heat of the room and the open tap of madness it also housed, Dwayne saw that in the corner of what was intended to be the living room the receiver to Metzger's landline phone lay off its cradle. Pouring from the porous plastic at one end, tiny holes in concentric circles, faraway screaming—Dwayne could hear them without the receiver anywhere near his ear, an old woman pleading for someone to stay away, to stay away, to stay away.

The screaming seemed to grow louder as his reaching hand approached, overloading the speaker. Shaking, he brought it to his ear and forced himself to listen to her. The few nights he'd stayed with her toward the end, she'd wake him sometimes, but never with sounds of such horror. He pulled the shirt down from over his mouth so she'd hear him clearer when he told his mother he was sorry. But before he could, the screaming shut away. A hard click and rhythmic clanging filtered in, thunderous and echoing, like a dryer with an unbalanced load.

Metzger said, "Doesn't feel good finding out someone's been recording your private conversations, does it?" *Click.*

Shoving his way through the stairwell door, Dwayne began his descent, maneuvering around the discarded furniture and the small mountains of bulging trash bags. He reached the fifth-floor landing, turned, rushed down the next set of stairs, turned at the fourth-floor landing, and rushed down to the next. His various puncture wounds—from needles, a rusty nail— no longer hurt. He detangled himself from the sling he'd made of his gun harness and flung it aside, his wrist misshapen and black. He turned the corner and stopped. Below, the second-floor landing was covered in blood. The former author, body still, lay with their throat cut so deeply Dwayne could see the yellow of their exposed vertebrae. Standing over them, thin arms slickened red to the elbows, was Gerald Metzger.

Rings chased each other across the standing blood as he turned on his bare heel, knife in his hand. Dotted with red across his chest and face, he looked up at Dwayne standing on the stairs above and the two regarded one another a moment under the stuttering fluorescent light. His face didn't change. There was nothing in Metzger's eyes. No connection there to be made. Gray and abandoned.

The knife—five-inch blade, pearl handle, nickel accents—clattered brightly to the floor. Metzger curled the long fingers of his now-empty hand toward himself. Come closer.

Anger falling away, something else dulled Dwayne's pain now—like the comfort and clarity that comes when a dreamer senses a nightmare, all its tools reddened, would soon be drawing to a close. The buzz of the stairwell lights faded and everything else seemed to dim and mute, leaving only him and Metzger upon the stair. He descended the last few steps, the smoke, the smell of the former author's blood, and the stink of poison that radiated from the chemist mixed to a single horrible, if not suitably complementary, odor.

Another gunshot rang out, closer than the others Dwayne had heard, but neither he nor Metzger paid it any mind. Once joining him to stand in the blood together, Metzger ran his small, busy eyes over the collapsing veins on Dwayne's neck behind his ear, then leaned slightly past him to study the spreading decay on the back of his arm.

"Do you know how many have come after me, either you, yourself, or people like you, or how many times I've chased you around and around?" Metzger said as he scrutinized. "The same amount, for both of us, that failed *without* fail." He met Dwayne's eyes. "I wanted to be a highly productive disciple of Lazarus and have everyone around me, everyone I knew, be able to work as much as they wanted without worry. I was over-eager, over-excited, and maybe that caused me to be a little hyperbolic in my wording when I asked for what I asked." His smile didn't reach his eyes, didn't warm them. "Careful what you wish for. It just might come true."

Dwayne said nothing.

"Leslie doesn't think it's Sam's time. But I'm tired. And so are you, by the look of things. This one may've run its course." As if satisfied with this ruin he'd created, project complete, Metzger issued a small nod, as if giving permission. "Whatever comes next," he said, placid, "I hope the boy gets further than I did."

Dwayne raised the blade.

Metzger closed his eyes.

7.

He EMERGED FROM the stairwell on the ground floor, laboring for breath. In the light of the fire raging out in the courtyard, he looked at the blood on the machete in his shaking hand, the clinging pink scraps, the pieces of hair, and the chips in the blade that weren't there before, from when he'd hit bone. He'd entered the stairwell one man on the sixth floor, left wearing a stranger on the first. Lever irreversibly turned, he could feel things rearranging around him, inside him. Lights going out, new tracks crashing as others fell away—one of which he'd forced, routing Metzger, one swing at a time, into nothingness. He considered what might have come if Metzger had been given the chance to reform, time to grow back things he'd lost or had stolen, to turn his own levers back to their original positions, original arrangements. He'd been somebody's son. Someone must've loved him, hoped he'd have a good life with little pain, little confusion. It was a waste of time to think about these things; the man was dead—Dwayne had checked for a pulse several times at several places, unable to discern what was still connected to what. Maybe this was the desperate bargaining of a conscience on its deathbed. Never again would a little voice suggest he seek temperance of clearer, cleaner paths. I am a murderer, alone in my act and now alone within myself.

The door to the courtyard stood ahead, the light of the pyre beaming through its glass pane onto Dwayne. Eyes adjusting as he stepped outside, bombarded by heat and smoke, he saw a line of paper people walking single file from the door opposite, taking turns marching into the flames. One would barely have gone ablaze before the next stepped onto its hollow back, climbing a little farther up before likewise being overtaken by the fire, and the next stepping through their cinders in turn. His neighbors no longer ranted and raved; they gave themselves to the fire mute of remark or protest.

Across the flames, like a ventriloquist had botched his wish upon a star, a flesh-and-blood boy sat on the lap of his armless paper father, dusted with ash and seated on a dresser hollow of its drawers. The paper man had a new, smoking hole on his forehead. The boy's eyes flashed each time another paper man fed the fire momentarily brighter, his expression flat as if miles away inside.

Without hands, the paper man used its chin to stroke the top of the boy's head.

"It's okay, Dad," the boy murmured emptily. "They'll move in again, like they were. You too. They'll all come back when they know it's time to leave Evergreen."

As Dwayne came around the side of the bonfire, the paper man's head swiveled sharply, the melting paint of its eyes snapping onto him. Ash fell from Sam's hair as he sat up in his father's lap. Lifting the stolen pistol in two hands, his small thumb struggled to draw back the hammer.

"She made me do it." The boy hopped down from the paper man's lap. Approaching Dwayne, his oversized jacket dragged behind him as he treaded the ankle-deep snow. "Connie and Jack were planning things behind my back, behind Mister Metzger's back, and *you* were helping, weren't you?"

"Sam, give me the gun."

The boy aimed up at Dwayne's head. "You're supposed to turn into my friend Mister Wells. I'm supposed to trust you, send you on missions for me. You're supposed to bring Jack here. I won't ever see him again if you don't."

Dwayne tossed the machete aside—it vanished into the snow. "That isn't yours, Sam," he said, his tone calm. "That belongs to me."

"And *you* belong to *me*," Sam said. Half of his face in shadow, the other given a volcanic cast by the fire, Sam smiled behind the gun. "You left Evergreen. In my kingdom, cheaters and backstabbers aren't allowed to stay."

Over the boy's shoulder, Leslie shoved his way through the line of paper people. Spotting Dwayne and Sam across the courtyard, he stopped, his face twisting. The boy hadn't heard him, too preoccupied with pushing the gun barrel to Dwayne's cheek, against his pressed-together lips, murmuring, "Here comes the airplane." Ryan's paper man screamed as Leslie grabbed it by the fragile throat he himself had given shape.

The gun barrel slid away from Dwayne's face as the boy spun away. "Dad."

Kicking the only limbs it had left, the flailing paper man could do little as Leslie turned and flung him onto the fire. The boy's screams bounced around the courtyard as he ran to the edge of the fire, but his father was already consumed.

"Why did you *do* that? I *told* him he could go last. We didn't say goodbye yet." The boy wiped his tears on his sleeve, and as if he'd forgotten he had it, scrambled to point the gun up at Leslie.

Snatching it away from him, Leslie scowled at it and tucked the gun into his tool belt. Shaking his head at Sam, he removed the same hammer he'd bludgeoned Dwayne with and weighed it in his hand.

"I'm sorry, Mister Leslie. Please don't be mad at me, I—"

Baring teeth, Leslie brought up the hammer. The boy screeched and turned his head away. Leslie swung. A resonant *crack*. The boy slipped trying to crawl backwards, blood pouring from his shattered mouth. Leslie stepped to stand over him and swung again. Dwayne yelled for him to stop, but the building manager, with a continuous motion of the hammer, drove the boy's head deeper into the blood-stained snow, deeper.

Dwayne reached them too late. The carnage was brief, exact. Steam lifted in pale strings from the unrecognizable mess lying cradled in a deep, red-stained hollow in the snow. Dwayne managed to get a half-step toward Leslie, hands ready to strangle him, but stopped, feeling cold metal grind against his ribs.

"He was a child."

That fleeting look of regret resurfaced on Leslie's lined face. "I didn't want to do that. I didn't enjoy doing that. But he was running fast, too ahead of schedule. Would've caused an unmanageable overlap." Behind him, the fire flared one final time as the last paper man climbed on. "A lot of work down the drain, right there." Leslie lowered the gun and looked at Dwayne. "Got anywhere to be right this minute? I could use a second set of hands with something."

* * *

With the building manager close behind him, Dwayne pushed open the stairwell door. Blood from the second-floor landing ran down the steps. The former author and Metzger lay together at the top, both gray, lifeless faces staring down at them. Dwayne couldn't stomach looking at what he'd done. Leslie nodded sidelong at the mess above. "You do that?"

"Only Metzger. The other one was already . . . like that."

"And you didn't think that was worth mentioning?"

Dwayne looked at him. He felt dead. He couldn't be sure he wasn't.

"I didn't have to kill Sam," Leslie said.

"I know. He didn't deserve that."

"He didn't. You're right. But, twenty-twenty hindsight," Leslie said, and groaned. It echoed up the stairwell and returned to them. "Always hated it when some asshole would say that to me. 'Twenty-twenty hindsight.' Good one, prick. Unless I'm not catching its meaning right, I hear that and it makes me think that no matter what anybody does, you're going to leave a trail of fuck-ups. Same as that one about if you want to make God laugh, make plans. Fuck that." He tucked the handgun into the holster for his power drill and removed the bloody hammer, taking his time wiping its steel head with a rag. "Things can be planned and those plans *can* work—if they're fucking followed. That's the hard part. Any machine with more than, say, two moving parts to it is a headache waiting to happen. Things wear down, things break, things that're fresh out of the box will just come apart because they apparently *feel* like it." He held the hammer in Dwayne's face—though clean, the coppery smell of a child's blood still radiated from it. "Case in point."

Feeding the hammer's wooden handle through the loop in his belt, Leslie's powerful sigh smoked, blueness obscuring his face. "This one ran longer than I thought it would," he said. "Feels like we almost had it this time, doesn't it?"

Dwayne had no answer.

"Still, if you'd spoken up about Gerry, we maybe could've beaten some sense into Sam and let things run, keep an eye on it, see how they might shake out. Still, no use bitching about it now. What's done is done is done." The building manager looked Dwayne over, bloody and trembling before him. "Either you were running ahead or behind a little. Can't say, but I'm fairly certain it was you, the problem for this particular go. But maybe not. The possum got impatient sooner than I would've thought. And the surgeon didn't sit there half the night trying to get the elevator to come down. She decided to go around to the other one almost immediately. Take matters into her own hands. Note to self—are you listening to me?—she won't let shit stand in her way every time. You can fill a hallway full of junk, she won't always care. Sometimes, she'll go barreling through it like that wheelchair of hers has four-wheel drive. Remember that."

"She's dead." Like everyone else in the building. Except us.

"How'd it feel?"

"I didn't kill her."

"Not the surgeon," Leslie said, stabbing a thumb over his shoulder, toward the stairs leading up to the second-floor landing. "Him. The chemist."

Dwayne couldn't look at the corpses of the chemist and the former author. The smell of blood was overwhelming. His disgust and shame crushed out all other thoughts to only a roaring, lonely silence.

"Inevitable? That how you might describe it, maybe?"

Lowering his eyes, unwilling to look at Leslie as he suggested these things, Dwayne saw he still had so much blood on him—from Connie, from Metzger.

"Seen my dog around?"

"I think Metzger killed it," Dwayne mumbled.

The building manager looked up into the chemist's stilled, bloody face lying with his left cheek pressing against the floor and sighed himself another mask of blue steam. "Housebreaking is always the hardest part. Tests the most patient heart when something you want to love goes and does exactly what you told them not to. Truth is, dogs aren't built to love. They'll respect you, sure, because you're giving them a home, feeding them. Really, they're parasites we invite in. But, same time, any ecology needs its small forms of life. Each got their own purpose. Do the work to keep everything above them running right. Provide. Shit is, whole time, they think *they're* the ones in charge." He faced Dwayne. "Own a watch?"

Askance, he held the building manager's stare.

Leslie tugged up a plaster-dusted sleeve and briefly eyed his timepiece, a wristwatch with a cracked crystal. Its three delicate golden hands were holding on twelve, the first notch past the one, and three—the second, minute, and hour were fixed, according to the watch. He nodded past Dwayne, to the stairs leading down. "Let's keep moving."

They passed the laundry room, a single machine canting forward and back. They passed the open metal box with the wiretap hanging out of it, suspended by its wires. They passed two parallel lines in the dust forming an equal symbol, the place where a wheelchair had once stood. Leslie drew out his heavy ring of keys to unlock a door marked MAINTENANCE and waved Dwayne in. A room barren, save for a rusty shovel leaning against the cinderblock wall. A bulb flickered to life above a hole cut into the cement floor no wider than Dwayne's shoulders, yawning with darkness within. An earthy smell hit him, making him yearn all the more for escape from this place, where something might grow if planted, not wither and gradually corrupt.

"Go ahead," the building manager said, handing him a flashlight. "Watch your head."

Dwayne looked down into the hole. He could see a dirt floor only a few feet down. He faced the building manager standing behind him, holding a shovel in one hand and Dwayne's gun in the other.

The floor to the basement of the basement was packed dirt with a clearance of less than four feet. It was colder than it'd been outside, the air stale. Crouched, Dwayne turned in place, unable to see any walls, only a plunging darkness that seemed to carry a cloying quality, always snapping in close after he'd train the flashlight elsewhere, and a silence more complete than any he'd felt himself mired within. He could hear the wet click of his own blinks, the blood surging in his temples.

Leslie dropped down, the thuds of his work boots echoing on and on. Stooped, the building manager motioned past him. "Over there, ten yards or so."

Dwayne looked at the shovel Leslie had brought down here with them. "I won't make it easier for you. I'm not digging my own grave."

Bent as he was, the veins stood out on the building manager's forehead. "That's not why we're down here. We're not burying something, we're digging something up. Take a look around, commit this to memory." He paused. "You don't remember me saying this to you, showing you what's down here?"

Dwayne only looked at Leslie. Nothing moved within his head; there were no attempts to dredge up any memories, no thoughts at all, just a cold resignation, things shutting down, lights dimming, a building silence save for acceptance whistling as it swept the floors.

"Before you decide to try anything," Leslie said, "I feel I should ask you something. If you were able to leave—which you aren't—what would be waiting for you out there?"

Dwayne didn't answer.

"Your wife's been out of your house for two years. At no point since then has she entertained the idea of coming back. I know you took a lack of divorce papers showing up in the mail as a good sign, but that's only because it was a financial thing with her—she's working that into the budget. Take it from me, divorces are expensive. And Jamie, sweet as she is, is going to be fine. Her mom's already met somebody. He'll be *good* to Sarah, and Jamie too. That kid of yours will grow up to do amazing things. You loaded her down with some baggage, sure, and she'll wonder once in a while what happened to you and why nobody ever found you, but trust me, you don't need to worry about her. It might be hard to accept, but she's better off without you in her life. Besides, you never really wanted a kid anyway."

"I love her."

"I know. I know you do, Dwayne. We all do. We've all been there, gone through it at least once, walked with those bones of yours, looked out from behind those baby blues."

"I'm me. Only I'm me."

"That's true. Right now that's the case, absolutely," Leslie said, with quiet condescension. "And there's no rule that says you can't hold on to that, how much you love your kid or anything else. If you get a flash later on, savor it. Even if you can only remember the *feeling*, that might help you get through the day, make it easier getting out of bed. Because trust me, at times it can get pretty goddamn monotonous around here. Listen, I can appreciate you're probably not real big on the idea of trusting anybody right at this moment, but I'm serious about this. Jamie is going to do great.

"And as far as whatever made you come running in here, obligation to your city or whatever you told yourself," Leslie said, "you got your man. You won, Dan. You came in after him, you caught up to him, and you got his ass—and how. Maybe he didn't spend the rest of his life behind bars, no. You didn't get to stand up in court and give your big, brave story about how you did it, no, but you got him. And how things are looking with solving this thing, not to be a downer, you'll probably get a few opportunities to get him again. Maybe do some things differently next time, see how they shake out. Where else can a person ever get a chance like that? Nothing's one-and-done here. Nothing." Leslie took a deep breath, checked his watch. "So, now that I've said all that again, are you going to give me a hard time or pull any shit if I happen to look the other way?"

"How did things end up like this?" Dwayne's question resonated and bounced around them, hitting his left ear, right ear, left ear, *like this, like this?*

"I'd suggest you ask the chemist next time you see him, but he'll likely tell you some rambling horseshit about unorthodox answers to unorthodox requests. He mentioned something to me once about how he damn near ODed and had a dream. Or it came to him after he crashed his bike as a kid and went ass over teakettle, or when he was in the hospital after jumping out the window at his parents' place. Once, he told me it was actually a friend of his, who, after someone stuck him—the friend—with a dirty needle at the laundromat, had a dream that told him exactly what he'd need to pass on to Gerry so he could make contact, make his wish. It changes." Leslie gestured at all that stood around them. "But the outcome's always the same. All roads, no matter how circuitous, eventually come together.

"I can appreciate that thinking of it in such terms might be, to you, same as throwing the baby out with the bathwater, but every mistake you ever made, it all goes out. That may not sound all that inviting, but for many of us who wind up here, it's a relief in disguise. Sure, you'll swing back around and get saddled with all that *you* again, but it's still nice having the occasional chance to step away. Gives perspective." Leslie checked his watch. "But unless we both want to end up on hold, we should get to it. You're not going to pull anything, are you?"

In Dwayne's silence and stillness, Leslie casually lifted the gun and thumbed back the hammer. There was nowhere to run down here. "I'll need an answer on that, Dan."

"I won't try anything."

"Glad to hear it." Leslie kept the gun on him, motioned with it. "Keep moving."

Shuffling ahead of the building manager, an irregularity in the floor's earthen smoothness came into sight ahead of the flashlight's stuttering beam. A slight mound, six feet in length, perhaps three wide. Spotting it, Dwayne stopped. "Who is that?"

Tossing the shovel out ahead of them, Leslie prodded the gun against Dwayne's bent back. "Pick it up. Dig."

The clang of the shovel hitting the packed earth continued to echo while he scraped away the clots of dark packed earth. Bringing the tool was almost unnecessary. The clumps came away easily in heavily damp portions that held the shape they'd been packed into, seemingly by hand. With the next portion Dwayne pulled away in his frostbitten fingers, a swatch of pale flesh appeared in the flashlight's sickly yellow glow. Even the slightest pause provoked the building manager to jam the gun barrel against Dwayne's spine. Continuing reluctantly, Dwayne pulled away another clump, revealing more of the body that lay beneath the pungent soil, revealing a portion of a perfectly-preserved face.

"Who is she?"

Leslie walked on his knees to the other side of the mound. He kept the flashlight trained on the partially-cleared face as he delicately swept the palm of his other hand across it, brow to chin. Moving away some more of the dirt, Dwayne saw Connie. Leslie swept away more, and Dwayne saw his ex-wife. A trick of the shadows, or the face really was changing. Another pass, his mother. It could be no one else. Another, a woman he didn't recognize, but one that gave Leslie fleeting pause. The building manager cleared his throat and hurried to brush his hand across this face. Now fully cleared, the wattle crinkled under the building manager's chin as he nodded, apparently satisfied by this final face. Eyes closed, expression serene, she looked more asleep than dead. Leslie turned on his knees and started pulling the dirt from over the buried woman's abdomen.

A round belly emerged. Under the top layer of her creamy skin, fractals reached and branched like purple lightning. A shape pushed out, weakly reaching for those that had found it. Life burned impossibly within the mother. The roaring silence in Dwayne's mind deepened as he stared at what the building now had to show him, buried at its lowest point and buried within its mother, ready to start its climb again.

From his tool belt, Leslie pulled his utility knife with its bright yellow handle. He turned it and reached across the rounded belly between them, offering it to Dwayne. He had no intention of cutting into the buried woman, but he accepted the knife, unable to look at or think about anything else—it felt inevitable, him accepting the knife. He held it, suddenly no longer feeling so alone. He felt himself here, many times before. Perhaps if he listened, he'd hear himself all those times before, saying the same things, doing the same things.

There was comfort available; he only needed to let it wrap around him, to stop fighting it. He'd gotten his man. He'd done his job. It didn't come about in any way resembling how he'd expected, but he'd done what he came here to do. Quiet initially, the promise of getting to do it again, to meet his purpose, filled him with a brightness—something he hadn't felt visit him in a very long time. To see out time that may've been stolen to its end, to witness a purpose being met, fulfilled, and to have a chance to relive that again and again, held an appeal. Preferring things ordered, structured, he could have that here. Though horrible at times and shocking at others, the world he'd left was no different. It had made sure he understood that. But here, at the very least, the bad times, when they came, might not hold such a surprise to him. He could grow to know this building and, in time, call it home.

The decision he'd made must have read in his face. Grinning briefly, knowingly, like a friend might over a shared inside joke repeated for the thousandth time, Leslie took off his wristwatch, set it in the dirt near Dwayne, and tucked the barrel of the gun under his chin, the metal making a sandy sound against his five o'clock shadow. Head back, he dragged in a breath, then looked across at Dwayne and smiled at him once more, again as one would at a friend. "See you around."

Dwayne didn't blink at the blinding flash that, too, felt inevitable. *See you around.* The gunshot rang—and rang, and rang—the echo never fading but, in its retained volume, serving as a driving beat as the things he needed to do next came automatically, hands on autopilot after years of muscle memory had been fixed into them, repeated task after repeated task. *See you around.* Pushing forward an inch of razor blade, it made a ratcheting sound, and he did as the echoes had suggested they, too, had done. *See you around.* As another innocent was pulled from non-existence, slippery and screaming in his arms, the second hand of the gifted wristwatch lying in the dirt twitched once, twice, and resumed its inviolable ticking. *See you around.*

8.

LIKE ANY OTHER THURSDAY, Dan got up, made coffee, got Keelut out of his kennel and walked the bouncy little puppy around the courtyard to yellow some snow. Keelut scratched at the ice encasing the flagstones, having sniffed out something underneath. With a screwdriver in lieu of an ice pick, Dan chipped out a torn strip of newspaper burned at its edges. A fragment of a headline, something about corruption within the state police, cops going missing. He balled it up in his gloved fist, not eager to study it anymore because he didn't want sad news to spoil his morning. Walking his dog back inside, he considered how he might need to make another sign to remind the tenants to put their trash where it belonged.

At nine, he went up to 418 and repaired a leaky bathroom sink for poor old Mister Pohl. And what a rough year it'd been for him. First his wife, Missus Pohl, suddenly moves out, then his oldest suffers some kind of break. Lately, the young woman just stands on the stairwell's third-floor landing morning to night, going like "he said then she said they said," on and on, the poor thing.

Dan went down to three and shampooed 308's carpets and collected the trash the previous tenant failed to take with them—among which was a rolled-up print of a creepy painting, a goat that looked like it was petting some dead kids and weird-looking women. Into the trash it went, done and done. As he steered the carpet shampooer into the next room, he heard rubber pop a second before a sharp pain assaulted the heel of his left foot.

Without anywhere to sit, he dropped to the wet carpet and tore off his work boot—and in the process, with it still stuck in the boot's tread, removed the hypodermic needle he'd just stepped on. He looked at it, speared through his boot. He could see it inside, the metal spike topped with a quivering bead of his blood. He peeled his sock off inside-out. Even though its invasion inside his skin had been less than a second, the site around the unwanted injection was already red and irritated. His head filled with questions that, without a trip to the doctor, could never be answered. He questioned every choice he'd made that had led him to this point, to working here, to managing this building, every moment stacking behind him and shoving him to right now, the day he stepped on a dirty needle. And he saw faces of two women, one young and the other early in her middle years. They were partly see-through, but seemed unbothered by this. They smiled at him. He felt he should know their names, but he couldn't recall them. They were nobody he knew, he was sure of that. He was good with faces.

And it was in this lack of knowing these two women he momentarily daydreamed deeper, remembering he had no one in his life. Only this job, managing this building, however long it'd been since he started working here. He didn't want to go to a doctor; he had too much to do, too many things needed his attention. He pricked his finger trying to pull the needle out of his boot's sole. Well, he grimly considered, if the needle was dirty it really didn't matter how many times he jabbed himself with it after the first time. Tossing the needle into his wheel-around trash bin, he tried putting his full weight on his injured foot, and was at least comforted that if he *was* sick, nothing hurt right now, and he could at least finish his day's work. He pulled his sock back on, then his work boot, and stood. If he was now at the genesis point of becoming sick, he'd rather go out while working instead of in a hospital bed jammed full of tubes, begging Death to change his mind.

He wasn't sure if it was his fear of falling ill worming into his imagination, but he began to feel a little strange. Something began to accumulate just off stage in his mind, inches from the spotlight of mundanely streaming thought, impossible to fully glimpse and grasp as known. The mental picture pulled more detail into itself, making him feel like he'd left the apartment altogether and was transported to a theater shrouded in darkness, with large windows that were oddly curtained outside, dark blue. And on the stage, in the shadow just left of the unoccupied spotlight, a mere suggestion of a person standing there, looking out at him. Their hand reached forward, into the burning beam, and curled long gray fingers toward the rest of its hidden self, beckoning invitingly—and yes, he did want to see what they had to offer him.

Returning with a whoosh of unreal wind, he found himself in mid-step, pushing the roll-around trash can out through the door to 308. He nearly collided with the knees of Leslie Rider in the hallway.

The young man was wearing this strange shirt with what looked like a nautilus shell covered in goop. The shirt had been washed so many times, it was like Swiss cheese. Despite the bright-eyed young man's choice of wardrobe, Dan asked if he'd made up his mind about school. Leslie told him he'd finally made his decision, that veterinarian school was to be his path. Though it felt a little awkward, and he didn't know why he did it really, Dan put up a hand for the young man to give him a high five. Young people still do that, don't they? Leslie tried to hide the fact he was laughing at Dan, which Dan appreciated. As he continued down the hall, with that natural effervescent skip to his stride that only people under thirty have, Leslie said, "Never change, Mister Wells. See you around."

After pouring some hydrogen peroxide on his punctured heel—which, somewhat concerningly, didn't burn—Dan spent some time cutting replacement keys for himself. He always enjoyed the musical sound it made when he threw the old worn-out ones in his key bucket. For lunch Dan had a handful of cashews and a reheated cup of coffee, then went out to salt the building's front walk. The car was still there; no one from the impound—even though he'd called them three times already—had come to pick it up. It hadn't moved in . . . well, he couldn't say exactly, but long enough it didn't need to be here anymore, taking up space.

Eyes drawn skyward by their calls, he paused to watch a group of seagulls glide over the parking lot, making him go lost in thought for a moment, but he couldn't pinpoint the thought. Maybe he just liked watching birds fly, drifting off toward the lake in the early afternoon fog until they became simple M-shaped silhouettes. For whatever reason, it made him think of the box of crayons sitting in lost and found that had never been claimed. He decided he'd give them to the little girl, Connie, who lived with her young father, Jack, if Dan remembered right, up in 406. The girl was a little strange. More than once Dan had caught her down in the basement, spearing dead mice with crochet needles and arranging her stuffed animals around them like *they'd* been the ones responsible. Maybe the crayons would be just the ticket, something to point that idle energy toward.

Behind the building, Dan found a big stack of old newspapers someone had thrown out. Though waterlogged and weighing a ton, he took them back to his own apartment.

After feeding Keelut, he turned on the episode of *The Price is Right* he'd programmed his VCR to record and sat in his recliner tearing the newspaper into strips. Next, he dunked the slips in plaster and applied them, with care, to the form he'd started last week. He paused, watching a young lady named Jolene jump for joy, having won a trip to Hawaii. Good for her, Dan thought. Returning to his work, he could already see his project complete in his mind. He wasn't sure why he'd taken up papier-mâché, or why he'd decided to start with something as complicated as the human form, but it was a relaxing hobby even if he didn't know what he was doing exactly or what he planned on doing with the art project when it was complete; but the doing of a thing, to him, didn't necessarily require a reason. It just felt right. And as far as the hand looking kind of malformed, who knows, this might just be the first of many he'd make and, like they say, practice makes perfect.

That night he got in bed with Keelut lying down by his feet and dreamed about finding himself in a house with beautiful parquet flooring in its entryway. There was a young man there who only had one arm but still smiled a lot, despite that. He told Dan to answer the phone he was standing next to. Seeing no reason to refuse, Dan answered it, and was asked by someone else to come downstairs. There were two lights by the basement door: one was green and the other one was red. The green one lit up, and he heard the door unlock. Dan obliged to descend, knowing nothing in the dream could actually hurt him in real life.

The floor was covered in long swaths of wires all neatly laid together and going the same way, almost looking the way muscle fibers did. They created a pattern, all joining together under a table in the center where a man with no bottom jaw, dressed in a cloak of some brittle, brown material, sat carefully steering a piece of carved wood around a board, connecting a nail sticking out of the planchette—was that the word?—to other nails that'd been hammered around the edge of the table. He recognized their hands. The person in his daydream of the theater, the figure that had been standing just outside the spotlight. Dan decided it might be best not to interrupt to bring this up to the jawless man. He wanted to see what might be shown to him.

In the table's center, in gorgeously detailed woodcut, was a five-pointed purple flower Dan didn't know the name of. Maybe it only existed in dreams, he considered. Each time the jawless man touched the planchette's nail to one of the other nails, a tiny spark would pop and machinery would grind in the walls around them and Dan would taste ozone in the air, like a lot of electricity was suddenly flowing. He was a little afraid of the man without a bottom jaw but, again, he knew it was just a dream. Plus, the jawless man didn't seem to have any ill intent to him anyway; he just seemed to want Dan to see this strange room. A place, Dan sensed, the jawless man kept very secret. So he watched the jawless man turn his ear to listen, like someone was whispering that only he could hear. Then he'd study each nail ringing the table's edge again, as if looking for just the right one, and guide the planchette to touch that nail, triggering more machinery sounds in the walls—like outside the house, enormous gears had been set to turning, the whole entire world shifting and reordering. Then, even though he didn't have any obvious means to speak, the jawless man still told Dan, "The new arrangement is set, the plenum recalibrated, and the synchronization retuned. Tell him to listen for me, to listen for Mtahsab Belsharh."

He woke up early the next morning a little confused. Tell who to listen? Maybe Dan needed to lay off the spicy food right before bed, he thought. He had to look up the word *plenum* in the dictionary, just to make sure it wasn't a word his dream had made up. It was in there. Turns out a plenum, depending on context, can be a gathering of all parties comprising a group or a committee, and it can also mean a space that's designed to be filled with matter. Like an HVAC or plumbing system, he thought, supplying scenarios relative to his occupation to bolt some grab-bars onto the idea, make it easier for him to pull in close as absorbed, understood. Still, Dan thought it was strange that while *plenum* was a word he was confident he'd never used or known before just this moment, his dream—ostensibly a story he was telling himself, as he thought of them—had chosen to employ it. Which meant he must've picked it up somewhere at some point, having a better vocabulary than even he was aware of. Well, better than learning you're dumber than you thought. Not a bad way to start the day.

After returning the dictionary back onto the shelf in its place between his copy of the good book and his copy of electrical system repair guide, seventh edition—in Dan's view, the only three books a man truly needs that cover all of life's bases—he started getting the coffee ready and pulling on his work boots. He stopped when he noticed something stuck to the tread of his left boot, something he must've tracked home from the day before. He peeled it off and saw it was a playing card, but not for any game he knew. A spangling cosmos on the reverse side, and its front showed a stone tower being struck by lightning, splitting it like a log. A real downer of an image, it gave him a matching grim feeling, as when he'd found that partly burned headline yesterday morning out in the courtyard about missing police officers and whatnot. Bad omens, albeit in pieces, were scattered all around lately, it seemed.

He'd barely deposited the playing card into his trash can when someone knocked on his door. He had to pull Keelut back, seeing how Dan hadn't taught the dog not to rush the door when company came. Standing in the hall was a man in his mid-thirties—mop of straw-colored hair, no coat despite the plunging temperatures—who appeared to either have some serious worries on his mind, or he'd been tasked with keeping a very big secret.

Dan smiled, eager to meet a potential new neighbor. "Can I help you?"

"Gerald Metzger," the young man said. "Nice to meet you. I called earlier?"

He wasn't sure why, but Dan had a good feeling about the new tenant. There was also a feeling that he had to tell him something that was very important, but he didn't know how that was possible, seeing they'd only just met. Maybe it was just that feeling one gets when things are fitting together, filling the plenum, finding their place.

Meant to be.

✳ ✳ ✳

The lonely tower stood with strip malls crowding the interstate to its south and a cemetery-like plain of dead factories to its north. Tenants within the Dunsany Arms building whose windows faced south could go on ignoring the sprawling deadlands. Out of sight out of mind, the wastes might not metastasize if they aren't regularly glimpsed.

ABOUT THE AUTHOR

Andrew Post lives in Minnesota with his wife, who is also an author, and their two dogs.